A
LITTLE
BIT
RECKLESS

A LITTLE BIT RECKLESS

COURT LEGACY: BOOK SEVEN

EDEN O'NEILL

Court High

They The Pretty Stars

Illusions That May

Court Kept

We The Pretty Stars

Court University

Brutal Heir

Kingpin

Beautiful Brute

Lover

Court Legacy

Dirty Wicked Prince

Savage Little Lies

Tiny Dark Deeds

Eat You Alive

Eat Your Heart Out

Pretty Like a Devil

A Little Bit Reckless

Dark City Royals

Sia

A LITTLE BIT RECKLESS: Court Legacy Book 7

Cover Art (People Cover): RBA Designs
Photography Credit: WANDER AGUIAR PHOTOGRAPHY
Cover Art (Discreet Edition): Ever After Cover Design
Editing: A. Jane Dove
Proofreading: Judy's Proofreading

CONTENT WARNINGS:

A LITTLE BIT RECKLESS is a dark new adult college romance recommended for readers 18+. Please see the author's website at www.edenoneill.com for all the book's content warnings.

CHAPTER
ONE

My dick disappeared into this dude's mouth, and my eyes rolled back.

About fucking time.

It took me forever to get hard, and, by the time I did, I was bored. I shoved him down hard on my cock. "Choke."

He did, his throat closing around my dick. He started to play with my balls, and I slapped his hand away. People tried to get fancy, and I just needed this dude's fucking throat.

Yes.

I gave in to the pleasure and finally got hard again. I didn't know if it would be possible, as it was getting increasingly more difficult to get out of my head these days.

I drilled into this guy's throat. His name was Brad or Chad or some shit.

"God, Wells," he groaned, choking on my cock. He tried to talk some more, but I held him down. I hated *fucking talkers.* Even still, he pulled back, and my dick fell out of his mouth with a pop. He gripped my hips. "Use me."

I smirked that people actually liked this shit, getting used.

I certainly allowed my clout to get me whatever partners I wanted. It was easy, so I did.

I dug my head back into my pillow as the dude swallowed me whole again. It should be weird doing this shit in my childhood bedroom, but it wasn't. These sheets got a lot of mileage in high school, but not so much since I went off to college.

Shit, I'm losing my boner.

My dick was literally going soft in this dude's mouth, and how was that shit fucking possible?

You know how.

Ignoring that shitty-ass thought, I rolled my head back more, until my gaze caught on to its intended target. I think most people thought I was into *The Lord of the Rings* because I was a guy, and that was a cool-ass movie. It *was* a cool-ass movie, but the giant poster of Orlando Bloom in full-out elven gear wasn't there because I was into battle scenes and glowing rings.

My hard-on back, I rammed my cock faster into this guy's throat. I guess I went through a little bit of a *Legolas the elf* phase in high school. Shit, I was still into that phase, considering my choice to dye my hair white blond.

When this guy attempted to leave my cock and angle up to kiss me (and touch my fucking hair), I shoved him off me. His eyes flashed. "Hey—"

His mouth was back on my dick. His eyes rolled back as I fucked into his mouth and, where I should be using the elf poster in my face as a visualization to get off, I wasn't. Another face came into my mind. One with a smart mouth, brown eyes…

My orgasm on the brink, I gripped the fucking Legolas poster in anticipation. I was almost there. One more thrust and—

"Wells!"

Shit.

I fell off the bed rolling away from this dude and I was glad I had because my pants were there. The guy on my bed popped his head over the side. He was a redhead. Go figure. He blinked. "Shit, man. Is that your—"

"Wells Ambrose, you better hope *to God* you're not up there, because your mother and I have a bone to pick with you!"

Fuck. Fuck. Fuck.

I assumed what the guy just heard answered his question about who was yelling my name. This was a modest-size town, but everyone knew the Ambroses. We were one of few families who built Maywood Heights into what it was. Everyone knew my parents. Everyone knew me.

That's the last time I bring a dude home from the fucking gas station.

I found his clothes and shoved them at him. He was only in his boxers.

I started to point toward the window for him to leave but heard footsteps on the stairs.

What the fuck!

I had no idea how my parents knew I was home, but since it was the weekend, that made sense. I often came back from college to do laundry and shit, and when the guy on my bed wasn't moving fast enough, I shoved his ass in my bathroom.

"Don't say shit," I bit out before slamming the door in his face. I had just enough time to get my pants back on before my door flew open and my father's face appeared.

I looked a lot like my father, which was something I took advantage of. He was what I called "funny guy" handsome. Like the "Ryan Reynolds that probably could have been a serious actor but decided to go the funny route instead" handsome. My dad liked to laugh, but he wasn't fucking laughing today.

He sneered at me, and my mother stood beside him.

I got my fairer features from her. She was a really tall lady with brown hair and a face that could fit right in with all those beautiful women from regency novels. Her personality also fit that era as she was hella proper and shy.

Honestly, I had no idea how my parents got together. Especially because they were technically stepsiblings. They didn't grow up together or anything weird like that, but, needless to say, I didn't talk about that shit a whole lot. I mean, who the fuck would?

Dad stood in his brown suit with his arms folded. Although he was in the food service industry, he worked in an office. He was a franchise owner of multiple locations.

Mom didn't work a formal job but she volunteered a lot in the community.

My parents were literally yin and yang, and maybe that was why they worked. My dad was the funny guy, and Mom was the one who laughed.

Again, there was no fucking laughing today, and even *my mother* was upset, which meant a red face indicating frustration, *disappointment*. That shit was almost worse than my father giving me daggers for eyes.

Despite the predicament I appeared to be in, my parents loved their kid and I knew how to work that shit. I also got the funny-guy thing from my pops, so I came over cool as a cucumber.

I put out my arms for hugs. "Hey, fam. What's up…"

My warm greeting was ignored when my dad marched around my ass to the bathroom. He ripped the door open so hard and fast I thought he'd pull it off the hinges.

"Out," Dad barked at the guy in the bathroom, and I palmed my face. My parents obviously fucking knew me.

I swear to God they had some kind of sixth fucking sense. They caught me more than once with a guy or girl in my bed. Sometimes there were both and those moments were really fucked up.

They also made my really vanilla mother cringe. I was sure my mom had fun in her own day, but no one was trying to walk in on their kid in the middle of a threesome.

My mom placed a hand toward the door. "Please."

Her face managed to get even redder as she directed my latest (almost) conquest toward the door. Her change in tint obviously came from the awkwardness of the situation. My dad's redness came because he was fucking pissed. I thought Dad might actually grab the guy and throw him out himself, but Chad or Brad was quick.

"Sorry," the guy mumbled to my parents before basically turning into Sonic the Hedgehog and racing out the door. The dude had the boldness to whisper "text me" to me before leaving. I probably wouldn't. Bro barely got me hard, and I had to look at an elf to keep me there.

"Wells, I swear," my dad started and took steps toward me before my mom got his arm. I mentioned my mom was tall, and Dad was too. He played sports in high school, and, if my parents didn't want me getting laid, they shouldn't have been as pretty as they both were. Mom was basically built like an Amazon and had an ethereal beauty that went with it. Dad had a more rugged look, and, even though he wasn't an overly huge guy, he was sturdy and could have played sports in college too.

Dad sighed. "Sit, please." He added the please because my mom was around.

Had she not been, he'd be frying my ass. I sat on my bed. "What's—"

Dad shoved a letter in my face. It had my name on the top but was obviously not in an envelope. That didn't surprise me, since my parents knew I didn't care if they opened any mail for me while I was away at school. All my mail was supposed to be forwarded to Pembroke, my university, but if something slipped through, I always had my parents open it so they could text me if something was important.

I made a mental note to revoke that privilege when I saw the big words "academic probation" stamped on the top of the letter. I took it. "See, um, Dad, the thing is…"

"Don't bother explaining. You've obviously been messing around in college like you do here at home," Dad said, and I assumed he was referring to the guy he literally just threw out of his home. Dad closed his eyes. "I'm done, Wells. You're fooling around on my dime, and you're not doing it anymore. Your mother and I are cutting you off."

Cutting me… off.

The words were foreign, and my brain didn't compute. My mouth parted. "Cutting me off as in…"

"No. *Money*," Dad emphasized, and my heart leaped. Dad nodded like he knew. "That's right. Starting today, consider the bank that is your parents done. That means no access to credit cards. No clothes, no trips, no cooking gear."

I swallowed. My parents knew I had a YouTube channel and social media where I did cooking thirst-trap content. I cooked with little clothing on and did some playful squeezing (or teasing) with the food. Nudity got you flagged, so I always wore an apron or kept my clothing tight. I used my face and body to my advantage, and I think that was why people watched, but they stayed for the food, which was the point. Yeah, I did a little mind trickery to get people to watch, but it was *always* about the food. Always.

I could get by without the clothes on my channel and socials obviously. I could also do without expensive trips with my friends. I'd hate that shit, but I could do it. But if I didn't have my cooking gear… I shook my head. "Dad, how am I supposed to cook if I have nothing to cook with?"

My parents didn't love that I did thirst-trap videos, but they respected the art of cooking and my love for it. That art required the latest cookware and, though my mom especially loathed the fact that her son was taking off his shirt for the views, she knew cooking was my life, my dream. I came from a long line of chefs and that passion must have been passed down. My grandmas owned several Michelin-star restaurants and, though my dad didn't, he did run a fast-food franchise empire. Jax's Burgers could be eaten all over the fucking place.

My dad's chosen career field was fitting. He loved food too, and that was the Ambroses. Our family cooked. That was what we fucking did. It was our lives.

Dad's eyes blazed. "You'll get by, and I'm also taking your car, so no more zipping around in your Audi."

My back shot up. "But how am I supposed to come home for the weekends and get around campus?"

Dad's eye twitched now. "Oh, do you mean how do you get around to classes you're clearly not paying attention in? My God, Wells, do you know how bad things have to get to be put on academic probation? That letter says if you don't shape up this semester, the university is kicking you out of school."

I said nothing. I think it was best not to in that moment.

Dad's expression turned grave. "I mean, are you even going to class?"

I wasn't. At least, not last semester, but I had my reasons. They were ones I couldn't explain to my father, but I'd never been awesome in school. Cooking had always been my thing, and I was good at that.

Again, I said nothing.

Dad pointed at me. "If you get kicked out of school, I'm definitely not paying for you to go to culinary school. I'm not rewarding that kind of behavior."

Fucking panicked now, I started to say something, but my mom did first.

She placed a hand on Dad's arm. "Honey, isn't that a little extreme?"

I wasn't surprised Mom came to my defense. She knew going to culinary school was always part of the ultimate plan for my life. I went to Pembroke University to play football and be with my friends. We were like brothers, but football and academics were never endgame for me like it was for some of them. I was always going to go to culinary school after college. After that, I planned to go the route of my grandmothers and ultimately own my own restaurant.

Dad shook his head. "I don't think so, Cleo. We just can't reward this behavior," he said, and Mom nodded. Clearly, she didn't want to, but she agreed with him. Dad frowned at me. "We *won't* reward this behavior."

My life was literally flashing before my eyes as I watched my dad take my mom's hand. He started to guide her out, taking my future with him, and I panicked.

I didn't know how I did it, but I got in front of them. I cut off their exit and I opened my mouth so fucking fast. "Dad, I have a tutor."

The words rolled out before I could stop them.

Again, I panicked.

I also said it loud, in fact so loud that my parents' heads shot back a little. Dad eyed me. "A… tutor?"

I nodded adamantly. I had like two seconds to get my thoughts straight, my lies straight. I swallowed. "Yeah, I've been working with one all semester. I've been trying to work on things. I don't want to get kicked out of school."

Dad didn't look convinced, but I didn't blame him. I mean, I was lying through my ass here. He folded his arms. "Really?"

No. "Yes."

I tried not to make it sound like a question on the end, and the surprise on my dad's face was legendary. He hadn't expected me to say such a thing. Hell, *I* hadn't expected me to say such a thing, and, to support the lie, I pulled out my phone.

"Look, I'm using Bow Reed's app and everything," I said, pulling it up. Rainbow Reed was my buddy Thatcher's little sister. She was brilliant like him, but I'd never let her know that shit. She also happened to design an app for high school and college students to find tutors and did so in high school herself *for fun*. She claimed she wanted to help people, but I knew that was phony as shit.

It was as phony as she was.

I knew that girl, who she really was, but those were thoughts for another day. Right now, I was using her accomplishments for my own benefit and had no problem doing so.

After all, she drew first blood.

My focus on my dad was the only thing that pulled me out of my intrusive thoughts about Bow Reed, and I was grateful. I needed clarity for all the lies I was spewing. Dad would believe me about Bow. He liked Bow. He was her godfather after all.

I wet my lips, refusing to give any more of my thoughts to that girl, and something inside me eased a little as I watched Dad. He didn't look so angry as he glanced at the app. The tension across his eyebrows even eased.

Dad's eyes flicked up. "You're serious."

"I am." I nodded. I put my phone away. "I wanted to be proactive about the probation. I want to do better in school."

I was going for an Emmy award with this acting at this point, but I held steadfast to my performance. I didn't like lying to my dad, my parents, but this was culinary school we were talking about. As far as I was concerned, I had no choice *but* to lie.

Dad rubbed his neck. "Fine. I'll hold off on the extremes. I won't cut you off *for now*," he said, and I released a breath. Dad pointed at me. "But I need you to fix this situation, Wells. You better take this tutoring thing seriously."

"I will, sir." And I would. I'd find a real tutor first thing. I'd do anything I had to in order to secure my future.

I finally released all the breath I had in my chest when my dad nodded. He left the room, but my mom stayed.

"I'm so glad you're getting ahead of this and using Bow's app," she said, grinning. She squeezed my arm. "That's amazing, honey. Really."

My mom hugged me, and I was sure the hug had to do with the first thing she said. She was happy I was taking school seriously, but, as she squeezed so hard and wouldn't let me go, something told me a lot of the hug had to do with the *last* thing she said.

Gritting my teeth, I hugged my mom back. I let her relish in whatever win she believed was occurring here. She clearly thought, in some capacity, I had no problem utilizing Bow Reed's services. I had no problem using *Bow* for help. This was a win for my mother and I knew why.

My mom loved Bow, like all my friends' moms did. They loved her because our families were close yes, but they also fell for Rainbow Reed's bullshit. In fact, I was sure everyone in this fucking town thought that girl walked on water.

But I was the only one who lived the soul-crushing truth.

CHAPTER
TWO

Bow

My phone buzzed with a number I didn't recognize. My heart in my throat, I sent it to voicemail, then added the number to my blocked caller list. I tried to ignore all the numbers that were already there. There were a lot, dozens.

"Excuse you."

The rude guy who spoke clipped me, and I stumbled forward. I'd been walking while texting, dumb I knew, but he was rude and didn't have to speak to me that way. I pocketed my phone. "Sorry. I wasn't paying attention but didn't go out of my way to run into you."

It was an accident and this guy didn't need to be a jerk about it.

He pivoted, as if to tell me off, but as soon as he made eye contact with me, his eyes flashed. He was a big guy and challenged the size of my brother, Thatcher, who was a huge football player. He lifted his hands. "Yeah, no."

Shaking his head (aggressively), he backed away and almost ran into someone while *getting away* from me. There was a lot of traffic coming out of the library. I was heading there myself.

"Tell Wells I don't want no trouble," the big guy mumbled, and, as soon as he said that, nearly everyone coming out of the library faced me.

They averted their eyes.

It was like I had an incurable disease after that. Everyone walked in the opposite direction and definitely made no eye contact.

God.

Used to that, I hugged my books. I shrunk into myself. Normally, people treating me like a social pariah made me sick, but currently, it worked to my advantage. I didn't want to be acknowledged, seen.

Darting my head around, I weaved through all the traffic coming out of Pembroke University's main library, then entered myself. This was the largest library out of several at my Ivy League, and I spent a lot of time there. It was easy to blend in and hide amongst all the shelves.

I was always hiding.

I didn't feel like I had a choice right now, and I was well aware of the phone burning into my hip. It hit my thigh every time my pleated skirt moved.

Why won't he stop calling?

I knew why. But the calls *would* stop, the texts. They'd stop because I was taking action and meeting someone who'd *make* them stop. He would without even having to do anything.

I just had to be brave enough to see him.

Forgetting about my phone, I headed toward the entertainment section of the library. They had all the media articles like magazines, movies, and music. It wasn't a great place to study, but I hadn't chosen the location.

Where is he…

There, at a table in the corner, and though I'd been seeking this person out, it didn't mean I didn't hesitate.

He always made me hesitate.

Wells Ambrose, my brother's best friend, took up a lot of space. He physically occupied a lot of the table he sat at, but he also consumed the entire environment he was in. All my brother's best friends did that, and they were known around campus as Legacy. All our parents donated a lot of funds to this school, and though I was considered Legacy too, no one bowed to me like they did my brother and his friends.

They simple avoided.

I was like a pariah everywhere I went and had been since high school.

Because of Wells.

Wells Ambrose sat with a stack of books around him, but not one of them was academic. They were all cookbooks, and I wasn't surprised. Wells was a great cook and came from a long line of them, chefs. I used to love coming over to Wells's house for his dad's omelets. They were always so good.

Walk toward him.

I had to tell myself this, and, though I did make my feet move, I also felt sick. People avoided me, but that was very much because of Wells.

Keep walking.

I had to, and that space he took up consumed me as I got closer. Wells was surrounded by cookbooks, but he had a graphic novel in his hand. That was fitting since he looked like he was plucked off the cover. He had electric blond hair he fashioned in a messy style, and the only thing that gave away he was a brunette was his roots. He was also jacked like an anime guy and was only missing one of those long swords out of *Final Fantasy*.

Just a few more steps…

This technically should be easy to do, but, with each step, I felt like I was walking into the devil's den.

I never actually made it to Wells's table before he glanced

up. It was like he knew I was approaching, and I immediately froze in place.

The way he stared me down had something to do with that.

An icy glare ignited his green eyes. Almost instantly, his focused gaze peered down the length of me. I almost wished I didn't wear a skirt, but I *always* wore a skirt. I was kind of into the dark academia aesthetic. I loved the romantic and polished look of a crisp, button-down shirt and knee-high tights. I wore both today, and they could be seen well beneath my open wool coat.

A muscle clenched in Wells's jaw when he noticed those knee-highs. I wore them with my heeled Mary Jane shoes, and he always made fun of me. He said I looked like a little schoolgirl out of a porno.

Wells was always cruel to me. Actually, he'd been doing that so long that I nearly forgot he hadn't always been that way. That was such a long time ago, though.

I could handle the heat of Wells's eyes, but when he sat back and crossed his arms, a smirk followed. Wells never laughed with me, only *at* me.

Bile heated my throat, especially when he placed his book down. He draped an arm across the chair next to him. "'Sup, Squeak?"

Squeak.

I *hated* what he called me. He also made fun of me because my voice cracked sometimes. It was high-pitched, and I couldn't help it.

Leave.

But I couldn't leave. I had to move forward.

Steeling myself, I strode right up to Wells's table.

"Hi." I took off my coat, then set my stuff up, ignoring the curious look he was giving me. I just took my books out and put them right next to his cookbooks.

His head cocked. "What do you think you're doing? You can't be here. I'm meeting somebody."

I knew he was meeting someone. I knew because I created the app in which he made a listing *to* meet someone. My tutor app was free, and I had no intention of monetizing it. It was something I made in high school. I just wanted a way to help people. I knew doing well in school didn't come easy to everyone. This included myself, contrary to what most people probably thought since I did do well. In actuality, it was really hard for me to get ahead in school. My ADHD made things difficult sometimes.

I ignored Wells by sitting down next to him. I definitely felt the heat of his eyes as I took my computer out. I started to open one of my textbooks but he slapped a hand on it. The sound radiated in the normally quiet library.

I didn't think anyone noticed me come into the library. Often, I went out of my way to avoid people. It was easier than *knowing* they were avoiding me. It hurt less, I guess.

But people noticed me now, and they always noticed Wells. He was a really popular guy and normally the fun one in my brother's group. Wells liked to joke and tease but the teasing stopped when it came to me. It was unusual the two of us were here *together*.

I went out of my way to avoid people. Wells Ambrose went out of his way to avoid *me*. In fact, we were only together if my brother's crew was around, though this put us together quite a lot since my best friend Sloane was dating one of Wells's friends, Dorian. Wells and I were never *alone* together though.

"You hard of hearing?" Wells cut, an edge to his voice. I heard it harshly, sharply. He leaned in. "I said you can't be here, so leave. *Now*."

I tried not to cower or shy away. Especially when his cool scent surrounded me. I knew that smell well. We'd been in each other's lives for so long.

It was funny. The essence of him used to be a safe haven for me so long ago.

Now, it only stoked fear.

Other people really were staring at us. Actually, every eye in this area of the library was on us, but I didn't falter. I didn't move.

Wells's eyes narrowed. "I'm warning you, Squeak. You need to get out of here. I'm meeting someone, so you need to leave. I'm not playing around."

I knew he wasn't, but I wasn't either.

Be brave.

I had to. It was this or something else and dealing with Wells was the lesser of two evils. I swallowed. "It's me."

"What?"

"It's *me*," I emphasized and tried not to be meek when I faced him. Wells had a way of making me feel so incredibly small, but I sat up in front of him. I sat tall. I folded my hands. "The person you're meeting is me. I'm your tutor."

CHAPTER
THREE

Wells

She had to be joking, but she wasn't acting like it when she opened a book that was for one of *my* classes. I knew this girl's schedule, and it wasn't the same as mine. Actually, her classes were more advanced, even though she was a year behind me. My jaw moved. "The fuck you talking about?"

Every eye in this room was on us. I was used to that shit with being me, being Legacy, but Bow Reed, aka "Squeak," got the opposite attention. Usually, people headed the other way when it came to her. They didn't give a shit about her, and that was her fault.

She knew that, which was why she never fought it. My best friend's sister could be a little spitfire. She could be *bold*, and she was talking some crazy-ass shit right now acting like my tutor.

"I accepted your listing on my app," she continued and very much wouldn't make eye contact with me. Bow had these blue eyes like a baby doll. She wanted people to think she was innocent, virginal, but I knew the truth.

I studied those eyes even though they wouldn't look at me. They were framed with dark eyelashes, her nose a pert little button, and her mouth full, pouty. They had a natural flush to them that matched her round cheeks. This girl couldn't *not* look like a fucking Kewpie doll, everything about her perfectly plastic from her lint-rolled skirt to the tightness of her bun. She always wore her hair up, and it exposed the rose tone of her neck. This girl blushed like a son of a bitch, and she certainly was now, with me.

My jaw moved. Bow kept ignoring my ass, and she was pulling books out of her bag like it was bottomless. Eventually, she stopped and placed her hands in her lap. She fidgeted. "Look at your phone. It's me. I'm your tutor."

My eyes narrowed. *No one* told me what the fuck to do. Least of all her.

Calm down.

I looked at my phone out of morbid curiosity, and my brow shot up.

What the fuck?

It was her name. Right there by my listing for a tutor on her app.

Rainbow Reed.

I pocketed my phone. "The fuck you playing at, Squeak?" She wasn't my tutor, at least not as of last night or even this morning. My eyes narrowed harder. "Where's Heather?"

I was actually looking forward to linking up with Heather Rodgers. We'd hooked up before, and I was banking on her giving me head after our session. Studying academic shit was hard for me, and I wanted the release.

"Heather Rodgers has a previous engagement," Bow stated, again not looking at me. She flipped pages in one of her books. "I got a notification this morning."

Bullshit, she did. Heather knew her assignment was me, and that meant her attendance was a given. Nothing short of a car accident would have kept that girl away from my dick.

I put my arm on the table. "What really happened?"

Bow was lying. *What are you up to, Squeak?*

Bow continued to fidget with her stuff, but I grabbed the anatomy book and threw it across the room. The thing slammed with a reverberating thud on the polished, wooden floor, and everyone in the room stopped moving.

The librarian even looked away.

She was an older lady, and even she knew better than to intervene with Squeak and me.

Squeak and me.

We had a history, and it wasn't a good one. Bow was manipulative, and it took only a moment for the world to see that. It took seconds for the world, but for me, it took eons. What she did ran in slow motion for me the day it happened. Rainbow Reed changed the trajectory of both our lives.

She changed *my* life.

The reality of that was something I had to live with, and if *I* did, she sure as shit would do it with me. She faced me. "Wells..."

I leaned in, getting close. My best friend's sister smelled like cookies and her innocent little schoolgirl act killed me. It was negative degrees outside, and this girl had her knees bare in those stupid little tights of hers. I sneered. "Tell the truth."

She had one more lie before I ended her, and, though I wouldn't physically hurt Thatcher's sister, there were other ways to make people suffer. There was a reason no one in this fucking library, or really, anyone on this campus, wanted anything to do with her. They knew what she did too.

"I canceled her acceptance for your request on the app," she admitted, her chest moving fast, her breath moving fast. She had dark hair like my buddy Thatch and pushed some of it behind her ear. Her hair was curly and a loose tendril of it had escaped her bun. She swallowed. "I heard our parents talking that you needed a tutor and were going to request one on my app so..."

Our parents were close, and she would have had ample opportunities to hear that.

So, she canceled with Heather, huh. I moved in closer. "Why?"

No way this girl would actually want to help me. She may be my best friend's sister, but Bow and I didn't do things socially beyond our group of friends. Because she was a conniving little kiss-ass, and it was only because of my friendship with Thatcher that I didn't do anything about that.

Thatcher tended to stay out of the drama I had with his sister. He had his reasons, and I kept things civil with Bow for him and him alone. He was like a brother to me.

Bow knew better than to have anything to do with me, and though I could see her brown-nosing to please our parents, I refused to believe she was that stupid.

"Why do you want to be my tutor, Squeak?" I asked, and she shivered. That was probably because I did get a little close, her ear close. Why the fuck did this girl smell like a bakery?

I shook my head, that syrupy-smelling shit only making me angry. I clenched my teeth. "You really that desperate to kiss some ass and please our parents?"

Bow didn't speak right away, and I lingered by her ear. One of her curls danced by her earlobe again. It was tiny, and my breath moved it.

A shallow breath lifted her chest. "I need something from you."

"Oh, yeah?" The loose curl distracted me. It was a flaw and proved she wasn't quite perfect. I smirked. "What would make you think I'd *ever* help you?"

She winced, and a sudden activity hit my dick. I got *hard*, and it had to be because of her discomfort. It certainly wasn't because of her, but knowing I got to her would do it. The fact I made her uncomfortable, broke her...

"It'd be a transaction," she said and finally slid those blue eyes in my direction. Her lips moved, a quiver moving through them. I terrified her in ways she probably didn't want me to see.

My cock twitched again.

She bit her lip. "I tutor you and you make the world see."

"See what?"

"Me." Her throat bobbed, and, glancing away, she wriggled. She acted so shy sometimes, but she wasn't. She was bold as shit when she wanted to be, deceptive... Her lashes fanned with several blinks. "If I'm seen with you... Seen publicly with *just* you, then people would know..."

"Know what?"

She glanced up, her jaw moving a little. "People would know that we were okay, you and me."

I sat back slowly. Did I know this girl or did I know this girl? "You help me and the world thinks I forgave you."

Called out, she fidgeted again. She huffed before nodding. "I help you get your grades up and your parents would get off your back. They wouldn't cut you off and would pay for your culinary school."

She knew everything, all my dirty details and family drama.

Of course she did.

If one looked up Bow in the dictionary, they would see many things. They'd see her truth. They'd see her bullshit.

I was only sorry it took someone getting hurt for me to see.

I managed to get even closer to her, and even though her smell made me want to punch something, I stayed there. I did it to watch that discomfort return, that bob in her throat. Her cheeks went red and mine heated. A red fury of anger surrounded me.

I didn't like people fucking playing around with my life, *my future*, and that shit went quadruple when it came to her.

"I'll give in to you this time, Squeak," I said, because, as much as I hated it, I did need her. My parents were on my back but by no means would I ever forgive this girl. *Ever.* My eyes narrowed. "To the world we'll look cool but behind the scenes shit will never change between us. Never ever, Squeak. You understand?"

She winced again, her expression pained. Like it truly bothered her that I'd never forgive her, and maybe it did.

I wished I cared.

Rather slowly, she nodded. "I understand."

That was the last word said before I leaned back and let her do her thing.

She opened textbooks and began exactly what she planned. She was helping me study, my tutor, and the effect was instant. People around us were blinking and chatting in hushed whispers. Especially when I nodded at them, then leaned into Bow.

But really, I'd never forgive this girl for what she did to me. I couldn't.

If I didn't get to forget what happened, she wouldn't either.

CHAPTER
FOUR

Wells

"You're letting my sister help you? You must be desperate."

I stopped curling my bicep to glance up at my buddy Thatcher Reed. He was a big motherfucker. Actually, he was the exact opposite of his sister, who was tiny as shit.

Snarling, I tried not to think about her as Thatcher sauntered up to me. We were at one of the university's gyms, and he nudged me with a sweaty arm which was gross as shit. He dropped a heavy bicep on my shoulder. "Maybe if you quit dicking around in your classes, you wouldn't need a tutor."

I wasn't dicking around in my classes. I wasn't *going* to classes. There was a difference.

I shoved him off me which made him chuckle. Dude and I had been best friends before we even knew what that shit was.

Not standing for the shove, Thatcher *attempted* to shove me back, but my ass was quick. I dodged it and our horsing around got the attention of one of our other friends who'd joined us today. His name was Bruno Sloane-Mallick, but we called him Bru.

Bru stopped his pullup after I dodged another attempted strike from Thatcher, his feet touching the ground. Bru was so tall he had to tuck his legs in tight just to make a pullup effective, but he started up again once he caught my eye. His gray sweatpants hung low on his hips, exposing his chiseled hip bones just briefly before his shirt covered them when he pulled up again.

Ignoring his next rotation, I shoved Thatcher, then got back to work. It wasn't football season anymore, but Thatcher and I liked to stay in shape. We both played for the university's team.

Our other friends, Dorian Prinze and Ares "Wolf" Mallick played for the university too, but they were having date night with their girls. It was weird to think they were shacked up considering what whores we all had been in high school. My buddy Thatcher had a serious girlfriend too, but she was a celebrity cellist. Currently, Aspen Davis was on tour, but that didn't mean we all didn't hear about her. My pal Thatch was in love, which was crazy.

I was happy for him. I was happy for all my friends, but it did leave gym days and general hangouts without one (or several) of my best friends. This particular gym day, I only invited Thatcher out, but Bru tagged along. He didn't play football. He hadn't since high school, but the dude liked to stay jacked.

Bru dropped from the pullup. He was a brunette who resembled Clark Kent in both looks and stature. I mean, he wasn't as pretty as me, but he got eyes across campus just like the rest of our group.

That kind of came with the territory of being, well, us.

Bru maneuvered his way over to his water bottle and his gaze slid to me before he sprayed some water in his mouth. He swallowed hard, then wiped his brow with his cut-off tee.

His core was just as strong and defined as his hips, and I shook my head before lifting my dumbbell again. Nothing against the guy, but he hadn't been invited today.

Nah, he hadn't been invited.

I really pushed myself with my weights and made myself look at everything but the mirror. It gave me views of things other than my workout, which was priority.

"What's your deal with Bow anyway? She's a sweetheart," Bru said from somewhere in the gym behind me. Did I mention that dude wasn't invited? "You're always giving her a hard time, and I don't get that."

He wouldn't, would he? Dorian, Ares, Thatcher, and I had all been friends since we came out of our mothers. Our parents were friends in school too, so that'd been natural. Bru and his sister, Sloane, entered our group later. Because of that, he didn't know my history with that "sweetheart."

Again, Rainbow Reed had the world fooled.

Because Bru *wasn't* invited, I didn't grant his question with a response. I just continued to lift my weights, and Thatcher nudged me again with his nasty wet bicep.

"He's just not her biggest fan," Thatcher said, which was nice of him. He didn't particularly love that I had beef with his sister, but he got it. He understood. My beef also kept dudes away from her, so there was that, too.

Yeah, there was that.

Rainbow Reed didn't deserve allies, let alone friends. She had none outside of our group, and that wasn't because of anything *I'd* done. It was a byproduct of bullshit she concocted all by herself.

I didn't feel bad for her, but, because Thatcher was like a brother to me, I did look out for her as needed. I did so for Thatcher.

Maybe Bru was about to ask something else about shit that wasn't his business, but Thatcher got a text and I took that as my way out of the conversation. It also marked the end of my gym session, because the text was from his girl-friend, Aspen. He felt compelled to call her after. He wanted to hear her voice, and as much as I was happy for my friend, I wasn't trying to hear all that. Their calls consisted of enough *babys* and *sweeties* for a lifetime.

No one was more deserving of an awesome girl than my buddy Thatcher, and Aspen was pretty awesome. She gave him a run for his money. She challenged him.

After gathering my things, I waved my goodbye to Thatcher, who nodded at me. He was so consumed in his call he barely even noticed I left which made me laugh.

I mumbled a short goodbye to Bru on my way out but that was all. I didn't think anything else was needed, and I didn't wait for his response before I headed to the showers.

I went there to get my head right.

I had a lot on my mind as I slid under the heat of the mist and one of those things was Bow Reed. Spending longer than necessary with her was the last thing I was trying to do, but she was brilliant. She could get me out of this scrape with my parents.

I only knew two people just as smart. One was Thatcher, who was completely consumed with his girlfriend. He'd offered to help with my situation, help me study, but I wasn't going to bother him with my problems.

The other smart person I wasn't going to think about. I refused, and, as I lathered my hair, I regretted not sticking around for a proper goodbye with Bru.

If I had, maybe he wouldn't have approached me.

I smelled him before anything else, his scent like oak trees and freshly cut grass. He smelled like nature and campfires and probably didn't actually smell like that last thing, but he reminded me of that, camping. He spent a lot of time outside. He liked to run and be around wildlife.

I knew too much about this guy, and, when he touched my shoulder, I should have shrugged him the fuck off. I should have tackled his ass down and told him to get the fuck away from me.

Instead, I let him squeeze my shoulder, his thick digits digging into my flesh. The lather from my shower gel ran over his firm fingers, and I growled.

He did too.

"Wells…" My name rumbled into my back, his chest pressing up against me. Reaching around, he grabbed my dick, and I sucked in a breath. For some reason, I let him work me, massage my balls, but not for long before I wised up and thew an elbow into his abs. That shit was rock solid and radiated hard into my joint, but that didn't stop me from doing it again. Bru didn't even move he was so big and me doing that would have *normally* sent a guy down.

It didn't affect Bru, and as if to emphasize that, the fucker locked me into a bear hug. He grabbed me tight against his chest, his hand pumping my dick, and I closed my eyes because I couldn't help it.

Fresh cut grass. Oak…

I'd come to hate that smell, resent it. Bru's hand went to my throat, and when he tried to kiss me, my neck, I shoved him off. I finally got my mind back.

I finally got the strength.

I turned around and that strength wavered a bit seeing Bru just as naked as me. The shower had taken his Clark Kent hair and flattened it over his brow. It curled a little. His jaw tightened and it worked when he noticed I was just as hard as he was.

And wet.

Bru's pecs glistened down to his abs, his dick, and he massaged it a little, looking at me. The action made my cock twitch. He rewet his lips. "Wells…"

I grabbed him, threw him against the wall, and he put his hands up instantly.

He submitted.

I felt myself go harder. In fact, I was fucking steel, and when I let go, I turned. I squeezed the bridge of my nose, and after, ran my fingers through my hair.

"Wells—"

"I told you to stay *the fuck* away from me," I growled, and when I pivoted, he blinked in front of me. My jaw clicked. "You had no fucking right to do that, touch me."

He didn't. I told him no.

Bru said nothing, his back still against the wall and his naked chest moving rapidly up and down.

I bared my teeth. "I told you. I'm not into this shit."

I wasn't *into him*, and when he walked toward me, I put my fist up. I'd punch his ass out. I didn't care if he was my fucking friend.

He put his hands up again. "Wells…"

If this dude said my name one more fucking time, like that… I pointed at him. "I told you. I'm not into you, bro. What? You didn't get the fucking message?"

I didn't know how I could have been clearer with everything that happened before this moment, but, when I said that, he laughed. *He laughed,* and I almost did hit his ass.

He gestured toward me. "I'm pretty sure that's not true."

His dark eyes scanned down to what he clearly saw as the evidence of that.

My eyes narrowed. "That shit is physical, bro. It was a physical response only and doesn't change anything."

It didn't, and so what I was hard? I got hard watching fucking *Titanic* and that was barely a flash of tits.

Once more, Bru said nothing, and I walked up to him. He was still hard too of course, but I ignored that. "I'm. Not. Into. You. We're friends, bro, and that's it."

It was, and what happened between us shouldn't have. I knew better than to kiss someone I considered a friend.

I knew better than to more than kiss my friend.

Bruno Sloane-Mallick and I had made a mistake. I was

aware that shit was on me. We started hooking up with girls at parties as a release for him. He always took himself way too seriously.

"We crossed a line," I continued, and I was aware of that too. I swallowed. "We both did, but we are friends and that's it, Bru."

That was it.

I stopped it before things got too deep, and I tried to before Bru embarrassed himself.

Bru scanned my eyes. "A line crossed is one time, Wells," he said, and my stomach knotted, tightened. He nodded. "*One* time. More than that is something else."

Something else.

"You must think I'm stupid," he said, lifting his eyes to the tiled ceiling. It was a wonder no one else was in here. I wished someone else was in here. He faced me. "But I'm not, and you're in denial. You're also failing and need a tutor *because of that* denial. Or did you think I hadn't noticed you stopped going to classes because of me?"

We had all the same classes last semester. I often had classes with my friends.

I didn't make that mistake this semester. Bru and I had zero classes together.

"You started missing them after what I said," Bru continued, and the breath punched from my lungs. "You stopped going to classes after I told you I loved you."

He loved me.

He didn't love me. He was infatuated with me like many people were once they got a hit. I had a lot of sexual partners I had to give the same talk to. I didn't do love.

Love didn't do me.

"Do me a favor and stop this," I said, backing off him. I shook my head. "Do it before there's nothing left of our friendship to repair."

We may not be able to get back to what we were after

everything that happened between us, but there'd be no possibility at all if he didn't stop.

Someone did come in, and, worried it could be Thatcher, I left. I didn't want to explain any weirdness to him. He was happy.

At least one of us was.

CHAPTER
FIVE

Bru

Bow Reed was on her phone when I approached her. I lifted my hand. "Hey."

She jumped. Like nearly a foot off the street, she jumped. She was in her running gear like me, her pink jacket zipped up to her neck and her earmuffs on. The holidays had passed, but it was still cold in the spring semester. She gripped her phone through her mittens. "Hi. Sorry. You scared me."

Clearly. I propped my hands on my waist. "You okay?"

She was kind of jumpy considering she expected me. I was late for our run but only by a few minutes.

Bow slid her phone into her leggings pocket. She'd been standing near a bench on Pembroke University's quad which was our meeting place for our weekly runs. We didn't do it as much since spring in the Midwest still got snow on occasion, but we tried to get out of the library when we could.

Bow and I were both a couple of nerds. She was the only person I knew besides me who studied when they didn't have to. She was brilliant and the little sister of one of my best friends.

She chewed her lip, a flush in her cheeks. She had her curly hair up in a bun and looked like an ad for The North Face with how coordinated and put together she was. She even matched her gray socks to her earmuffs, but that was Bow. She was always polished with rarely a hair out of place. She wrestled with her hands a bit, her smile wobbly. "I'm good."

"You sure?"

"Mmhmm." Her face managed to get even redder, but it was cold out. "You ready?"

I was, so I allowed her to lead the way. We picked up our feet, and I knew this would be a nice release.

Especially after yesterday.

I had so much shit going on in my head right now, and it was nice to get a run in with a friend. Thatcher's sister and I were good buddies. She was the only person I could relate to in regards to school and stuff, and she was just incredibly kind. The exact opposite of ninety percent of the people in our friend group.

My friends weren't bad people. Many of them were just dudes, and I found I got along much better with girls in general. Another one of my best friends, Fawn, was a girl.

I really pushed the run with Bow today. We took some of the more elevated areas through campus, but I made sure to keep my strides slow. Bow was the exact opposite in regards to Thatcher in size and general stature. She was barely five feet, if that, and it took her several strides to catch up with my one.

"Come on, Bru," she laughed, sprinting ahead of me. She was a ball of energy, and I felt stupid for trying to take things slow. My legs may have been longer, but Bow could talk and move a mile a minute.

"Hold up," I said, easily catching up to her. Once I did,

she charged off, and I got nothing but her back. It seemed we both needed the run, because the pair of us were thoroughly exhausted by the time we wrapped around back to the quad, and later, to my car.

We sat in my Audi and warmed our hands on the vents.

It was so weird I had such a nice car. It was so weird I had paid tuition and never wanted for anything. My parents, the Mallicks, were incredibly generous.

There was a lot of history there with the Mallicks. They adopted me after finding my sister, Noa Sloane-Mallick. She was their biological daughter, and, though I wasn't their biological son, they took me in too. I had a family again. My sister and I both did after we tragically lost the people who raised us.

I could write a book about tragedy, but every day I found the past more and more behind me. I found I didn't dwell on it so much and embraced my future.

It was easy to do with people like Bow, Fawn, and all my other friends in my life. I was grateful to say I had very few worries these days, but the ones I did I was reminded of often.

Bow and I were barely in my car before her phone buzzed, and she had it out again. Her face shot up in color once more and very few people in her life made her look that way after hearing from them.

"That Wells?" I asked, though I shouldn't have asked. "I heard from Thatcher you're tutoring him."

I didn't get that almost as much as I didn't understand why he seemed to have an issue with her.

That's none of your business.

It may not be, but Wells Ambrose was pissing me off these days, and I had no problem getting in his business.

Bow froze before slowly lowering her phone. She gazed up at me. "It's not him, but I *am* tutoring him."

"Why?" I asked, forgetting about who she was texting. She and Wells had my attention now.

Keep your mouth fucking shut.

I should but I wasn't. My eyes narrowed. "He's not very nice to you, Bow."

Truth be told, Wells wasn't nice to many people, but that was just the dudes in my friend group. They were aggressive. *They were guys*, but Wells in particular seemed to single Bow out. He always had. Even in high school he appeared to have a distaste for her.

Why is he your every thought?

He wasn't my *every* thought, but he did piss me off, and Bow was literally the nicest person in the world. She didn't deserve his aggression.

You don't either.

That was neither here nor there, and I watched as Bow slipped her phone in the pocket of her jacket.

"You're right. He's not," she said softly. Her small shoulders lifted. "But he's not a bad person. He's not, and I understand."

"Understand what?"

"Him I guess." The wobble returned to her smile. "We've known each other a long time, and it doesn't help being mean back. I mean, what's the point?"

What's the point.

My back hit my seat, her sweetness, her *kindness* too much. She was giving Wells way more allowances than he deserved.

You are too.

I swallowed. "You're a good person, Bow. You are, and you shouldn't let anyone push you around."

Truth be told, *I loved* being around this girl. She was like a breath of fresh air in a world that could be full of bullshit, pain...

I never felt pain around Bow. I always felt good, and,

honestly, I always felt like a selfish fuck for stealing as much of her time as I had since I came back home.

I got kicked out of my old university for fighting. Clocking dudes had been my way of not dealing with shit from high school. My sister, Sloane, and I had a background of violence and pain, and fighting was how I dealt with it. It obviously caught up with me, and, after lots of therapy and support from family and friends, I was happy to say I was back on track. A large section of that support came from Bow though. Rainbow Reed and her relentless optimism. Rainbow Reed and her copious amounts of joy and beautiful spirit. She was a fucking unicorn.

"You're so beautiful," I said, the words coming out before I could stop them. I realized how they probably sounded, but I wasn't talking about how she looked. I mean, she *was* fucking gorgeous with her dark hair, blue eyes, and a tiny exterior that made a guy just want to hold her…

Protect her.

I did want to protect her, and if I couldn't protect myself from Wells and his bullshit, the least I could do was step in and let her know she didn't have to be the bigger person when it came to him. I got what it was like to be around Wells. He was an unyielding force, and it was easy to get crushed under the waves. It was easy to let him push you around.

It was also easy to want him.

I didn't *want* to want him, and my life would be so much fucking easier if I could fall for someone like Bow. Neither one of us deserved how Wells treated us, and I was thinking about that when a soft scent moved toward me.

I was thinking about that when Bow kissed me.

I didn't know what was happening at first. A warm mouth touched mine, and my eyes closed.

Though only briefly.

I froze, and, when I backed away, Bow's eyes shot open.

"Sorry," she said, her cheeks *even more* flushed. She touched her mouth. "I didn't mean to. I mean…"

"No, you're fine," I said, blinking, and she blinked too.

That was when she kissed me again.

She ended up on my lap, my best friend Thatcher's little sister. I was in shock. I was in more than shock, especially when I didn't stop her right away.

I didn't stop her at all.

My hands braced her trim hips, and it was different than kissing Wells. It was less angry and aggressive.

It was more Bow.

It was soft, delicate, and I let it go on for longer than I should have when I tasted her lips. They tasted like cherry lip balm.

What are you doing?

I was kissing my best friend's sister, and that was so fucking wrong. I was also really confused because, not a day ago, I was kissing someone else.

Stop.

My hands followed the thought. I braced Bow's hips but for a different reason this time.

I returned her back to her seat.

The air filled with Bow, her soft, feminine scent. Her fragrance reminded me of a fruit cobbler. Had she always smelled so sweet, good…

"Bow," I started, literally shaking the thoughts out of my head. They were inappropriate, and *this was Bow.* I huffed. "Bow, I'm so sorry."

I didn't know what I was apologizing for. For kissing her back…

For liking it.

I did like it, and again, I was confused. Bow and I were completely platonic. We were friends, and this was Thatch's little sis.

Bow's blinks were rapid. She looked like Snow White with

her dark hair and flushed lips and cheeks. She eased back in her seat. "But you said I was beautiful."

I did say that. I closed my eyes.

Fuck.

"Bru…"

I opened my eyes, hearing the strain in her voice. I felt punched in the gut by what I saw. Bow was curled up in her seat, wincing.

And she had water in her eyes.

There was a visible sheen there before she looked away, and my stomach tossed. I reached for her. "Bow, I'm…"

Again, I wanted to apologize. I *had* called her beautiful, but it wasn't in the way she thought.

I messed up.

Bow didn't let me touch her again. In fact, she all but recoiled when I got close. My throat tightened. "Bow—"

She scrambled out of my car.

"I'm sorry," she said before slamming the door in my face. She sprinted away, and I assumed she was heading back to her dorm. She lived close by, but I didn't chase after her. I had no right to. She may have kissed me first, but I kissed her back. I also led her on, but I wondered how much as I sat there. I called her beautiful, but I also meant it.

And I definitely liked kissing her, too.

CHAPTER
SIX

"The fuck's wrong with you, Squeak?" Wells asked me, and I blinked. He shook his head. "I called your name like three times."

Had he?

He sighed from across the dining room table. I was helping him with his math homework. He was in a junior class, and, though I was a sophomore, I'd learned many of the concepts in his class already. All my classes in high school had been accelerated.

Wells eyed me with a heat that hadn't let up since I came over to his house. He shared one with my brother. Everyone on campus called it Legacy House since all my brother's friends—Wells, Dorian, Ares, and Bru—lived there. It was always the hotspot for parties. I gripped Wells's math book thinking about Bru.

Wells angled back in his chair. He was getting increasingly frustrated as the night went on, and I think only part of that had to do with the fact that he was locked into studying with me. The school stuff wasn't easy for him, and that clearly annoyed him. He stamped out his big legs. "You're supposed to be helping me, and you're not even fucking here right now."

"Sorry," I mumbled, my face hot, when my brother came into the dining room.

I jumped when my brother smacked the back of Wells's head. Wells shot forward and jumped out of his seat.

Wells growled. "What the fuck?"

"Don't talk to my sister like that, you fucker," Thatcher said, and Wells lifted his eyes. I knew the dynamic my brother had with his friends for a long time, so, honestly, them hitting each other wasn't exactly foreign to me. They were like two colossi, and, even though Wells was lankier than my brother, he was faster. I'd also seen him clock my brother to the ground enough times to know he could hold his own with him.

Apparently, Wells chose not to today, and, as he rubbed his blond head, his white tee lifted. It exposed the first section of his abs, and when he caught me looking, he smirked.

My gaze darted away. Wells always liked to tease me and probably did that on purpose. Obviously I'd look, because he put them in front of me.

Feeling dumb, I put my head down but looked up when Thatcher nudged Wells. Wells shot up a fist, like he would hit my brother, but he didn't. That was just a part of their dynamic.

Chuckling, Thatcher shook his head at Wells before facing me. My brother looked a lot like our dad and was a similar size as well. Thatcher frowned. "What the hell is wrong with you? You did kind of look weird in the face when I let you in the house earlier."

I did? In what way?

Gosh.

My face shot up a million degrees. I didn't know what

Thatcher meant. And suddenly, the dining room was filled with half the house. The dining and living rooms were connected, and my best friend Noa Sloane-Mallick—Sloane, to me—and her boyfriend, Dorian Prinze, entered the living room.

Sloane and Dorian had been on the couch watching TV with Ares Mallick and his fiancée, Fawn Greenfield, only seconds ago. Ares was also Sloane's twin brother.

"Leave her alone, you ass," Sloane said, her lips turned down. She was always on my team, and we'd been best friends since high school. She was also gorgeous, with dark hair and a natural tan, and was easily a foot taller than me. Most people were taller than me, but I never felt small around Sloane. She always lifted me up and bolstered my confidence with hers.

Thatcher looked like he might say something back to Sloane. She never stepped down from anyone, even though my brother and his friends could be crazy intimating. Hands on her hips, Sloane looked ready to take whatever my brother shot back at her, but then Dorian got between them.

He was kind of the leader of my brother's friend group. A tall blond, Dorian shot Thatcher a look like he dared my brother to say something to Sloane. Dorian and Sloane had been dating for forever, and we all knew they'd get married someday.

Thatcher put his hands up in front of Dorian. They were both huge football players, and, though my brother was also bigger than Dorian, he respected him. Thatcher laughed. "Chill out, man," he said before facing Sloane. "And my sister did look weird earlier. Like all spacey-eyed."

Oh my God.

I had no idea I'd looked that way, but I also knew I hadn't been completely paying attention during my study session with Wells.

I'd been thinking about that kiss.

I felt sick after I kissed Bru. He called me beautiful but obviously hadn't meant what I thought he meant.

"Bow, I'm so sorry."

He'd actually apologized to me, and I probably looked so pathetic. I *felt* pathetic.

My fingers curling on Wells's book, I sat there with it in my hands. My tutoring session with Wells had been surprisingly easy, considering the circumstances in which we were working together. I wasn't Wells's favorite person, and definitely not after I basically manipulated a situation to get him to do what I wanted.

"What would make you think I'd ever help you?"

I tried to ignore his voice in my head. He always had a way of making me feel like the worst piece of scum on the planet, and I knew he believed that I was. He thought I was lower than scum, probably.

I caught Wells's eyes on me after what Thatcher said, like he was trying to analyze me and figure me out. He was so good at that, *great* at that.

Wells had his thick arms crossed in his tight, white tee. I refused to look at how the fit hugged his biceps and made him look more intimidating than he already did. He was probably doing that on purpose, too. He liked making me uncomfortable. He liked reminding me of the power he had over me and my life, but he didn't have to do that.

I was well aware of it on my own.

"I need a break," he mumbled before dropping his arms from across his chest. I may have been distracted tonight, but I was also aware he'd taken a lot of breaks during our session. Wells pushed back his dyed locks. "I'm going outside to smoke."

I cringed. It was like he couldn't stand being around me more than fifteen minutes before he went off to smoke weed. Like it was all he could do to stomach being around me.

My stomach tossed, tightened. I didn't want to work with Wells either. He was so mean to me, but I got it.

I got it.

There was a history there, and it made me just as sick as what I was doing now with this whole blackmailing-him-into-letting-me-tutor-him thing. I was sure Wells thought I was an excellent manipulator, and I hated that I was proving him right.

Wells grabbed his Pembroke Football hoodie off his chair before exiting the room, and, once he had, Sloane shook her head.

"How is he being toward you?" she asked, taking his seat. Dorian and Thatcher headed back into the living room and plopped on the couch across from Ares and Fawn. It looked like they were all watching a Japanese anime.

"Not bad," I said, watching their small group. Ares and Fawn were hugged up on the couch watching TV, and Dorian would be too if Sloane was over there. If Thatcher's girlfriend, Aspen, was in town, they probably wouldn't even be in the room at all. They didn't see each other a lot since Aspen was on tour. She was a professional cellist, so, when she was in town, they basically took every opportunity they could to be together alone.

My brother and his friend group were my whole world, which was a big reason I lived in a dorm by myself. I also didn't have a choice, since no one would room with me. Sloane would have of course, but she and Fawn were with the guys all the time. I probably deserved to be alone anyway.

"I have no idea why you're doing him a favor," Sloane said.

I just smiled at Sloane. She sounded so much like her brother Bru. He wasn't her biological brother, but they were still so similar, kind. I hugged my arms. "He's not that bad."

"You're being nice, little rabbit," she said. She called me little rabbit because I always talked and moved a mile a minute. I blamed it on my ADHD and always loved that I had a friend to give me a nickname. Sloane wasn't scared of Wells, and, even if she found out about my history with him, I knew she'd still be my friend. Even if I probably didn't deserve it.

I hadn't gone out of my way to talk about my past with Sloane. We became friends in high school, but that was after everything happened with Wells. It was something none of us involved liked talking about.

It was something I didn't like talking about.

Maybe a part of me was as terrible as Wells believed I was. I was selfish when it came to Sloane. I wanted her friendship. *I wanted a friend*, and, even though I knew that wouldn't change if the past came out, she may look at me differently.

Sloane hugged me. "I swear you're just too much of a sweetheart for your own good."

But I wasn't though, not really.

I eased my arms away from her, knowing I was in this situation with Wells because of something else I'd done. Maybe I was just as bad as he believed, evil and manipulative. I bit my lip. "Where's your brother?"

I obviously meant Bru since Ares was in the other room and another wave of shame hit me that I hadn't told her about what happened with him in his car. I doubted Sloane would care I kissed her brother. She wasn't like that. But I didn't tell her what happened because I was embarrassed.

I had a feeling Bru hadn't told Sloane what happened either, but that didn't surprise me. Bru was such a good guy, and he saw how embarrassed I was in the car.

I thought I was going to be sick all over again. Especially when the front door opened, and Bru entered the room. He consumed it, since he was so big and all-encompassing.

He was also gorgeous.

I always found my best friend's brother attractive. Truth be told, *all* of my brother's best friends were good looking, but I grew up with them, so that basically made them brothers. *Most* of them were like brothers. The ones that didn't hate me.

Bru wasn't like a brother, and I certainly noticed how much space he took up in the room. I also noticed how low his jeans hung and how well they fit his, quite frankly, tree trunk–sized thighs. He was nearly as large as my brother, Thatcher, but had a golden retriever energy about him that was only emphasized by his large brown eyes and tousled dark hair.

He hugged Sloane right away. He had a messenger bag on his arm and slid it to the floor to fully hug his sis.

"Speaking of," Sloane stated, hugging her brother real tight back. They looked nothing alike. Bru was white, and Sloane was a mixture of races. Even though they weren't biological siblings, they were raised together.

Sloane dropped an arm around Bru. She wasn't as tall as him, but definitely had height on her. She was one of the tallest girls I'd ever known personally. She grinned. "And excellent timing. We were just talking about you."

Having been acknowledged, I popped up, but that was hard considering how I completely embarrassed myself in Bru's car.

You idiot.

I couldn't believe I kissed him, but I'd been vulnerable, going through stuff...

That wasn't an excuse, but after Bru came away from the hug, he smiled at me. He gave me his warm, *kind* smile when *I* hadn't been kind. I'd been stupid and I threw myself at someone who'd always been nice to me. Bru was the only one of my brother's friends who hung out with me, and, whenever we were together, I knew it was because he actually wanted to be. He genuinely liked spending time with me.

Perhaps that was why I gave in to the delusion that anyone like Bru could actually be into me. I took his kindness for something else.

He lifted a hand. "Hey, Bow."

I sat there trying not to be weird because Sloane was here, and she always knew when something was wrong with me. I waved back. "Hey."

"You guys were talking about me?" he continued, and it was so nice because he completely switched his attention to Sloane. He didn't put any pressure on me after what happened by staring awkwardly at me, not like I was at him.

Sloane nodded. "Yeah. Bow just asked where you were and then you came in."

"Ah," he said, keeping his focus on her. It truly made me hate myself for making things so awkward between us, kissing him…

"And it's good you just came in. Dorian and I were talking earlier about getting pizza," Sloane continued. "You guys want to come?"

Sloane had asked Bru and me both, and I said yes after he did. It would be weird if I didn't go. Whenever our friend group went out, we all did.

"Brilliant," Sloane said, squeezing Bru's arm, then mine when she passed me. She called to Dorian and the others about pizza, and they all gave their version of *hell yeah*. The loudest had been my brother, who could easily eat his way through a pizza house.

"I'll text Wells what we're doing," Dorian said as he reentered the room. He had his phone in his hand and dropped his arm around Sloane. Dorian wanted to grab a jacket, so Sloane went with him. Thatcher headed to his room to change, and that wasn't surprising since he spent more time in the mirror back home than I did when we were growing up. Ares and Fawn decided to head out and wait in Ares's truck, so that left Bru and me.

It *awkwardly* left Bru and me.

"Um, I gotta clean up my stuff." My study session with Wells was obviously over.

I was very aware I was under Bru's gaze and that we were now alone together for the first time since I got stupid and kissed him. I gathered my things up in quick time. My declaration was also giving Bru an excuse to leave me to my misery, but he didn't for some reason.

"Bow." He placed a hand on mine, and his rough touch burned into my skin. It should have burned because of embarrassment, but that wasn't the reason. I mean, I was embarrassed being around him, but him taking my hand and raising it up elevated my heart rate for different reasons. The contact of our hands coursed lava through my digits and that molten heat chased up my entire body and into my chest, my breasts…

I had to be delulu, and I knew I was, because I didn't get a whole lot of physical attention from boys. I didn't get any at all, really. I shook my head, unable to meet his eyes. "Bru, you don't have to."

I knew he was going to address what happened. It was a mistake. It was *my* mistake.

I bit my lip. "I'm sorry I kissed you."

It ruined everything and made things awkward now.

I had definitely been going through things at the time of the kiss. I was *still* going through those same things and absolutely none of them had anything to do with him.

I started to slide my hand out of Bru's, but he didn't let me. I released a harsh breath. "Bru—"

"I'm not."

I blinked.

"I mean, I should be," he continued, scanning my hand. He flipped it over. "You're Thatch's little sister and what happened shouldn't have been okay. But…"

His rough digits dragged down my palm achingly slow. His fingers only skimmed my flesh, but it felt like he was touching me all over.

I opened my mouth to say his name, but I couldn't say

anything. I was one hundred percent trying to focus on breathing.

"I should be sorry," he said, closing my hand. He gave it back to me, and when he did, he took a step back. His eyes narrowed. "I shouldn't have liked it, Bow."

I shouldn't have liked it.

It took me a second to mull over what he said. I didn't think I heard him right.

"You liked it?" I didn't know what to say. This wasn't real, but suddenly, Bruno Sloane-Mallick was inches away from me. He was breathing his own harsh air into the room, and I didn't know what was happening.

He touched my chin. "I shouldn't have liked it, Bow. For a lot of reasons," he said. He closed his eyes. "I think there's someone else."

Of course there was.

Of course.

There was no way a guy like him, someone so kind and wonderful, was actually available. I glanced away, but he brought me back. He pinched my chin. "I'm fucked in the head right now, and it wouldn't be fair to you. That, and you are Thatcher's little sister."

It was like the waves of reality crashed into me. I hung on to that last part more than what he said before. There was always something. If I wasn't evil, there was something else that made me not worth it. I wasn't worthy.

I was nothing.

I stepped back and the door opened yet again. This time it was the smell of sea breeze and ocean waves that entered the room.

I used to love the way Wells Ambrose smelled.

I used to love Wells Ambrose.

I'd had a little kid crush. But that was before he hated me.

Wells had his hoodie on, his hands in his jeans pockets. A smoky smell lingered in the background of his clean scent, but not in a bad way, never in a bad way. His head cocked at Bru. "What's going on?"

He glanced over at me next, and I guess it did look kind of weird. Bru and I were just staring at each other. I'd put distance between us, but we still looked like we were having some kind of intense conversation.

I mumbled nothing before wrestling around with the study materials again. I jammed my stuff into my book bag, and, when I glanced up, Wells and Bru were staring at each other. Wells had his eyes narrowed, and Bru did too.

Bru's eyes narrowed harder.

"Yeah, it's nothing," Bru said before leaving the room. He mentioned something about heading downstairs to wait in the truck with Ares and Fawn, and, though I said something similar about our conversation meaning nothing, it felt different when Bru said it, harsher.

My insides tightening, I swallowed, but I was forced to push everything away when my phone buzzed.

Unknown: Stop ignoring me.

Unknown: Come back to me.

"You high in demand or something, Squeak? I find that hard to believe since you barely have any friends."

I glanced up to find green eyes studying me, analyzing me. There was no way Wells saw my text from across the table. He was just being mean.

His head cocked, his stark blond hair passing over his eyes. Wells was just as beautiful as Bru, but in different ways, and I hated that he lost who he was. He became someone else because of me. He became darker and completely different than who he used to be when we were growing up. There had been a reason I loved him.

I said nothing to him, and, apparently bored with me, he started to leave the room. I took a step toward him. "Can we have our next tutoring session on the quad tomorrow around two o'clock? The forecast says it will be warm enough to study outside." The Midwest had weird weather like that. One day it was scorching hot and the next blistering cold. Especially when seasons changed from winter to spring. I gnawed my lip. "The quad's out in the open and people will be able to see us there."

He would be able to see us.

My phone buzzed again, but I ignored it as Wells stepped up to me. He towered over me and looked at me like I was the worst person in the world.

He wasn't far off.

I'd never be able to take back what I did to him, and I knew that as he analyzed me as if I was a piece of crap. Like I was worthless. His nostrils flared. "I'll meet you. But remember, I'm playing your game because I need you. But, like I said in the library, no amount of looking buddy buddy *will ever* make me forget what you did, Squeak. It won't because I know you, Squeak. I *see* you."

He did see me, and in the next moment…

He looked right through me.

I couldn't remember the last time Wells saw me as a person. I may have been Thatcher's little sister to Bru and a great friend to his sister, Sloane, but, to the rest of the world, I was the girl who screwed Wells Ambrose over.

I was the one who killed a girl.

CHAPTER
SEVEN

"God, Wells has no business being that fine," my friend Leigh said.

I glanced up from my lounger, picking at the plastic beneath me. I sat cross-legged, and it didn't take me long to spot Wells from across the pool. He twirled a whistle around his finger in a pair of red swim trunks, his abs flashing in the summer sun, and I immediately gazed away.

"Summer's definitely been treating him right," Leigh continued beside me, giggling. She was always talking about how hot Wells was. Him and my brother, Thatcher, which was complete ick. Thatcher wasn't lifeguarding today thank God, and, really, none of my brother's friends were spared from, well, *my* friends. My brother had three best friends, Wells, Ares, and Dorian, and my friends talking about them got worse since I started high school.

I supposed the guys had developed.

My brother and his friends didn't have baby faces anymore like me, and Wells certainly didn't. He had a jawline that didn't look like a boy anymore. It was chiseled, just like his abs, and was golden just like the rest of him. He was even getting facial hair now like Thatcher, but he shaved it. I caught him once.

My nail continued to pick at the lounger, noticing Wells grinning at a girl in the pool. He hunkered down to her, her arms on the side of the pool. She kicked her tanned legs and had way bigger boobs than me in her bikini top. I had no boobs. Not really. Not yet.

Shifting, I cut off my stare when Jasmine tapped my shoulder. She was on the other side of me in her own lounger.

"Don't talk to Bow about Legacy," she said, referring to what basically everyone called my brother and his friends since coming to high school. Our families had all been going to Windsor Preparatory Academy, my school, for a long time, and people gave Thatcher and the other guys that label. We were the next generation, and I guess technically I was Legacy too. Jasmine laughed. "It's like she has blinders to the fact that her brother's friends are hot."

I grimaced, my brother's friends like brothers to me. We'd all known each other since we were in diapers, and she was right that I didn't see them that way.

Mostly.

Chewing my lip, I tried not to stare at Wells, who was life-guarding today. My brother and his friends all did that summer, but only Wells was out here today.

He smiled at me.

It was subtle, but the wink he gave in my direction wasn't. It made my stomach spasm and flutter, and I started to lift my hand and wave, but the girl in front of him splashed him. She sent a strong current of water in his face, and Wells laughed.

He was always laughing.

The water completely drenched him, but all he did was splash her back. He then rubbed her head like a puppy, which was cute and flirty. He was always flirting. He was easy to flirt with. He was so nice.

I hugged my legs, studying him and that girl. He'd forgotten about me now, but he didn't usually. Out of all my brother's friends, he always made sure to include me in things. He even stood up for me when the others treated me like a little kid sometimes. He never babied me or treated me like one.

My butterflies left as Wells sat on the side of the pool. He put a leg up, his muscled arm on it. He had lots of muscles since he and the other guys played football for Windsor Prep. The girl continued to kick her legs in front of him, clearly flirting. Wells had flirted with a boy earlier today. He was always flirting because people flirted with him, but he typically didn't for this long.

My cheek touched my knees, my stomach tight. My feet touched the wet concrete. "I'm going in."

I did before my friends said anything, rushing. I didn't plan on getting wet today since Wells was lifeguarding. I didn't know why, but I didn't care about my hair or anything else when I got in the pool.

I ended up sinking.

I could swim just fine, but I let myself fall, my eyes closed. I let my arms extend in the water. I didn't want to open my eyes. I just wanted my stomach to not be so tight.

It was so tight.

A rush hit me when a hard body slammed into me, held me. Firm arms came around me, and the next thing I knew, air filled my lungs.

Wells.

He'd brought me to the surface and was yelling something. People were screaming too, girls, guys. Two of the girls sounded like Jasmine and Leigh, but it was like my brain turned off. Like I couldn't hear them anymore because the only thing I was aware of was Wells's voice.

"Bow," he said, swimming so hard with me in his arms. His arms felt good, warm. "Bow, hang on."

He cradled me like a small child, and my eyes closed. I felt drunk, euphoric. He ended up carrying me out of the pool in his arms, my legs dangling, and I held on to him like a bear cub.

He felt *so* warm.

"Everyone get out of the way!" Wells said, and he laid me flat on the wet concrete. He hovered over me, and I saw that right before his mouth touched mine.

Oh, God.

My eyes closed again, air from his mouth breathing into mine. I'd never touched my mouth to a boy's, but it didn't feel icky. Not like it would with Ares or Dorian.

No, this didn't feel icky.

Wells's breath was warm, and he tasted like syrup. He was always eating sweets, and he gave me sweets too. Buttercups and fruit chews.

"Bow?"

My eyes shot open. Wells's green eyes were on me. He had eyes like green quartz or jade. He frowned. "Bow, are you not..."

He didn't finish his sentence, scanning me. He'd clearly thought I wasn't breathing, but that wasn't the case. I could breathe just fine. Kinda.

It was hard when his mouth touched mine, and, seeing I was breathing, Wells sat back. He lifted my head. "Are you okay? You were at the bottom of the pool and you weren't moving."

He thought I'd been drowning.

"I'm... I'm fine. I..." It was still hard to breathe, my mouth still warm from his, tingling. I fought touching it. "I wasn't drowning. I was just..."

I didn't know what I'd been doing underwater. I just knew I didn't like seeing him with that girl, and I was shutting off my system to all of it. Like being in one of those salt tanks where you couldn't hear anything or feel anything.

"You *weren't* drowning." His blond hair dripped water droplets on me. He dyed his hair, but I always liked it brown. He forced all that electric blond back. "Why would you do that? Why would you—"

Another scream came and splashing. It wasn't Jasmine or Leigh who were beside me with red faces and dropped jaws. They'd watched the whole thing, as well as what seemed like everyone at the pool. There was a healthy crowd around Wells and me, and no one was watching the other side of the pool.

Because if we had…

The screaming, the flailing ceased when a girl disappeared beneath the water. It was the girl Wells had been talking to, and, without another thought, he left me. He ran, diving back into the pool, and people around me started to scream.

"Oh my God, she's drowning!"

"Oh my God…"

"Wells, get her!"

People were freaking out, panicking, and it was like I was watching it from a bird's-eye view. I'd left my body. I *froze* when people left me and went to the other side of the pool. When they watched Wells drag a limp girl's body out of the water…

When they watched him try to resuscitate her….

A similar crowd formed but this time around Wells and the girl. I was there too. Though, I didn't remember how I got there. I just knew I was standing there, wet and helpless, as I watched my older brother's best friend legitimately try to save a girl's life. She lay there unmoving on the concrete just like I'd been. I didn't know how long I watched Wells try to breathe life into her. I didn't think any of us did.

But I think we all knew when he ultimately stopped.

CHAPTER
EIGHT

Me: Consider our deal officially off, Squeak.

Me: I've decided I'm making other arrangements for a tutor.

Me: I think you know why.

Me: Also, don't ever try to blackmail me again.

Me: You'll severely regret it if you do.

My thumb hovered over my last text to Bow.

I deleted it.

I didn't know why. That shit would have been more than fucking valid. I waited over an hour in the quad for her to show up for our tutoring session, and she didn't.

Still waiting there now, I gazed around, my hands in my hoodie's pocket. It was warmer today in Queenstown Village, but it was still colder than shit. Others were out on the quad studying in jackets despite that, and I would have spotted Thatch's little sister anywhere on the quad. She was tiny, stood out.

Needing to get high, I decided to text Thatcher to see if he wanted to go to a party tonight. He probably wouldn't get high himself. Thatcher and his hard partying days were pretty much over since he got a girlfriend. A part of me was happy about that though. He used to party harder than me before he met Aspen.

Thatcher: Can't. I have to study, and I'm video chatting with Aspen after.

Thatcher had gotten way more responsible since he found his girl. No one deserved what he had with Aspen more than him. Thatcher had a pretty rough go of it before she came around. She completed him, made him happy, and I loved that for him.

Thatcher: You should see if some of the other guys want to go though.

I probably wouldn't. Ares and Dorian rarely came out since they found their own girls. That left Bru, and that shit wasn't happening.

I hadn't heard from Bru since I'd last seen him, and that wasn't much of a conversation at all. Actually, it *wasn't* one. He'd given me a death stare, and Squeak had been between us.

That moment had been weird to walk in on. Like they'd been having some intense conversation, but something I knew about Squeak was that she had a way of getting under a dude's skin. For all I knew, she was pulling her little manipulative shit with Bru, but that (like him) was none of my business.

Nah, it was none of my business.

Bru had once again crossed a line with me. We were good friends, and he was ruining that shit.

I was ruining that shit.

Really needing to get high, I decided to go party myself later that night. I always knew what was going on around campus. I got what felt like a million texts a day from people asking me to appear at their parties or events. They knew if people spotted me, shit would pop off. Their parties would be the it places to be, so my DMs were constantly flooded with requests. Especially since I was basically the only one in my friend group who really partied anymore. My friends all got boring once they were tied down.

It made shit get lonely. I used to have Bru to hang out with.

I needed to fuck.

I did *badly*, and the moment I crossed the threshold of the house I decided to appear at, I grabbed the first girl I saw. She came willingly with me, and even offered me a blunt.

I lit it as she felt me up through my jeans. We were in some bedroom in the house now, but, when she tried to kiss me, I forced her in the direction of my cock. I rarely kissed, and when I did, it was generally guys. I didn't know why.

Trying to will my high to come faster, I zoned out. I took another hit on the blunt while the girl kissed me through my jeans. Growling, I yanked her ponytail back. "Pull me out."

The bitch was too busy playing around.

The unzipping of my jeans hit the air when she finally got done screwing around. I just wanted her hands, her mouth. She reached in, and as soon as her clammy (cold) hands touched me, I sucked in a breath.

Fuck.

It was like I got the ick the moment her hand wrapped around me. She opened her mouth to take me in, but before she could, I shoved her away.

She fell to the floor with a thud, and her eyes flashed wide. It was the first time I noticed she was a redhead. Cool. She shook her head. "What's wrong?"

Ignoring her, I put myself back in my pants. "I changed my mind."

I didn't know why, and I wasn't even hard when I opened the door. It was like what happened in my bedroom with that guy, and really, every time I tried to fuck since then.

Every time I tried to fuck, I couldn't get hard without a lot of effort.

Not every *time.*

I hadn't even had sex the last time I got it up, and I shook my head in an effort to get the thoughts of *why* out. What happened in the shower with Bru had plagued me since it happened, and I didn't want invasive shit like that playing around in my head.

I needed to get drunk.

I was doing what I usually did when I wasn't trying to deal with something. I got high. I got drunk and partied/fucked my way out of my feelings. There were full days if not weeks of high school I didn't remember when I went on a bender. Being stoned against one or several warm bodies was an easy way not to remember shit. It was an easy way to block out the screams of someone who needed me at the pool while I paid attention to another. While I looked for blue eyes and the feeling it felt not to see them for once. I was always aware of those eyes, so when I didn't see them…

"I guess I'm not surprised to see you here."

I pushed smoke through my nose, closing my brain off to more shitty thoughts, memories. Bru couldn't have come at a better time, his voice.

The head fuck got worse when I turned around and looked at him though. When I studied how his jeans hung low, and the visible bulge he had through the dark denim. Dude wasn't even hard I bet. He was just *big,* and I knew that from personal experience.

I wet my lips. It was almost distracting how his university sweater stretched across his broad chest and hugged his biceps. Dude literally was built like Superman, and I was so fucking into Superman. Especially the last couple of castings.

The thing was, I didn't even know Bru was into dudes before something happened between us. If I knew that, I would have come at things differently when it came to our friendship.

Nothing happened between us.

It didn't as far as I was concerned, and Bru smirked when he caught me checking him out, sizing him up. It made me want to sock his motherfucking face in. I frowned. "What are you doing here?"

He never partied before we started partying together. He was too busy in school. He was like Squeak in that regard.

Why the fuck you thinking about her?

I took a swig of the beer in my hand as my former friend walked up on me. Former, because he was really messing with that friendship now.

He was checking me out too.

Bru did a visible once-over on me. His dark eyes definitely lingered over the fit of my Pembroke Football hoodie and where my low jeans sat as well. His attention rested on my cock, and it twitched. A fucking *semi* followed, and it was effortless.

Fucking hell.

I didn't like that shit. I didn't like that I *thought about shit* the moment Bruno's scent was in my nose. The first time we kissed, I thought it'd been an accident. It wasn't the first time a seemly straight dude went to experiment when we were fucking a chick together. I seemed to have that effect on people, so it happened a time or two. Dudes got caught up in the thrill of a threesome, but I never had any desire to be anyone's gay awakening. That shit had happened too, and, with Bru, I thought us brushing lips during a threesome had been an accident. I hoped it was because we were friends, and I didn't think either one of us wanted to mess any of that up.

But then more happened.

My best friend and I deep dived into something we had no business venturing into. I may have been gay, but I only ever saw my friends as brothers. Ares, Dorian, and Thatcher were my brothers, but I wasn't feeling like that with Bru. It wasn't like that with Bru *at all*, and each time shit went down between us, I knew this wasn't some experiment or gay awakening for him. Bru knew how to touch. He knew how *to suck.*

And he also knew how to submit.

Like he knew I was thinking about all that, he smirked again, and that shit heated my blood. What I wouldn't give to take him into a room and teach his ass a lesson.

I had before.

"I guess the same thing as you," he said, answering my previous question. My eyes narrowed, and he bumped a laugh from his Superman chest before taking a drink. I knew this game he was playing. Shit, I taught him how to play it. We fucked a lot of girls together before anything happened between us.

Bru lowered his beer. "How'd your tutoring session go with Bow? Sloane mentioned you guys were meeting today. Bow told her."

And for some reason he thought that was his business.

I shook my head. "I wouldn't know since she didn't show up today."

That really surprised me too. Her motivations had been clear. She was using me, and though that may surprise someone else, it didn't me. That was that girl's MO. She was drama, and she was also selfish.

Bru's cocky expression wiped away. He gazed down at his beer, sloshing it around.

I tipped mine at him. "What's your deal?"

I knew Bow had him fooled too, like she was innocent, flawless. She may fool everyone else with her sweet-little-girl act, but she didn't me.

She never would.

I had to live every day with that shit that happened in high school. I had to see a girl drown and therapy couldn't even help relieve those images in my head. A family lost a daughter that summer, and I died that day too. I had to in order to cope and freaking function every day.

Bru's attention turned to me about the same time the bottle went tight in my hand. I thought I'd crush it in my grip, but his focus on me distracted me. He shook his head. "I wish you'd lay off her, and honestly, I have no idea why she's helping you." He took another drink, his swallow hard. "You're an asshole."

That last bit was under his breath but not enough that he didn't want me to hear it. I approached him, and the bottle left his lips. I put a finger in his chest. "You don't know shit about that girl, and you definitely don't know shit *about me* and that girl."

He didn't, and though I put it in my past, daily, it kept cropping up. It had last night, actually. I had another fucking dream about it, about how I was too late. About *how I failed* and also something else I'd never talk about.

I refused to talk about the itch in the back of my mind that day. It was a recurring thought I had. A feeling hit me that day when I found out that girl who drowned wasn't Thatcher's sister. It was a deep feeling, a hard pulse in my chest, and, though it should have been about Thatcher, it wasn't. I wouldn't talk *or think* about that feeling I had that fucked-up summer, that relief.

If I did, it'd make me as fucked up as Bow Reed.

My finger was making an attempt to drill a hole in Bru's chest. I stabbed into the fucker hard, but for some reason, that didn't faze him. His lips turned down. "Wells?"

Wells.

"Did something happen? Between you and Bow, I mean," he asked, suddenly scanning my eyes, and I hated that shit, his concern. Dude liked to fuck with me, but he also cared about me. The feeling was mutual, as much as I hated to admit it. He touched my arm. "Wells?"

If this dude didn't stop saying my name like that...

I moved my arm out of his hand. "I'm getting another beer."

Mine was still pretty full, but I had a feeling I'd need another, maybe several.

"Wells?"

By the time Bru called after me, my back was already turned. I shot through the house toward the kitchen where the beers were, but a scream sounded. It made me pivot, and I instantly became aware of the people gathering on the stairwell to the next level of the house. People were clustering like a motherfucker on it and damn near trampling each other.

"Rainbow Reed's going to jump!" one of them said, and my eyes flashed.

Bru's did too.

I didn't know how we found each other. We were on opposite sides of the room, but our eyes managed to find each other in that moment. Right away, Bru dashed toward the stairwell like the Superman fucker he was, but I was The Flash I think.

How else would I have beat him there?

CHAPTER
NINE

Bru

I'd never seen Wells in such a way…

He was shoving people over the banisters.

Wells was literally tossing people off the stairwell, and I was helping him. Someone mentioned Bow. She was jumping off something?

That didn't make sense.

It didn't, and, what also didn't make sense was Wells's reaction. He seemed to be blind as he plowed through people. I supposed this *was* Thatcher's sister, and all of us protected her. Wells did too, whether he liked it or not. He would on Thatcher's behalf, so I guess that made sense.

Wells grabbed a dude. "Get the fuck out of the way or I'll literally end you." Wells tossed the guy before growling to the crowd. "That goes the same for all of you motherfuckers. Get. Out. Of. The. *Way!*"

The response was immediate. People started flooding off the stairwell and those who were going too slow both Wells *and* I handled. We were a tag team, and soon, I found myself as his wingman. I was clearing people out of the way so he could go faster. We played football together in high school, so I knew he was quicker than me. He could get to her sooner, faster…

I didn't know what was going on, but so much fear hit me. Whoever yelled Bow was jumping off something had to have been mistaken.

"Where's Bow Reed?" Wells asked a girl at the top of the stairs, and she pointed ahead. The hall was still packed with people trying to get to wherever the alleged action was taking place but, with one bark from Wells, they cleared again. The whole hallway of partiers literally parted, and, when people started to follow us, I made my own threats. I didn't know what was going on up ahead, but no one else needed to be privy to it.

Especially if it involved Bow.

My last conversation with her played over in my head. I hadn't wanted to leave her. I only wanted to hold her, *kiss her,* and that didn't make sense for many reasons. I was still trying to figure out this shit with Wells, and there was still the fact that Bow was Thatcher's little sister.

None of that seemed to matter in the moment when I talked to her. I forgot about everything else, but I also rejected her. I did because I was fucked up, and she didn't deserve that.

No one was ahead of Wells and me anymore, or behind us. Between the two of us, we got the job of a cleared path done. Folks had been attempting to get into a room that appeared to be locked.

"She's in there. On the balcony," someone said, pointing toward the door. It was a girl with flushed cheeks. I didn't know if that was from panic or booze. She flailed. "People can see her from the street."

What. The. Fuck.

Again, Wells and I made eye contact but only briefly before we both kicked in the door. It was quick, easy. The door shot open with a snap, and, right away, people started to flood inside with us.

"Stay back, or you'll regret it," I gritted out. I wasn't typically a violent person, but I had my moments. I could definitely be fucking violent, and I was sure everyone on this campus knew that. Everyone knew everything about my friends and me, and I had a rep. I could hurt someone.

And I would.

The threats worked when people stayed back, and I realized right away that I was by myself. Wells was already inside the room. It was dark in there, and he stood frozen at the entryway. He stared off toward the sliding door of a balcony. The door was opened, and we both appeared to be in a bedroom in the house.

I froze too, staring in the direction of the balcony. It was Bow out there.

She was dancing.

Her small feet glided along the thin banister of the balcony. It was one of those wooden ones connected to the house, and she was out there in her jacket and bare feet, her heels kicked off to the floor of the balcony.

I couldn't breathe, noticing a drink in her hand. Bow *didn't* drink, and she was dancing on that banister with her eyes closed. There also wasn't any music, like she was moving to her own internal beat.

Wells was already moving. He did so slowly, carefully, and I did the same after closing the door from the prying eyes I knew were behind us.

What is she doing?

Wells and I moved as one toward her, and that wasn't the first time we operated together. I didn't want to think about that, *our history* right now because, currently, our best friend's little sister was out on a balcony. She was out there *dancing* barely even a day after I rejected her.

I swallowed. "Bow?"

I made it to her first, Wells in the back of my mind. I couldn't focus on him right now, and that went double when Bow whipped around so fast that she nearly stumbled.

I rushed toward her. I did so to catch her, but I barely made two steps before her hand shot up.

"No," she said, her mouth turned down, sad. She shook her head. "No, Bru."

No.

I didn't know what to say. I didn't know what *to do* and could only watch when Bow took the beer she had to her lips. She was too young to drink, and, though that had never stopped any of my friends in the past, Bow Reed was a rule follower. She was a good girl who never got into rowdy shit.

Her cheeks shot up in color, the red reaching to her hairline. She had her hair up in one of her tight buns but some of her curls had escaped. They swept across her eyes but also across her flushed lips. Her throat moved. "I don't want you here."

She didn't... want me.

My chest did something I didn't expect. It caved, hollowed out, and I'd felt something similar before. It was the way I felt after I expressed my feelings to someone else. That someone else was somewhere in the room but Bow had obviously not seen him yet. Her focus was on me, but only briefly before she stole another swig of her beer.

I couldn't look for Wells. I was too focused on Bow. I could imagine he was doing the same thing as me right now. I couldn't move in that moment, scared to. My mouth parted. "Bow—"

"And nobody wants me," she said, a crowd forming on

the street below her, though she didn't appear to notice. I could see them in the distance behind her. They were calling out, and some had their cellphones out.

Bow wiped under her eyes. There was a shine to them, tears. She sniffed. "No one likes me, and I guess I don't blame them. I suck."

I had no idea what she was talking about, and though it did sting, her telling me not to come closer, I would if it kept her safe. I put my hands up. "I'll stay put. I just need you to come down."

"No, Bruno," she said, wincing. Her voice actually screeched and that reminded me of what Wells called her. I always thought that was so cruel. Her voice was high, but it wasn't squeaky. "You shouldn't want to be around me either. I don't deserve it."

Deserve it?

Her lips quivered. "No one likes me, and I don't blame them. It still hurts, though." She rubbed her chest like there was pain there, an ache. "No one wanted to be around me tonight when I came to this party. No one likes me."

She kept saying that, but that wasn't true. She had my sister, Sloane, and the rest of our friend group. She *had me*, but, before I could emphasize that, Wells stepped forward.

He lifted a hand. "Bow."

Right away, she pivoted in Wells's direction, and she went so fast, too fast. She even backed up on that thin ledge and absolute terror twisted Wells's expression.

I never saw Wells scared. The guys in our friend group were pumped to shit with so much testosterone and rarely shed emotion. They didn't give it freely, but, in that moment, Wells didn't hold back how he felt seeing Bow get closer to that ledge. I saw it all over his face.

The expression had to match mine, the horror, the fear. Bow obviously hadn't known Wells came with me. More of that sadness touched her pretty face upon seeing Wells there. The sadness nearly turned to anguish. She winced. "Archer?"

Archer?

I watched Wells's expression change yet again. Something flashed across his face, but then he went stoic. His features went incredibly hard, and I had seen that before. He used that shit with me all the time. He liked to pretend he didn't feel anything. But he did. I'd seen it. I'd felt it.

His jaw moved. "Yeah, it's me."

I had no idea what was going on here, but his acknowledgement of her name for him caused her to waver on the ledge again. I saw that *something* flash on Wells's chiseled features again, and my heart felt too big for my chest with its rapid beat. I physically squeezed my fists not to run, grab. If I spooked her, and she fell…

That same conflict Wells was obviously feeling as well, because his fists also tightened. It was like he was doing everything he could to stay in place. He wet his lips. "It is me, and I need you to come down from there," he said, then eyed me. "I need you to let the kid help you."

I was closer.

All my friends called me the kid. It was a nickname my brother, Ares, gave me, but Wells stopped acknowledging me at all when things started happening between us.

He stopped being my friend.

A lot had changed between us recently, but, when it counted, we had each other's backs, and the asshole and I needed each other right now. We needed to get Bow down, and she apparently needed Wells's words.

I knew that because she let me help her off the edge.

Bow allowed me to come closer, nodding at me, and I didn't hesitate before approaching and taking her hand. Bow squatted in her pleated skirt and tights, and I slid my arms beneath her. I took her off that ledge damsel-style and didn't return her to the ground. I didn't trust she'd stay there on her own, but, also, I was selfish.

It was Bow's heat, and her remarkable ability to smell like an entire bakery. I brought my best friend's sister close, and, when I passed Wells, I studied him. He didn't say another word before pivoting and leading us all out of the room, then out of the party. I didn't put Bow down, even after we all left.

I guess I couldn't.

CHAPTER
TEN

Bru

My phone was blowing up by the time we got back to the house I shared with my friends. Wells's and Bow's phones were, too.

Our friends had seen the video.

Wells, Bow, and I got the video from completely different sources. Then, the three of us started hearing from our actual friends. I heard from my sister, Sloane, my brother, Ares, and the other guys. Thatcher was furious. The only reason he hadn't come to the party was because I texted him that Wells and I were on our way to Legacy House with Bow.

Everyone was there.

Dorian, Sloane, Ares, and Fawn all sat on the couch. Thatcher was in an easy chair, but he leapt from it the moment Wells, Bow, and I entered the house. It was all I could do to convince Bow to come home with us. She shouldn't be alone right now, and she was achingly quiet in the backseat of my Audi. Wells and I hadn't bothered her, and I wouldn't have let Wells, even if he wanted to give her a hard time. Bow looked miserable and defeated as she stared drearily out the window, her head against the glass.

"The hell were you thinking, Bow?" Thatcher barked at her. The rest of the gang was right behind him, but he'd gotten to the front door first. His face blazed in color. "Have you lost your mind? You could have killed yourself."

"Thatcher, back off." If Sloane hadn't said that, I would have. It wasn't helping the situation, and I was sure Bow already felt like shit. Both physically and emotionally. She wouldn't look at Wells or me in the car.

"I don't want you here..."

Bow's voice played in my head still. She hadn't wanted me there, and I'd be a fool if I didn't think her drunk moment had anything to do with me.

She drank tonight, and she mentioned people not liking her. Had she meant me? She might have. She had to have.

As if she knew my thoughts, Bow finally made eye contact with me. She winced, the contact brief, and I felt like I was going to throw up. This was my fault, and I opened my mouth to say that to the group that was now surrounding her. Our friends (as helpful as they were trying to be) crowded her, and I entered the circle. I got in front of Bow and held a hand out toward our friends. "Actually, guys, what happened tonight was—"

"Completely my fault."

I turned around, and the group's attention drifted away from Bow. *Bow's* attention drifted away from Bow, and she blinked in Wells's direction.

I did too, confused, and not for the first time. Truth be told, Wells Ambrose was more than a head fuck. He was confusing as shit and often sent mixed signals. It was just something I was starting to pick up on about him, but his latest head trip had involved Bow tonight. He'd gotten her to get off that banister. He'd gotten her *to come to me,* and that hadn't made sense.

Wells slid his hands into his pockets, and, though the attention was all on him, he kept his sight on Thatcher. He approached Thatch. "Tonight was on me, bro."

"What do you mean?" Thatcher asked him. He tucked his thick hands under his armpits, confusion lacing his wrinkled brow.

He wasn't the only one confused by what Wells said. Everyone in the room was looking at each other, exchanging glances.

Wells's attention pivoted to Bow, and she blinked again. Wells's jaw moved. "It was my beef with her. I gave her a hard time like I do and took things too far. It was my fault, and I take full responsibility for what she did tonight. She was drinking and partying and wasn't acting like herself."

Silence blanketed the room, and Bow went completely white.

Wells wet his lips. "She was doing that because of our beef, but it's squashed now. It's all over now, right, Squeak?"

Bow's mouth parted in his direction. Blinking once more, she faced the group before redirecting her sight back to Wells. Her face glowed red. "I guess I was dumb."

"Dumb because of me," Wells said. Wells apparently had beef with Bow, and, though I didn't know what that entailed, he'd obviously covered for her just now. At least, it felt like he had.

He'd said he hadn't even seen her today. She hadn't shown up for their tutoring session.

"That beef shit better be over, man. I've told you for years how stupid that shit is," Thatcher said. He stepped over to Bow. He placed a hand on her arm before looking over at Wells. His jaw tightened. "My sister could have died, bro."

Those words played over Wells's face. I once again noticed a flash of something before he schooled his features. Wells nodded. "I know, man. It's over now. I promise."

I was so confused. There were a lot of things going on

here, and I didn't seem to be the only one in the dark. Right away, Sloane made eye contact with me. She was beside Bow and, when she eyed me, I shrugged my shoulders. What was this beef and why, for years, had Thatcher not agreed with it?

Those answers obviously wouldn't be coming to light now. Not in that moment.

Wells said he needed a smoke, so he left, and Sloane advised Bow to get some sleep. It was too late for Bow to go back to her place tonight, but I didn't think any of us would allow her to go there anyway.

"Come on. I'll get you set up in a guest room," Sloane said, putting her arm around Bow. She and Bow left and Fawn, Ares's fiancée, went with the pair. That didn't surprise me since Fawn and Bow were pretty good friends too.

"I'm going to make sure she's good and settled," Thatcher said, then followed. He was immediately going into big-brother mode and any of us would have done the same thing if that'd been our sister. Our friend circle was incredibly close.

The text messages were still flooding in about the events tonight. I received several texts of the same video and each one that came in made me cringe. People wanted to know if I knew what happened, like it was any of their business, and Dorian and Ares were getting the same.

"Looks like phones are going off tonight," Dorian said, pocketing his. He was a huge blond and currently lounged on the couch. He, Ares, and I headed to the living room after everything settled. Dorian shook his head. "It'll be by the grace of God if we can keep our parents from finding out about this shit."

It was probably only a matter of time. I didn't know how word or that video would get back to our parents, but people liked to get into our business. All our parents were powerful people, not only in our small town of Maywood Heights, but on this campus. Word would most likely travel back home, but my friends and I might be able to do damage control.

I wasn't thinking about that right now. I was thinking about Bow and everything that happened tonight. I was thinking about how she looked on that ledge and what I would have done if she'd fallen. I didn't even want to entertain that shit.

"What beef were Wells and Thatcher talking about?" A lot of frickin' stuff happened tonight, but one thing that never made sense was how Wells treated Bow.

Nor why she seemed to have a visceral reaction to him tonight.

She also called him by a name I'd never heard, and both Dorian and Ares exchanged glances after what I said.

My brother, Ares, sat back on the couch. We all called him Wolf because of how crazy he was when he played for Pembroke on the football field, and he was grizzly like one. His hair was wild with shaggy curls, and the guy definitely resembled a werewolf with his five o'clock shadow. He sighed. "It's not really our place."

My brow popped up at the same time Fawn and my sister entered the room.

"I want to know too," Sloane said. She started to take her own seat, but Dorian got an arm around her waist. He made a seat right on his lap for her, and when he asked her how Bow was doing, her lips turned down. She messed with her hands. "She seems okay. She and Thatcher are talking right now."

"We decided to give them a moment," Fawn said. If Wolf was a werewolf, Fawn was his princess with her edgy look and her miraculous ability to tame him. She was getting so many tattoos these days and nearly had full sleeves on both her arms. Wolf didn't have nearly as many as her, but the two complemented each other. Fawn was also one of my really good friends, and we've known each other for a while.

I loved that both my siblings were happy and had found someone. Though, I wouldn't lie, it was hard sometimes being around them. Especially when our parents were equally as happy. It was lonely sometimes.

"Like Wolf said, it's really not our place, little fighter," Dorian said to Sloane. That was his nickname for her since high school. Sloane eyed him though, and he laughed. His head cocked at her. "What are the odds either of you guys let this go?"

"How about slim to none," Sloane said, then faced me.

I nodded. This not only concerned Bow, but Wells too. I *needed* to know.

I needed to know about both of them.

Tucking my feelings down, I waited. Wolf tipped his chin at Dorian. I assumed he was passing this off to him.

Dorian scrubbed into his blond hair. "Wells and Bow used to be friends."

My mouth parted. "What?"

"They actually used to be thick as thieves." Wolf made his own lap a seat for his girl. He wrapped his long arms around the curves of Fawn's waist once she sat. He frowned. "Until that girl died."

"Died?" Sloane looked at me, but I was already looking at her.

"What happened?" I asked, and Dorian pushed a breath through his nose. He told us a story about how Wells was lifeguarding one summer. Apparently, it was something all the guys used to do before Sloane and I moved into town. Dorian explained it was during that summer that a terrible accident happened.

"That girl died on Wells's watch, and he's never forgiven himself for it," Wolf said. Sloane, Fawn, and I were silent while both guys spoke, and I think equally stunned. All this happened before the three of us came into the picture. The Ambroses, Reeds, Mallicks, and the Prinzes had all been friends for a very long time.

Wolf wet his lips. "His focus had been on Bow and her friends at the time."

"Wells believed Bow had been drowning. She'd been underwater, and it was an honest mistake," Dorian explained.

I shook my head. "It wasn't Bow's fault, though. It wasn't Wells's fault either."

It wasn't anyone's.

What happened was tragic, but it was one hundred percent no one's fault.

Wolf faced Dorian. "Tell that to Wells."

So much was starting to make sense now, and, though I didn't know what part of what I said Wolf addressed, I had a feeling Wells definitely believed what happened was Bow's fault. He treated her like crap, but I also knew something else. He'd come to her rescue tonight, and he looked absolutely terrified.

CHAPTER ELEVEN

Bow

My phone pinged, and I opened the message.

I wanted to be sick.

It was a video of me on a balcony at that party, but it wasn't the video itself that made me sick to my stomach. It was the message underneath, and I knew who it was from, even though, I once again didn't recognize the number.

Unknown: I'm assuming he caused you to do this. You see how toxic he and your other friends are? If they cared about you, they'd protect you from him. Come back to me, Bow. It'll be different this time.

Shaking, I deleted the message. I immediately pulled up Sloane.

Me: Hey, can I stay at your place again tonight?

I never thought I'd be asking her that so soon after staying there. I spent exactly one night at my brother's place and left the next morning before anyone woke up.

I couldn't face anyone.

Feeling sick again, I waited for Sloane's text. I really didn't want to text her, but I didn't have a choice. I didn't feel safe at my dorm by myself. I mean, he knew where that was so…

Sloane: Sure!

Relief swept me, but then, Sloane texted me again.

Sloane: Dorian and I aren't home though. We're back in The Heights visiting my parents. Ares and Fawn came too.

Crap. Maywood Heights was my hometown.

Sloane: You're welcome to stay back at the house though. Bru, Thatcher, and Wells should be there.

I never *ever* thought I'd intentionally put myself in a position to run into my brother. He hadn't been happy after what I did at that party but even dealing with him was better than accidentally running into Bru.

Or Wells.

I liked to say I didn't know why I'd decided to go to some random party and get drunk, but that'd be a lie.

You see how toxic he is…

Ignoring the voice in my head, I texted Sloane back.

Me: Thanks.

Sloane: No problem. I'll text Bru and let him know you're coming. You got your key, right?

I did have a key to their house and slid a hoodie on before venturing out of my dorm and into the darkness of Pembroke University's campus. I knew how to travel in a way that kept me from attracting attention. I stayed off the main paths.

I kept my head down.

I knew how to blend in, which was the exact opposite of what I'd been intending to do through my study sessions with Wells. For those, I needed to be in high traffic areas. We needed *to be seen* by everyone.

I supposed that was all over now.

I screwed up that plan too, and I thought I'd be sick by the time I got to Sloane's house. I'd be as sick as I was the night I decided to get drunk because of the way Wells looked at me. I thought I could use his hate for me to my advantage, but all my plan did was make me feel like crap. It made me feel guilty, and that message on my phone was wrong.

Wells wasn't the toxic one.

I was.

I was, because I was the reason Wells got distracted that day at the pool one summer. I was the reason *a girl died*, and it was also me who used Wells after the fact for our tutoring sessions because I didn't know what to do. I was scared and desperate.

"I need you to come down from there."

Wells saved me again when he didn't have to. He once again thought I was drowning. He was Archer again, *my* Archer, and I spent so much time that night throwing up. I'd been drinking, yeah, but it honestly wasn't that much. I was just a lightweight, so any alcohol made me not act like myself.

But it was seeing Wells as my friend again as he tried to save me on the balcony that made me sick.

I was the reason I lost his friendship, me.

Bru also being there the night I screwed up only made things worse. He had rejected me, and he shouldn't have been there. I used him, too, in a way. I used his comfort on the regular. My best friend's brother was always nice to me. He was such a genuine person, and I'd mistaken that kindness for something else.

The first thing I did after sleeping off my drunken state was leave before anyone could see me in the morning. The moment I got back to my dorm, I locked myself inside it.

Not nearly enough time had passed before coming back to my brother's house tonight. The multilevel home known as Legacy House sat up on a hill in a wooded area of campus. It overlooked pretty much everything; my brother and his friends like gods among men. They had parties here all the time, but, thankfully, things were quiet tonight.

Using my key, I snuck inside. I didn't have to worry about security alarms since others were probably home, but I checked them anyway. I checked the security alarm panel and saw it wasn't armed, so that meant someone was here.

I made myself be brave. The house was big and I could easily sneak into a guest room without being detected.

"Seriously, man. What the fuck?"

I froze. I gripped my bag at the front door. It'd been Bru who'd spoken.

Taking a few steps from the entryway, I eased a look into the living room. That was the direction his voice had come from, and it was dim in there, the TV on.

I froze again once I saw Bru. He was sitting on one of the couches with his denimed legs crossed, but he wasn't alone. Wells was in there with him. Wells had his leather jacket on like he'd just gotten home and the television remote was in his hand.

"Dude, what the fuck? I'm watching TV," Bru ground out. He was usually so calm, so seeing him grit his teeth at someone was different. His strong jaw clenched as he reached for the remote in Wells's hand, but Wells was standing. Wells also had an extended reach, so he easily got it away since Bru was sitting.

"Not anymore," Wells said. He threw his long body on the opposite end of the couch Bru was on. Wells worked his jacket off, his t-shirt intentionally ripped across the front and exposing his chest. He'd call that fashion, but my brother would probably call him a show-off. He liked to expose his body a lot. Especially on his YouTube channel.

I watched Wells's cooking channel more than I liked sometimes. I couldn't help it. I watched one video and, ever since, others came up in my feed.

Wrestling with my hands, I ducked my head. The boys sounded like they were about to squabble, which was good. That meant they were both distracted, and I could sneak into a room undetected.

"Watch in your room or something," I heard Wells say. It

was silent after that, but I looked over when I heard move-
ment. I panned just in time to see Bru rip the remote out of
Wells's hand, and, when Wells went to grab it, Bru switched
the remote to his opposite hand. Bru had a broad frame, so
Wells wasn't getting the remote unless he got up or tackled
Bru.

Wells bared his teeth. "I said watch in your fucking room."

"Nah. Not happening." Bru proceeded to lounge back on
the couch. He switched the channel back to whatever he was
watching. "I was here first."

"You were here first," Wells singsonged before his eyes
narrowed into slits. "What are you, five?"

"You're one to talk about acting like a five-year-old.
Coming in here and throwing your weight around." Bru
continued to change channels. His lips went tight. "Asshole."

The word had been light, but Wells obviously heard it.
Wells shoved Bru, and when Bru shoved him back, my
stomach dropped into my butt.

Fists started flying.

It didn't take much to set Wells off. He got in physical
fights all the time with my brother and their other friends.
That was just their dynamic, but Bru tended not to lift his
fists as much as the rest of them. I knew this probably was
because of a history he had with fighting. He didn't like to
do that if he could help it, but something about this argument caused Bru to engage the moment Wells swung
at him.

Wells missed, but Bru didn't, and he clocked Wells in his
jaw. Wells's eyes went wide, and he didn't miss this time,
when he socked Bru in the stomach.

Bru reared back, his own eyes wild before he shot a fist
directly at Wells's face. Wells dodged and a scream bubbled in
my throat when Wells drew back his own fist. I was going to
do anything I could to stop this, but my shout silenced when
Wells released his fist. He folded a hand behind Bru's neck

and kissed him with so much force that Bru fell back into the couch.

Oh. My. God...

I couldn't breathe. I couldn't think, because soon the guys' tongues were dancing outside of their mouths. Wells was biting Bru's lips, and Bru was biting Wells's right back.

My hand wrapped around my throat. I didn't know if I was trying to squeeze out the breaths or what, but if I had a necklace around my neck, I knew I'd be clutching it. The guys proceeded to make out, but then Wells started messing with Bru's pants.

"What are you doing?" Bru panted. He was still tasting Wells's tongue, and this time, Bru was forcing the kiss. He had his hand shoved into Wells's dyed locks to keep him there, but Wells forced Bru away. Bru lifted off the couch a little, and, after Wells worked Bru's pants down, Wells started messing with his own pants.

I backed up, but stopped when Wells forced Bru to turn over on the couch. He spit into his hand, then took Bru's ass in a hard grunt. He fucked him so hard the couch moved.

It creaked.

Both guys grunted, Bru's hands gripping the couch while Wells's hands braced Bru's hips. Bru was grabbing the couch so hard his biceps flexed, and Wells wasn't looking at him. Wells had his eyes closed, and when they opened, they were rolled to the back of his head.

"Fucking *yes*," Wells called out, and Bru reached back and grabbed Wells's hand. Bru put Wells's hand on his own chest. He placed it right over his heart, and my own heart raced. It beat with the fury of a thousand drums, and my legs quivered.

They weakened.

I thought I'd fall, my legs were so weak and my heart beat so hard. I put a hand over my stomach, where Wells's hand moved on Bruno. Wells forced his hand under Bru's shirt and exposed his abs. The shadows of whatever was playing on the television screen danced across both guys' mighty forms as they grunted, labored. Bru called out, and I reached beneath my skirt.

I squeezed my sex.

I came as Bru did, his eyes shut tight, and Wells was both literally and figuratively right behind him. A couple hard thrusts, and Wells was filling Bru's ass. He did it with so much force and vigor that he ended up collapsing on top of Bru.

Bru held Wells's hand while his own body sagged on the couch. His fingers laced with Wells, and Bru attempted to put Wells's hand over his own heart again.

Wells didn't let him this time. *This time,* Wells let go.

Wells pulled up his pants, and Bru closed his eyes before glancing back at Wells. Bru's mouth turned down. "That's it?"

Wells didn't grace Bru with a response. He simply reached over and grabbed a box of tissues off the coffee table. He then handed it to Bru, but Bru shook his head.

Bru shoved the box of tissues away before working up his pants and leaving the room. I backed into the shadows, but it turned out I didn't need to. Bru left the room in the opposite direction of where I hid.

A door slammed somewhere in the house. Wells ripped the box of tissues in half. He threw both halves across the room before plopping on the couch, and I left after that. I faded back into the shadows, my essence sticky between my legs as I quietly padded to a guest room. I immediately went to the bathroom, feeling guilty again.

I wasn't supposed to see what I just saw, and, as I cleaned myself up, I was confused why it affected me the way it had. I liked Bru. I more than liked him and should be devastated that he said there was someone else, not turned on.

I guess Wells was that someone else.

CHAPTER
TWELVE

"I still don't know how the dads found out about all this," I said, unstrapping my seat belt in Thatcher's ride. He drove a Range Rover and pulled us up in front of a local theater in our hometown, Maywood Heights. Everyone entering sported tuxes and other fancy shit, and that was exactly the attire my buddy Thatcher and I rocked tonight. My bow tie choked the fuck out of me, and I hated wearing such tapered shit, but it was necessary.

We were going to the ballet.

Mind you, this wasn't our choice and something our dads had been doing for what felt like the beginning of time. Whenever one of their sons fucked up, our dads took us to the ballet. Ballet outings were for *special* fuckups though. If my buddies or I crossed a woman (or in my case, a partner), our dads made us all suffer through an entire night of tights and boring-ass shit. Our dads also suffered through it, so we all knew they were doing this to teach us a lesson. The whole thing was something about reminding us to be better men to our partners. The guys in the ballet were delicate with their ladies or whatever.

It was just all a giant snoozefest for me, and I knew this *particular* time it was about me. I didn't know how the dads found out about everything with Bow, but I knew they did. I heard it from both my mom and my dad. Mom's response to everything was sweet as pie of course. She could never even yell at me growing up, but she had expressed how disappointed she was with me in several texts. That felt shitty as hell, but it was better than when my dad contacted me. He *called me,* and he never called.

Still hearing his rant in my head, I faced Thatcher. He went James Bond tonight with a white jacket and black pants. He didn't take out his earrings of course, and his spiked crosses dangled when he unstrapped himself. He left the car running since we were using valet. He frowned at me. "I called this one in myself, bro."

My brow had to have jumped to my hairline. I pushed back my hair. "What?"

I knew he was pissed at me after what happened, and rightly so. Bow was his sister, but he'd never tell our dads about our shit. Not on purpose anyway.

At least, I thought he wouldn't.

Thatcher came around the Range Rover after handing the keys to the valet, and I got out of the car too. He pressed a finger to my chest. "I told your ass to stop this shit with my sister years ago, so yeah, I'm still pissed."

He hadn't spoken to me the majority of our ride to the theater. I obviously knew he was still pissed, but I was giving him his space.

Sighing, Thatcher shook his head. "I let this shit go on for too long, so maybe a part of me called this in for myself, too. I was too complacent."

I knew why he did go along with it. My vendetta against his sister meant no guys wanted to be around. Thatcher was doing the older-brother thing by cockblocking.

He obviously was regretting that now. Our other friends made their appearance when they pulled up in Wolf's Hummer. I wasn't surprised that Dorian, Wolf, and Bru traveled together. Dorian was dating Wolf's sister, and Wolf and Bru were brothers.

It still wasn't easy to see Bru. What happened on the couch last night was too fresh.

All three guys looked pissed stepping out of Wolf's Hummer. I could imagine Dorian and Wolf just didn't want to be there. They hadn't screwed up in a while since they had steady partners they both loved and respected. Everyone knew this shit was on me, but it was only Bru who looked like he actually wanted to kill me. Dorian and Wolf might just rough me up a little, but Bruno Sloane-Mallick gave off like he'd finish the job and then some.

Bru had his hands in his pockets and his suit was just as tapered as mine, his shoes shined. He looked sexy as fuck with his hair moussed back, and I hated that he looked sexy as fuck. I hated that he *bothered me* and took me to my limits.

I wanted him to stay last night so I could watch my cum seep out of his ass. I wanted him to stay so I could push it back in and watch the face he made as I did it.

I wanted him to stay.

He hadn't of course, and that made sense.

He flanked Dorian, who wore his own suit. Dorian Prinze was Pembroke U's quarterback, and he rocked a black-on-black suit tonight. Wolf was right behind him once he handed his keys to the valet.

Wolf looked like he belonged in an Armani ad with his height and his wild curls ponied up. I might be in that spread with him, since I took some creative license and wore a patterned tux. I kept it classy with a jacquard black pattern.

Dorian and Wolf mumbled low hellos in my direction after shaking my hand. They both snapped their fingers after the greeting, but there was nothing warm or inviting about those handshakes.

Bru didn't shake my hand at all. I got barely a chin tip, and that was probably only out of formality. He followed the guys toward the theater.

"Kid, hold up," I said to him, and he sighed before turning around. The others went on into the theater, and I wasn't even going to touch that one. Normally, we all had a quick smoke before our dads arrived. It was the only way we could get through this shit, but no one even bothered tonight.

My friends loved me, but they were obviously pissed at me.

I allowed Bru to stay on the higher step when he turned, and, when I offered him a smoke, he waved it off. I let out a breath. "Bru…"

"Nah, don't bother," he said, starting to turn back toward the theater, but I took the high step, cutting him off. He sighed again. "What could you possibly want? I think you said all you needed to say last night."

I lit my joint but didn't smoke it right away. I stood there, and Bru laughed.

He shook his head. "You're confusing as shit, Ambrose."

I was sure that was what it looked like to him, and I was questioning myself. I told him to stay away from me, keep things platonic, and then I fucked him. I fucked him hard. I fucked him *good*, and we both enjoyed it.

We always did.

It was always easy with Bru. It was until things changed. That was on him, but last night was definitely me.

I took a hit from my blunt. "I'm sorry."

I *was* sorry. I was sorry I confused things and went back on what I said. I did just want to be friends, but I was just coming off all that bullshit with Bow.

"Archer."

Bow had gotten in my head with all that. She brought up old history, and yeah, that fucked me up. I may not look like I had a soul, but I was human, and she'd been so fucking stupid that night. She had no business getting drunk and getting up on that balcony.

It just showed how starved for attention she was. I got out of my head when Bru got too close. That outdoorsy smell that came off him worked itself into my nose. It riled me up, made me growl.

"I think you don't hate Bow as much as you want to," he said, causing me to blink. What the fuck was he talking about Squeak for? He nodded. "I know what happened between you guys. I know how you used to be friends and I also know why you're not anymore. The guys told me about that girl who drowned in high school. It came up that night Bow was on the balcony."

So, my friends had been talking behind my back. They'd brought up old shit that I'd been doing everything I could to forget.

"Archer."

They got it wrong that Bow and I used to be friends. I may have tolerated Thatcher's little sister, but I was *never* her friend, and she let me know that the minute she decided to do her fake drowning shit. She'd pretended to go under the water that day at the pool to get attention, *my attention.*

That was how it went down that day, and that would always be how I saw it. I would.

I swallowed. "Bow's the reason that girl died. She pretended to drown, and I really don't know why you're bringing that up."

It was some dark shit, and he had to know that it was hurtful. That it *killed.* That girl died on my watch. Mine.

"I think that's what you want to believe," Bru continued.

"That it was Bow's fault. But I definitely don't believe you hate her. You covered for her that night with the guys."

I did because it was true. I had said some shit to her earlier that day. I hadn't gone too far though. In fact, what I said had been completely fucking warranted. I put a finger in Bru's chest. "I covered because it was hurting Thatch."

"I'm sure that was part of it, but I saw how you reacted when we both thought she was in trouble. It was like you snapped, and you were also able to talk her off that ledge." His eyes narrowed. "She trusted you."

She was stupid to. Bow Reed shouldn't trust me anymore than I could trust her. "I told you that night that you don't know anything about that girl and me."

"I know you don't hate her. People who hate each other don't look terrified when they think the other may fall off a ledge, which you did. I was there, Ambrose. I saw it. You also fucked me not long after it happened. Like what went down got you up in your head. Like *she* got in your head."

I bristled. I didn't know what he was insinuating, but whatever it was, he needed to step back. He was crossing the line, just like he'd done with our friendship. My jaw moved. "I got her off that ledge for Thatcher."

"I'm sure that's what you're telling yourself, and, believe me, I know what it's like to be confused." He rubbed the back of his neck. "I need to tell you something about Bow."

I blinked. He got my attention quicker than I wanted him to. He got my attention *period* which I didn't like, and it took effort not to react to what he said.

It took effort not to feel something.

Bru opened his mouth. I assumed that was to speak, but an arm came around him, and once it did, I hid my blunt. The arm was his dad's, Ramses, and my dad was with him.

All the dads were with him.

"You guys are looking intense," Ramses said, squeezing Bru's shoulder. Ramses was Bru's adoptive dad. He looked nothing like him, but Wolf was like the man's clone. Ramses towered over both Bru and me, just like Wolf did. Ramses glanced between Bru and me. "Everything all right?"

I wasn't sure.

Bru avoided my eyes suddenly, with his dad there. Mine narrowed, but I let up when my dad made eye contact with me. I might look more like him if I didn't dye my hair platinum blond and grow it out. He and my mom were both brunettes, which was my natural hair color.

"I'm sure Bru isn't happy he's being punished because of my son," Dad said, eyeing me. I averted my attention to the ground. Dad may have shot laser eyes at me, but it wasn't his focus that hit me right in the gut.

Knight was beside him.

Knight was Thatcher's dad, which made him *Bow's* dad. He was also huge as fuck like Thatcher and could easily pummel my ass. It didn't matter if he had twenty years on me.

Knight, aka Mr. Reed, had nothing but a grunt for me once he entered the circle of dads. All the dads were here now, except for Dorian's dad, Royal, and my god-dad, LJ. LJ didn't have any kids, but he was good friends with the other dads. Anyway, in the group text with my friends, Dorian let us all know his dad and LJ were out of town on business.

"Where's my son?" Mr. Reed growled lowly, borderline sneering at me.

Shit.

Answer fast.

"Inside with the other guys," I said and did try to smile a little at him.

The sentiment didn't work.

The sneer became deadly, and I shot my sight to the ground again. I'd be a submissive little bitch if I had to. Thatcher's dad didn't play.

I was only glad he wasn't *my* dad in that moment. My dad

was already close to cutting me off, and I think the only reason he hadn't was because he hadn't gotten to it yet.

I wasn't about to remind him of that shit though.

I started to stay behind so I could talk with Bru. He definitely was about to say something to me, but my dad got my arm.

He tipped his chin toward Mr. Reed. "You're sitting with Knight this evening."

Fucking brilliant.

Dad's eyes narrowed. "And he's also taking you to the restaurant after the show."

My mouth parted. We always went to one of my dad's fast-food chains, Jax's Burgers, after the ballet. It was one of the only highlights actually. Not the conversation, of course, but the food. "Dad—"

He started to walk off. That signaled the end of the conversation.

And so my nightmare was just beginning.

I didn't have a chance to talk with Bru. I was mashed between my dad *and Mr. Reed*. Mr. Reed simmered beside me the entire show and the only thing worse than that was the *actual* ballet. I didn't know what this one was called. I didn't fucking care, but it would have at least been tolerable with my cellphone.

My dad took it.

Mine was the only one he took, so I just had to sit there between two pissed fathers. The only break I got was intermission, and Mr. Reed followed me to the bathroom. Of *course* he had to go to the bathroom too.

I was barely able to pee once I got there. Even breathing around Thatcher's dad took effort. I screwed over his daughter.

And he definitely knew it.

I wrapped up my intermission quickly, then it was back to the show. I caught a glance from Bru during the second half at one point. He had that look in his eyes, telling me again that he wanted to say something to me.

What's this about, kid?

I attempted to ask him with my eyes during certain points of the show, but whenever I did, I got *a look* from Mr. Reed or my own dad. I also got occasional glances from my friends which were equally angry. Those were bad, but Thatcher couldn't even *look* at me. His attention remained forward like he cared about this shit, and I could see him well since we were all in a private booth. The dads always arranged for us to have the best seats in the house. They didn't want their sons to miss anything.

I wasn't.

I was well aware of everyone looking at me all night. After the show, all I had to look forward to was a drive with Mr. Reed, but I thought my dad would be there as a buffer at least.

He wasn't.

Dad literally left my ass at the curb when the valet pulled up in Mr. Reed's Escalade. I slid my dad a pleading look on the street. "You're not coming?"

"Oh, we'll have plenty of time together, son. Don't worry about that," Dad said. He patted my back, and I was left alone. The other guys had already gone off with their dads toward their own cars.

"You getting in?"

I turned to find Mr. Reed already at the wheel. He faced forward as if he hadn't spoken.

But he had, and I felt the energy of his words when I got into the Escalade. Outside of my own dad, I'd spent the most time around Mr. Reed when I was younger. Thatcher and I were really close, so that was a given.

Because I spent so much time with him, he had no problem treating me like he would his own son.

Our fathers were all incredibly close, so their sons were raised by a tribe of strong men. I always admired our dads, especially Mr. Reed. He was the badass CEO of several companies.

I felt some kind of way sitting beside him and definitely didn't like disappointing him. He was like a father to me.

"I don't know what to say, Wells," he started, and I sighed. We'd barely gotten on the road.

Honestly, I thought he'd start with yelling. He was like a bear in a cave when Thatcher screwed up. My lips parted. "Mr. Reed—"

"I mean, you used to protect my daughter."

I faced him, not expecting those words.

His hands gripped the wheel. "I obviously know what happened between you two and why you fell out with one another. That summer was terrible, tragic."

I swallowed hard, saying nothing.

"But I know you know that summer was no one's fault."

This time I refused to speak for Mr. Reed's benefit. He didn't want to know what I had to say about that. He didn't want to know *how I felt* because if he did, it'd make things so much worse. Instead, I chose to sit with my anger and frustration with *his* daughter. I held my fucking tongue, but I couldn't help but look at him when he said what he did next.

"I urge you to stop all this, but not just for my daughter. *For you*, Wells," he said, his lips turned down. "You're hurting her, but you're also suffering."

You're also suffering.

It was like his words were amplified in the air. This man cared about me just like my own dad.

Mr. Reed faced away, silent after that, and I studied the road too. I didn't say anything, but my mind was screaming. I did use to protect his daughter. But that was because I was laboring under false pretenses. I'd been the fool. His daughter made me the joke the moment she decided to play her little trick at the pool, and I made a promise to myself that day. I wouldn't be the fool. Rainbow Reed wouldn't get anything else from me.

Even if I had fallen for it again that night she was on the balcony.

CHAPTER
THIRTEEN

Bow

A book hit the grass in front of me, and I jumped, shrieking.

I almost shrieked again.

I couldn't help it when Wells Ambrose lowered his lengthy body to the ground with me. He may have been tall, but he was also thick and took up quite a bit of surface area in front of me.

Others noticed.

In fact, everyone within eye sight of us noticed Wells lounge his lengthy body in front of mine. Wells played football but was built more like a swimmer with a long wingspan, legs, and chiseled torso, which he revealed a little when he took his hoodie off. His shirt almost always rode up when he did that.

Trying not to notice, I curled my hand around my pen. I'd been trying to study. It was a bit warmer today, so I was outside on the quad. I didn't even have to wear my jacket over my button-down shirt. I'd tucked it into my twill skirt. I gazed up at Wells. "Um, what are you doing here?"

He shouldn't be here, and I was honestly scared that he was. Did I do something?

I hated that *that* was my first thought. That I was so intimidated by him that I couldn't help thinking that him being around meant I did something to him.

You did do something.

I supposed I had, and I still didn't know why he covered for my stupidity at that party. I didn't mean to start drinking. I just…

Wells's hair was messy when he tugged off his hoodie. It almost appeared intentional since, the majority of the time, that was how he wore his dyed locks anyway. He pushed them back. "This is our time, isn't it?"

My eyebrows had to have shot up to my hairline.

He frowned. "You said to meet on the quad at this time, right?" He lifted his hands, gazing around. "Well, I'm here. You're supposed to tutor me, so get tutoring."

I didn't understand. I didn't show up to our last tutoring session *because* of my stupidity. I'd gotten depressed and closed off. I ended up going to that party, and he knew what happened next.

"I thought you said to forget about our arrangement," I said, referring to the text message I read after I sobered up. I got why he sent it. I mean, I stood him up.

"By the grace of God, my dad hasn't cut me off yet," he said, lounging back. His shirt lifted again, revealing his tanned abs, and my eyes averted. I came back to find him smirking at me. He shook his head. "They're just abs, Squeak. Focus. It's the least you can do considering I covered for you with your little drunken balcony incident."

But why? He had no reason to.

His mouth thinned into a firm line. "I'm not giving my parents a reason to cut me off by getting behind in school. Therefore, I'm here for you to tutor me, and again, you owe me at least that after what you did."

He always had a way of driving the dagger, making me feel small, and, though I couldn't blame him, that didn't mean it didn't make me angry.

Wells made me want to hate him, and I didn't hate anyone. I also didn't want to tutor him, but I knew I didn't have a choice.

I gazed around. "Fine."

He smirked. "You're saying fine like I'm not the one doing you a favor. Or have you failed to notice that everyone sees us together out here."

As if to drive that point, Wells placed his sight on the quad. I glanced around.

A few students even smiled at me.

It was weird being acknowledged in a way that was positive instead of negative. I supposed that was the power of being in Wells's good graces.

I glanced around for another set of eyes but ended up being cut off when I caught Bru's. He took up just as much space as Wells did, but in a different way. Still several feet away, Bru lifted his hand as he strode toward Wells and me, and my stomach flopped remembering the last time I'd seen him.

Remembering the last time I'd seen *both* of them.

"Fucking brilliant." Wells sliced the words through his teeth. He obviously noticed Bru coming toward us with his messenger bag. He also wore dark slacks and a teal polo that revealed a sliver of his brawny chest. He looked like a young professor, and, for some reason, Wells didn't want to see him.

I didn't want to see him either.

Truth be told, I'd rather avoid both of them right now, but that wasn't because Wells hated me and Bru rejected me. I mean, that didn't help, but walking in on them hooking up was worse. I thought it'd hurt seeing the reason for Bru's rejection, and it did, but only at first. It was what happened *after* that initial sting that made me want to avoid them both.

It was me in the bathroom wiping myself off after watching the two of them together.

It was witnessing the cum between my legs.

It made me ashamed and feel, I don't know, dirty? I mean, I should have felt dirty. I should have...

"Hey, Bow."

I jumped again, even though I knew Bru was coming, and both guys looked at me weird. Bru had merely greeted me, and I nearly jumped out of my skin again.

I pushed back some of my curls. They always escaped my bun. "Hey."

"Hi." Bru lifted his hand again. It was a little awkward this time, but that made sense. I mean, a lot of awkward things were happening lately. He quite literally and figuratively helped me off a ledge recently. Bru pocketed his hands. "Ambrose."

"'Sup." Wells avoided Bru's gaze, but he couldn't once Bru sat down. Wells's head cocked. "What do you think you're doing, kid?"

I forgot Wells called Bru that sometimes. It was a nickname Bru's brother, Ares, gave him.

Bru apparently knew exactly what he was doing because, once he sat with us, he started taking things out of his messenger bag. Things like his MacBook, an actual notebook, and various writing materials.

"I'm here to help Bow tutor you," he said, and both Wells's and my eyebrows shot up. Bru frowned. "I'd rather avoid another trip to the ballet I guess."

My heart sunk. It was well known that our dads took both of them on a punishment trip to the ballet recently. It was something my dad and his best friends Royal, LJ, Jax, and Ramses usually did when one of the guys messed up.

I wanted to be sick. Bru and Wells being punished was my fault this time, and that was well known too.

Why did Wells cover for me?

I didn't know, and I certainly didn't ask him to. He may have said something to me that took me over the edge that night, but it wasn't his fault I got there. Truth be told, I got there all on my own.

I gazed around again. I was looking for someone in particular. Someone I didn't see, even though he always came through the quad around this time.

Swallowing, the tension in my body moved toward the sudden environment I found myself in. Wells stared at Bru. Like stared *daggers* at him for some reason, and Bru was acting like he didn't even notice. He just kept arranging his materials, and, once he finished, he glanced up at me. "So, what's with the Archer thing?"

That gave Wells pause again, and me, too.

My heart thudded. "What do you mean?" Of course, I knew what he meant, but I was still in shock. I was just like I had been when I heard the name come out of my own mouth that night.

I shouldn't have said it then, just like it shouldn't be addressed now, and Wells sharpened those daggers he stared in Bru's direction.

Bru shrugged. "You called Wells that, and I was just curious about it."

I said nothing. I didn't know what to say, and honestly, I'd already said too much, bringing up old things. It was weak, but all I did was look at Wells. He wasn't saying anything either, but he did look like he wanted to tackle Bru.

Wells's jaw moved. "It's just a dumb thing made up by our parents," Wells said, and my stomach dropped. It plummeted.

He faced me. "Squeak used to always get herself into scrapes. The girl would literally fall over her feet, so I helped her out from time to time. Looked out for her for Thatch or whatever."

"So how does the Archer thing come into play, then?" Bru

pushed, and I wished he'd stop. I wished this all stopped. That history was ringing in my ears, and it hurt, my insides burning, caving.

Wells's expression cooled. "It was a play on our names. I was protective, and my middle name is Archer. Our parents joked that I was the archer, and she was my bow. The archer and his bow."

The archer and his bow.

"Anyway, the term stuck, and Squeak started calling me that," Wells continued, saying that history as if it was nothing, and I supposed it *was* to him now. His mouth formed into a hard line. "Like I said, it was dumb."

It *was* dumb, and I felt like a fool for calling him that for as long as I did. I was just a dumb kid, a stupid kid.

Bru focused on Wells, frowning.

When Bru finally let up and veered his attention to me, I was looking at our books. I wanted to get our study session done and get out of there.

I wanted to disappear just like those nicknames.

CHAPTER
FOURTEEN

Bow

Things surprisingly weren't awkward during my tutoring sessions with Wells and Bru. They should be, gosh should they be, but they weren't. Things were naturally easy between Bru and me normally. We got along really well, which was why I liked him so much.

I expected to lose that with everything that happened between us recently, which would be my fault. We didn't though. We seemed to pick up right where we left off with our ease. Maybe that was because he was taking things seriously by tutoring Wells. He didn't want to go to the ballet again.

Bru seemed to forget about everything that happened between us with the kiss, and, though that stung a little, I was glad. It kept things less awkward and the return of our ease seemed to transfer to Wells. He was also taking his tutoring seriously, which was crazy. He wasn't much of a serious guy when it came to anything. Let alone school. With Bru and me tutoring him though, he was trying.

Wells showed up every day on the quad for our tutoring sessions. He participated and appeared to be a sponge for the information. He didn't always get the concepts Bru and I attempted to show him, but he worked at it until he did. He must really not want to be cut off by his parents.

It was easy to forget that was the reason we were hanging out when we were together. Wells wasn't only on board with learning, but he was civil to me. He *respected* me, and that was something I hadn't felt since we were younger.

It was something I hadn't felt since before I screwed up.

When the three of us were together, it was like none of that had happened, but gosh, those first few days had been weird. The boys had this weird tension, but I supposed I got that. After they hooked up, all Wells did was hand Bru a tissue box. It was like Wells didn't want anything to happen between them but something obviously had.

That was where my own awkwardness came in. I'd witnessed something that happened between them, but I had to keep all that to myself. I thought things would be weird for me being around them because I had kissed Bru and also got drunk. I made things weird for *all three* of us, but I found that what I thought about most was the night neither guy knew I'd been watching them.

It was the time I came only several feet away from them.

"Come on. You got this, Ambrose," Bru said. He was sitting on the couch with an Algebra textbook in his hands. It was Wells's textbook, and Wells himself sat on the armchair across from Bru. Wells had his long body draped across it while he tossed a stress ball in the air. Bru frowned. "You know this. Now tell me what you got for x."

Wells sighed. He continued to toss his stress ball, which was something Bru gave him around our third tutoring session. Bru and I both noticed Wells liked to work his hands when he was thinking, which made sense. Wells really enjoyed cooking, which was honestly the only thing he took seriously outside of football.

The three of us normally didn't have tutoring sessions at Legacy House. Wells knew I liked to be out on the quad, especially since it'd been warmer. Our group could be seen there, and he knew I wanted that for our deal. People stared at me now, but not in judging ways because it looked like Wells was cool with me. People smiled at me, and some even said hi. The power of Wells Ambrose was something I hadn't felt in a positive way for a long time, and once upon a time, that would have meant everything to me. I wanted to be acknowledged, be cared about.

Now, I was only grateful for his presence, and, though I would prefer to be outside, it was raining, so we had to stay in.

I sat on the floor of the guys' living room, waiting for Wells's answer too. I crossed my legs in my dark leggings. I had another one of Wells's textbooks on my lap. "Come on, Wells. I know you got this one."

It was a complicated equation but Bru and I had taught Wells hacks he could use for some equations that wouldn't require paper or even a calculator. We found that Wells was perfectly capable of doing the work but sometimes got lost in the numbers. Many equations did need to be written out, but the one we were working on now didn't.

Wells continued to toss his ball. His legs were so long they were basically touching the floor and the room smelled so much like both boys. I noticed that Wells's scent was fresher. He smelled like a tidal wave, whereas Bru gave off a more oaky smell. Bru was like the forest and Wells the sea. I thought of both when I was around them.

I shouldn't have been thinking of either boys' smell. It was weird, so I focused as I waited for Wells's answer.

Wells caught his stress ball. He popped one of his high-tops on the arm of the couch Bru sat on, his eyebrows scrunched. "Uh, 149?"

Bru and I exchanged a glance, my insides fluttering that Wells got it. Bru shot Wells a grin. "Uh, yeah, dude."

"You're fucking kidding?" Wells dropped his ball. He'd been tossing it again, and the ball hit his face before tumbling to the floor. Wells popped up. "You're joking?"

"He's not. You totally got it, Wells." I clapped, so excited for him, and I was thrown when Wells launched off his chair and grabbed me. He pulled me up off the floor, my feet pedaling beneath me. The tall football player did this as if I weighed nothing, and, after he put me down, he grabbed Bru too.

He grabbed us both.

Wells hugged us both, and soon, I found myself sand-wiched between both guys when Bru stood. I was surrounded by the forest and hit by that tidal wave. I was both drowning and dizzy in the breeze of both of them, which didn't seem possible, but it was.

It was.

"Fuck, yeah," Wells said. His arm was beneath mine but also around Bru. I was right, Wells had the wingspan of a swimmer. Wells's cheek touched the top of my head. "Thanks, Squeak."

Thanks, Squeak.

"Of course," I said, and soon, I found myself hugging him. I squeezed him, and I realized I hadn't had my arms around him since that day in the pool that summer. His embrace had been so warm then, solid.

"Don't know how I would have done that without you and the kid," Wells continued, and I noticed he didn't let go of me. He didn't even though he had to know I was squeezing him tight.

I almost felt his body relax under my embrace, and it definitely did when Bru reached around and squeezed Wells's shoulder.

"That was all you, dude," Bru said. His force hit my back, and I might have been crazy, but I believed I felt his cheek touch my head too. That or his forehead or something I didn't know. I was too busy swaying in the forest…

I was too busy drowning in the sea.

"Yeah, but without you guys there's no way I would have gotten this shit. No way." The sea was suddenly pulling away. Wells's shirt had rode up a little. It always did when he extended. A sliver of his abs disappeared when he tugged the shirt down, and he wrestled with his hair before pointing toward the kitchen. "I'm going to go make you guys an omelet or something to celebrate."

He was always making food. He was always making *Bru and I* food. The three of us usually met in the quad, and Wells showed up with some kind of peace offering. It reminded me of when we were kids, and he used to bring me candy, sweets.

Food was definitely Wells Ambrose's love language, and I tried not to think too hard about that. Things weren't like old times. Wells didn't like me.

Wells hated me. And Bru didn't like me either. At least, not in the way I wanted him to.

Bru studied Wells's back as Wells left the room. A deep frown was etched in Bru's face, but it disappeared by the time he faced me. I think Bru really did like Wells, and, like me, he was fighting an attraction he couldn't help. And I knew for a fact that Wells Ambrose wasn't easy to love.

I knew because I once loved him.

It was a love I had to let go, of course. It was too painful to love someone when they hated you.

"I guess while he's doing that, let's watch something on TV," Bru said to me, smiling. It hurt to look at his handsome smile. To have feelings for someone when they clearly were into someone else. Bru sat back down on the couch. "You think *Jeopardy* is on right now?"

We used to always watch game shows together and keep our own scores. Winner would often take control of our study playlist or something equally as silly.

I so missed Bru. He was such a good friend. I always did screw up my friendships, and it was a wonder his sister was still friends with me.

"It might be." I sat beside him but not close. It hurt to be too close to him just as much as staring at his smile. He was always using it. Great at it.

"Let's see what we can find." Bru draped his long arm behind me. The hairs on his arm brushed the back of my neck, and I fought the chill in my body. A chill in a great way.

He's not into you.

He wasn't, and it didn't matter what he said that day at Legacy House. He'd said that he was into me, but there was someone else. Even if there wasn't, I'd be delusional to think someone like him could actually be into me. He was perfect, and I screwed things up.

Jeopardy turned out to not be on, and Bru ended up turning the TV to some regency show. Wells had dropped eggs into a skillet by then. I could hear the sizzle coming from the kitchen and whatever he was frying up with the eggs smelled heavenly.

Wells was such a great cook, and he really didn't need to do his thirst-trap content. His cooking skills could be respected without it. *I* respected him without it.

Wrestling with my hands, I forced myself to remain focused on what was in front of me. I think Bru gave up on finding something to watch because he ended up keeping it on the regency show. The couples were dancing in fancy ball-gowns. I brought my legs up on the couch. "It'd be cool to dance like that."

"Dance like what?" Bru asked, distracted. His dark eyes

were back toward the kitchen, which could kind of be seen from the living room. The only thing separating the kitchen from the living room was the bar, and Wells was in there dancing to his own internal beat while he fried the eggs. No music was playing or anything but the stuff on TV.

It was shocking to me how I didn't notice there was something going on between them. I mean, I *saw that now*, Bru's eyes on Wells and that... tension. My stomach tightened before I pointed to the TV. "Dance like that."

Bru faced forward. As I suspected, he wasn't really watching TV. His eyes narrowed on the screen. "Dance in that ballroom style, you mean?"

I wished that were the case. I shook my head. "No, I mean dance in general I guess. Dance with someone in general."

Bru was completely focused on me at this point, and I kind of wished he'd go back to paying attention to Wells in the kitchen. His mouth parted. "You mean to tell me you've never danced with a partner before?"

No, not really. My face grew hot. "I mean, I've danced with you guys."

"Yeah, but that was in a group," he said, probably referring to the high school dances we all went to. His head cocked. "You've really never danced with someone else before? Never danced with a girl or guy?"

Did his sister count?

That wasn't what he meant though. He meant romantically, and, when would I have had the opportunity? I was into guys, but my brother and his friends made sure any romantic prospects stayed away over the years. They were really protective over me, and, even if they weren't, Wells's hate for me kept guys away. I sort of got male attention from guys at other schools, but once they found out about Wells, that faded away. My track record with guys wasn't the best.

In fact, it was terrible.

"Come on." Sometime in my thoughts Bru had stood. The

regency scene continued to play in the background on the TV, but it was suddenly white noise with Bru standing in front of me. Bru with his big hands and large frame. Bru with his handsome grin. He put his hands out. "I'm going to help you fix that right now."

What was he talking about? I didn't move, and he laughed.

He waved me forward with his fingers. "Dance with me, Bow."

Shocked, I still didn't do anything, so Bru decided to take initiative. His large hand slid into mine, and it was a wonder he could be so gentle when he tucked me into him. He was so big.

His hugeness enveloped me once I was against his broad chest. Did people normally dance this close?

I didn't care about my question once engulfed in Bru's heat. His scent surrounded me, and I closed my eyes until he dipped me back.

I laughed when he brought me up. "You're going to make me lightheaded."

I was already lightheaded.

"Not my intention, but I'm happy to make you smile," he said before spinning me around. He extended my arm before bringing me back. He placed a hand on my waist. "And every girl should be able to slow dance at least once in her life."

There was no mistake this time when he pressed his cheek to the top of my head. He held me close. "I'm happy I get to be this first for you, Bow."

My eyes closed again, my stomach tight. I *loved* this.

I loved it too much.

This boy wasn't mine and could never be. I knew that, but I was delusional enough to hold him closer. I brought my arms around his waist but let go when a throat cleared.

"What's going on?" Wells had a plate in his hand. It held a huge omelet, and beneath the plate were three empty plates. I assumed he was going to divvy up what he made, and he placed the plates down when Bru finally let go of me.

"Bow had never danced with a partner before," he said, then pointed at the TV. The people on the screen had stopped dancing, but they were still in their regency attire. It was a rather tense scene where several characters were talking but the orchestra's music still played in the background. Bru pocketed his hands. "I was just showing her how."

Wells's eyes narrowed. He glanced between Bru and me, and, for some reason, Bru crossed his arms. In fact, Bru got visually bigger, standing up taller, and Wells did the same. Wells crossed his arms too, and what was happening reminded me of something in the wild. Like two male lions challenging each other, and I wasn't sure what that meant.

"Not like that you aren't," Wells said, then stepped behind me. I didn't know what he was doing, and, judging by the look of Bru, he didn't either. Wells waved Bru over. "Put your hands on Squeak's waist."

My mouth parted, and Bru's eyebrows shot up.

Wells shrugged. "I'm the one who's actually had etiquette classes thanks to my mother, and you aren't showing Squeak how to dance right," he said, and I almost laughed. He was right. Actually, my brother and the majority of his friends had etiquette classes when we were younger. I think our parents wanted the guys to have good foundations when it came to girls.

I think it kind of fell on deaf ears considering how they treated girls in high school, but I never said anything about that.

Still behind me, Wells waved his hands. "Come on. I'll show you both how."

Bru had his head cocked, his expression curious, and I didn't blame him. Not a second ago, Wells looked like he'd been about to challenge Bru for whatever reason.

Bru released the tension in his arms when he dropped

them to his sides. He studied me. "That okay with you, Bow?" Bru asked me, but he had his eyes on Wells. The guys still kind of seemed like they were in some kind of standoff, and I'd somehow gotten between them.

"Okay," I said, not knowing what else to say. It was all kind of weird. Especially when Wells reached around me. He didn't touch me or anything but grabbed Bru's hands. I watched as Wells gripped them, bringing them closer to me.

"Now put this hand on her waist," Wells said and physically guided Bru to do that. I thought Wells would let go after that, but he didn't. He kept one hand there at the position of my waist while he directed Bru to fold his other hand with mine. Wells nodded. "And hold this one."

Hold this one.

Like the hand at my waist, Wells kept hold of Bru's other hand, the one folded with mine. Wells then began to sway both Bru *and me.* Wells wasn't touching me at all, but it almost felt like he was.

It felt like they both were.

They were, in a way, and though there was no music playing, it was like we were kind of making our own.

"Don't let go of her. Guide her," Wells said from behind me. His heat moved in closer. "Make her feel secure. You're the one directing this ship. Remember that."

It felt like Wells was directing us. Bru's fingers dug into my waist. I noticed a heat was flushing his face as he shifted his attention between Wells and me. Bru gripped my hand. "Got it."

He certainly had, his direction firm. Bru's fingers moved, and suddenly, Wells's fingers were between the spaces. Like Wells was fighting for real estate. Wells's fingers brushed mine, and I sucked in a breath.

"Don't let go," Wells said, his voice an octave lower. Pressure moved into my waist, and though it was Bru's hand, I wasn't quite sure if the action had been made by Bru. Wells eased out a slow breath, the warm current sending tendrils of awareness across the back of my neck. "Hold her steady, bro. Firm frame."

"I'm not letting go." Bru's voice had deepened too. It'd gotten *husky*, and, even though he was talking to Wells, Bru was looking at me. Bru's hand moved, and, suddenly, it was at the small of my back. This meant Wells's hand was too, and Wells stilled.

We stopped moving.

It was like I was frozen in a Bru-and-Wells sandwich but tendrils of awareness hit me again when Bru's finger played at the space where my top brushed my leggings. There was a sliver of skin there, and Bru managed to find it. My nipples beaded as his index finger touched my spine. This meant *Wells's finger* touched my spine because both boys' hands were definitely still together.

It was Wells that sucked in a breath behind me. His hand instantly gripped Bru's, but he didn't let go.

"I guess your hand can go there too," Wells said, his voice gruff, and I fought the gasp in my throat when he pressed Bru's hand to the small of my back. "Just like that."

Something of a low rumble occurred in Bru's chest, but I may have been the only one who heard it. Bru was right in front of me, and his pupils had dilated, his eyes hooded, lidded. He looked nearly sex drunk, and I wondered if that was because Wells was touching him. He was looking at me though... Bru wet his lips. "Mmhmm."

Wells continued to put pressure into my back and swayed us again. Wells wasn't touching me. He'd only done so that one time, and that had obviously been an accident. "You're doing so good."

Warm heat moved the top of my hair. Like Wells had spoken those words down *toward me*, but that wasn't possible.

"Um, this is interesting."

Wells put distance between Bru and me. In fact, he was

halfway across the room when the three of us were joined by not one but two people. My brother, Thatcher, had spoken, and he wasn't alone.

Aspen Davis, his girlfriend, was with him. She was beautiful, with dark skin and hip-length locs that framed her heart-shaped face. She had one of those sweet faces and also had an amazing sense of fashion I could only hope found me in the next life. Her wrap dress hugged her shapely curves, and, even with her stiletto heels, she didn't quite reach my brother's height. He had his arm around her, but he dropped it upon studying Wells, Bru, and me.

Thatcher's head cocked. "What's going on?"

My brother's look was curious between his friends. He kept looking back and forth between Bru and Wells, but it was Wells who stepped forward. Wells pushed a hand through his hair. "Bru and I were just teaching Squeak how to dance."

Squeak.

And just like that we were back. I was the kid sister who annoyed him. I was the pipsqueak he hated.

I was the girl who ruined his life.

Casually, Wells leaned back against the wall. He tucked his hands under his arms. "You know our parents made us take all those etiquette classes." He lifted a shoulder. "I was just helping out I guess."

Nothing about what he said was false, but it just shot reality into what I was to him. I just caught him in a brief moment of kindness. He'd been happy I helped him out with his math and made me an omelet and taught me how to dance. Nothing had changed. He didn't like me and never would.

"Yeah," Bru said, and I didn't know why that hurt more. Maybe because Bru didn't hate me. But he didn't like me either. He liked Wells, and that was why whatever weird tension had just happened between the three of us. Bru braced his arms. "Bow and I were watching a show, and she mentioned not being able to dance."

"So you two were teaching her." Thatcher directed a finger between both of his friends. He looked hilarious standing next to Aspen, considering his mighty size. He was built like our dad, which basically meant he was the size of a small truck. Thatcher fastened his attention to me. He had two earrings in his ears, and they dangled when he eyed me. "That true?"

I nodded. My brother smiled.

"Well, that's good," Thatcher said, mostly to Wells. My brother actually *grinned* at Wells. "Really good. Nice."

"Yeah, I told you things were different," Wells continued. He was such a good liar, and I almost believed him.

For a second there, things did feel different. It wasn't just that he didn't hate me though. It felt like something else, something *more*.

You're dumb.

I was surprised to see Aspen. I thought she was on tour.

I smiled when she waved at me, then hugged her. I missed her. She was so sweet and made my brother happy. I was also a huge hugger, and she laughed when I got her in a big, tight one.

"I missed you too," she said. She was such an awesome match for my brother and balanced him so well. Thatcher could be insane, and Aspen was so level-headed.

"What are you doing here?" I asked, and returned her to my brother who quickly put his arm back around her. It was so weird to see my brother in love. He'd definitely been a huge ladies' man in high school.

"Snowflake took a break from the tour to visit me," he said. I didn't know what it was with my brother and his friends. They seemed to always give their girlfriends nick-names. I didn't know why Thatcher called Aspen "snowflake," but the term of endearment never failed to bring the joy out on her pretty face. He brought her close. "I guess she missed my ass."

"Hardly," she said, teasing when she jabbed him. She looped her thin arms around his large waist. "Your brother basically begged me."

"Yeah, I did. Because I missed *your* ass and *this* ass." He caught her butt in his hand which made my face hot and his friends roll their eyes. Wells actually groaned. He mentioned something about not wanting to see all that, and Thatcher flipped him off.

"Fuck you," Thatcher said, then picked Aspen up by, well, her ass. She squealed and he smacked it. My brother grinned. "Anyway, if you need us, Imma be letting Aspen know exactly how much I missed her in my room."

"Thatcher, come on!" Aspen kicked, but she definitely giggled. Wells groaned again, and Bru laughed.

"Yeah, I'm not staying here tonight," Wells said after Thatcher and his girlfriend disappeared down the hallway. Aspen continued to giggle the entire way. Wells cringed. "Fucker and I share a wall, and I'm not trying to hear that shit all night."

Wells grabbed his hoodie off the chair he'd been sitting on this evening. Apparently our tutoring session was over, and he wasn't even staying to eat the celebratory omelet he made.

Wells tugged his hoodie down over his shirt, then pushed up the sleeves. "I'll probably couch-surf with a friend tonight."

He didn't say it, but that *friend* would probably be one of his casual hookups. He most likely would be bedding with a girl or guy tonight, sans couch. His evening might even include both knowing him.

I didn't know what impulse made me move my feet, but a burst of panic hit my chest thinking he'd hook up with someone tonight. I followed him to the door.

"You can stay at my place." The words tumbled out of my

mouth before I could stop them. Before I realized how weird and stupid they were.

Wells turned around. He'd been at the door and had a joint pressed between his lips. His eyes narrowed. "What was that?"

I supposed I had spoken kind of fast. I mean, I panicked. *Why had I panicked?*

I didn't know, but with those words out there, I had to follow them up. My shoulders rose, my body suddenly feeling small. I messed with my hands. "I said you can stay at my place."

Wells's blinks were rapid before his head shot back. "What are you talking about? And where would I even stay?"

The *where* was easy. I may have had a one-bedroom dorm, but I had a futon. My heart raced. "It's just you said you needed a place to stay and I have that futon and everything so…"

It was dumb. So dumb, and I wished I hadn't said anything.

Immediately, I thought to backpedal, but when I opened my mouth, Bru stepped forward.

"I think it's a good idea," he said, surprising me. He shrugged. "It makes sense, and anyway, if Wells doesn't take the offer, I will. Thatcher and I share a wall too."

"Nah, I'm taking the offer." Wells flicked his joint to the other side of his mouth. He stepped right up to Bru. Wells's eyes narrowed. "If you're gonna come too, you can put your ass on the floor and sleep there."

Bru's expression cooled. "Fine."

"Fine," Wells said.

I glanced between the two of them and that lion comparison came to me again. They were like two peacocks showing off their feathers, but that didn't make sense. No, it wouldn't make sense.

At least when it came to me.

CHAPTER
FIFTEEN

Wells

"Wells, she's drowning! Wells, save her!"

I jumped into action, panicked. I swam like my life depended on it.

It did.

I put that out of my mind and spotted Bow at the bottom of the pool. I grabbed her arm and pulled her to me.

Don't die. Please don't die.

I breached the surface with her frail little body in my arms. She smelled like nutmeg and cinnamon buns. She smelled like Bow.

Don't die. Don't die. Don't die.

She was limp when I pulled her out of the water. She wasn't moving, and she was pale.

People screamed around me. Her friends cried. Everyone was freaking out, but I couldn't. I was her only hope.

I pressed my mouth to hers, giving her my life, my breath.

Come on, Bow. Come on.

This wasn't right. She wasn't the girl who drowned. She wasn't the girl I couldn't save.

"Bow!" Water dripped from my hair across her face, her skin ghost white when she was normally rosy red. This girl blushed like a motherfucker, and I always wondered what it would be like to touch it. To drag my finger across the tint and see what it did. Would she blush more?

Would it last?

I never got the chance to see what it would do. All color had drained from her face, and my repetitions to bring her back to life weren't doing anything. She wasn't coming back, no matter how much I tried. My best friend's little sister drowned, and it was my fault. I couldn't bring her back.

I couldn't save her.

Bru

Wells called out, and it jolted me from my sleep. He was thrashing on Bow's futon, and I got up off the floor. Bow had set up a makeshift bed for me there.

"Breathe, goddammit! You have to. You have to…" Sweat lined Wells's brow, and he gripped the blanket that'd been covering him. Bow had given that to him too. Wells sucked in a breath. "If you die, I'll die. I swear to God…"

An ache hit the guy's voice, and it ripped its way through me. I'd never seen him like this. I shook him. "Wells?"

"Please, wake up. Please!"

I shook him harder. "Wells!"

Wells jolted awake, and I thought he'd punch me in the jaw since he'd woken so violently. The color drained from his face. Wells gazed around. He looked panicked or in some kind of crazy daze.

I squeezed his arm and my hand came away damp. His cut-off tee was drenched as well around the neck. I ignored it, searching for his eyes. "Wells?"

His green irises focused on me, and right away, he sighed. It was like seeing me brought him some kind of relief.

I wouldn't let it affect me that my presence did that. I couldn't get wrapped up with him like that again. Things had been bullshit between us for weeks.

"Bru," he said, and didn't call me the kid. He didn't call me anything else at all.

He just kissed me.

I froze, his masculine scent filling my nose, and the next thing I knew, he was messing with my sweatpants. He managed to get a hand inside, and I pulled that shit right back out. I shoved his hand away. "What are you doing?"

Ignoring me, he shoved me down to the floor. His mouth returned to mine, and it was just like that day he came onto me at our house. He was all anger, all *heat*, and I winced just like I had the last time this happened. This shit hurt like a son of a bitch.

"*Stop*," I gritted, my heart racing, but then he bit me. Groaning, I felt the heat rush to my cock the same time I got a hold of his shirt to push him away. This wasn't right, and I wasn't going to let him do this shit to me again. I only joined in on his study sessions with Bow to see what was going on with him and her. He acted like he hated her, but he didn't that night she was on the balcony. In fact, the only other time I'd seen him that scared was right before I woke him up tonight.

"No," I growled, forcing him back, away. It took effort, and even though I was stronger than him physically, that didn't matter. Mentally, this asshole had me in a headlock.

He wasn't the only one.

How quickly I took up Bow's invitation to come to her house tonight and definitely used her brother as an excuse. Yeah, I probably would have been able to hear Thatcher and his girlfriend fucking, but a set of earplugs could have corrected that. I lived in a house full of dudes who had serious girlfriends. Having a good set of earplugs was a given.

I took Bow up on her invitation because I wanted to be close to her, and I also didn't want Wells around her. For some reason, I got territorial seeing them together. I think it was because I did know they were friends, and it didn't matter whether Wells passed that off or not. I saw the way he looked when he had his hands on her tonight. Technically, it had been *my* hands, but I merely felt like a conduit. Like he was touching her *through me*, and the heat that backed his eyes confirmed that, the way he stared down at her…

"Don't let go… Hold her steady, bro… Just like that…"

Wells had said similar things while we were in bed with a woman. He told me what to do, how to treat a partner and how to fuck her within an inch of her life. He did that so beautifully. We did that *together*.

"Don't let go of her. Guide her…"

There was something… happening, and it wasn't just between Wells and Bow, Bow and me, or even Wells and me. It was *us*. All three of us because the heat in Wells's eyes only ignited when it returned to mine. Honestly, I thought he'd punch me after seeing how being so close to Thatcher's sister affected me. He'd do that on behalf of Thatcher whether she annoyed him or not, but that's *not* what happened. Wells's grip on my hands increased. Like he didn't exactly mind I was touching our best friend's little sister.

It didn't make sense.

My confusion about his actions only outweighed the confusion about my own. When the evening started, I didn't want Wells having anything to do with Bow. I was into her, and I was jealous of Bow's history with Wells for some reason. *I* wanted to be her fucking friend, but in the same thought, I also wanted Wells. It was so fucking confusing, but when the three of us were dancing together tonight, it wasn't. It'd all felt natural.

It felt right.

It felt just as good as Wells Ambrose shoving his tongue down my throat now, but I couldn't do this with him. I couldn't let him do this *to me*, not again. I gripped his arms, attempting to shove him off me.

"Don't fucking fight me," he growled, his tongue flicking mine, and I groaned. He also returned his hand to my sweatpants. With a skilled hand, Wells felt me up from the outside and a charged noise left my throat. My head rolled back into Bow's rug, and I felt so fucking weak. Wells gripped my jaw. "Let me own you."

Why was I? Why did I let this dude get to me every fucking time?

Fighting his draw, I reared back. My fist connected with his perfect jaw, and he bit my lip before separating from my mouth. The immediate taste of metal filled my mouth, and Wells laughed upon seeing it before crowding me and tasting the blood himself.

Fuck.

"No." His hair was in my hands, but I wasn't pushing him off me anymore. My hands were embedded in his scalp, but I wasn't pushing him away. Why wasn't I pushing him away? "Wells, I swear to God…"

My threats were empty because when his chin dipped, I let him pepper kisses across my jaw, then my neck. His hand slid into my sweatpants, and my back instinctually lifted off the floor.

"Please," he said, all laughter in his voice gone. He was begging me, and Wells Ambrose didn't beg. His teeth sunk into my neck the same time his relentless fist got a hold of my cock. He pumped, and I immediately swelled inside his grip. I didn't want to be affected by his touch. I just couldn't… help it. He pressed his mouth against my neck. "Bru, I need to fuck you. Please let me."

Again, Wells never pleaded with anyone, and definitely

not me. In actuality, he typically got off on being able to control me.

I felt like the one who was in control in this moment, and that ache his voice had when he'd been sleeping, dreaming returned. He sounded like he needed me and not whoever he was thinking about in his dream.

He sounded like he wanted me.

"Fuck," I gritted, completely giving in when I grabbed his face. I forced him closer, and he kissed me harder, deeper.

"Shit," Wells ground out and somehow we both ended up back on the futon. I didn't know who grabbed who but we both ended up falling on it.

The legs buckled.

I thought that shit would seriously break with both of us on top of it. We quickly became a sea of dueling tongues and aggressive kisses. Wells lost his shirt, and we collided against each other like crashing waves. We were two tsunamis fighting for dominance, and there was nothing like kissing this guy, fucking him. I'd always known I'd been into guys as much as girls, but I'd never been with any guys until I'd gone overseas for college. I had a few male partners here and there, but it was different being with Wells.

It felt different.

I tried not to think hard about why it was, the emotions I felt, the feelings. I just let Wells turn me over and tug down my pants.

Yes.

Wells spit into his hand first. Then he shoved his cock to the hilt inside me. I bit my arm to keep from calling out, and he bit my neck.

Fuuuck.

Wells's hips slammed against me, relentless as his dick when it drove into me with piston-like precision. He grabbed my throat, his other hand on one of mine to keep his momentum, and I had both hands on Bow's futon just to keep us upright. It was so fucking fucked up we were doing this on Bow's couch, and I didn't even *want* to do this. I didn't want Wells, and I definitely didn't want to do this with Wells.

Tell my body that as I let him fuck me. Tell my balls that as they surged and my dick felt on the cusp of unloading. I fought hard not to touch myself, to give in.

"Come on, Bru. Let me fucking own you, bro," Wells taunted. Releasing my neck, he fisted my dick, stroking and playing with my balls. He bit my neck. "Give in."

I grabbed the closest thing I could find. That turned out to be Wells's shirt because there was no way I was letting this dude make me come all over Bow's couch. I also wanted some fucking payback after he tossed me a box of tissues last time we were together.

"Fuck, Ambrose. *Fuck.*" I bit my arm, filling his shirt with my cum. My eyes rolled back as I unloaded, and at the same time, Wells's momentum picked up. His hips slammed into me once, then twice before he filled my ass.

"Yes," Wells said, his dick surging inside me. I shook while he did, so fucking full before he pulled out. His cum dripped out of my ass, and I felt him push it back in. He even parted my ass cheeks to do it, and I wanted to turn him around. I wanted to own *his* ass. He kept making me the bitch in more than one way. His forehead touched my back. "God, Bru…"

He sounded so much like he needed that, like being with me did something for him, and that made me feel more than pathetic. I'd given in *again.*

I started to push Wells off me, to say fuck this guy, but he got off me first. In fact, he shoved me away from him, a curse under his breath.

I glanced up and froze.

We weren't alone.

Wells and I probably hadn't been quiet. I'd been doing what I could by biting my arm and had the welts to prove it but that obviously hadn't worked. Bow was standing in front of us now, behind the futon.

Our best friend's sister was in her nightgown. It was sheer and an outline of dark circles were beneath. I'd never seen Bow's nipples before, the peaks like Hershey kisses…

Bow's face drained of color. Her dark hair was down over her shoulders. The waves actually intercepted with her arm because her hand was inside of her nightgown. She had a pinkie on the edge of one of her areolas.

Like she'd been touching herself.

A face that had been drained of color suddenly had so much. Bow's flashed the tint of a fire hydrant before she rushed away. Somewhere in her dorm, a door slammed. Then Wells was moving too.

"Fucking, fuck. *Fuck*," he growled before working his pants up. I blinked, still in shock by everything, but once that faded a little, I managed to get my pants up too.

What the fuck just happened?

Neither Wells nor I talked about it. We just got ourselves together and I barely had my pants on before Wells was out of Bow's dorm. The front door slammed with a snap behind him, and he hadn't bothered to put his shirt back on. I guess I didn't blame him.

It was filled with my cum.

Christ.

Grabbing his shirt, I took it with me to the front door. I shifted back and forth on my feet. I was at war on if I should go check on Bow or not.

In the end, I opted to leave too. Though, I didn't do so as dramatically as Wells. Bow's RA was probably aware of enough noise coming from Bow's dorm without me adding to it.

Goddammit.

After closing the door softly behind me, I headed back to Legacy House. I guess I'd be sleeping there tonight and didn't regret not talking to Bow before leaving. I didn't want to make things more awkward for her than they already were, and I knew why I'd chosen that option the longer I thought about it in my own bed that night. It wasn't just that Bow had walked in on Wells and me together. I mean, that was embarrassing, but then there was what she'd been doing watching us. I saw clear as day what she'd been doing.

And it affected me just as much as seeing my best friend's little sister's tits in a nightgown.

CHAPTER
SEVENTEEN

Bow

"Babe, are you sure everything is okay? You normally love going to taco night at the Ambroses."

I glanced up at my mom. She was staring at me from the front seat of my dad's Escalade, and my dad had also stopped the car. Apparently, we'd arrived at our destination in the time I'd been spacing off.

Crap.

I unstrapped myself. Dad was staring at me too, but he wasn't saying anything.

I bit my lip. "I'm fine."

"Are you sure?" Mom reached back and put her hand on my forehead. She was small like me, but she was blond and had way more confidence than I had. My dad was a big guy. He was literally like three of her, but he became a puppy dog when it came to my mom. She was confident and beautiful, wonderful. Mom's head tilted. "You don't feel warm."

That was because I wasn't sick. At least when it came to a cold or the flu or something.

Mom pulled her hand back. "We can take you back home if you're not feeling up for tonight."

Mom had been asking me about the state of my health since before we left the house. She was right. I normally loved taco night at the Ambroses. Jaxen and Cleo Ambrose were my parents' best friends. My parents had a lot of good friends but my family saw a lot of the Ambroses due to Thatcher and Wells. Thatcher and Wells were really close, and Jaxen and Cleo Ambrose happened to be Wells's parents.

Which was why my mother thought I was sick.

Wells never went to our family's taco nights. Not since he and Thatcher went off to college, anyway. I guess the boys never felt like making the two-hour trek back to Maywood Heights, but I always came.

"I'm sure Jax and Cleo will understand," my dad said. He frowned. "You don't have to put on a brave face if you're not feeling well."

My dad was even more protective of me than Thatcher and his friends. Let's just say that, if guys actually paid attention to me, they wouldn't because of him. My dad could be very intimidating, but he was just as much of a puppy dog when it came to me. I was his little girl.

I shook my head. I wore a long braid and nice blouse for dinner tonight, and I played with the braid on my shoulder for a second before I realized how nervous that probably looked. I smiled. "I'm okay."

Dad didn't look like he believed me. Neither did Mom, but, in the end, Mom grabbed her dish of taco meat, and Dad grabbed the Crock-Pot of refried beans. Mom liked to make her own beans for taco night.

He's not going to be here. You'll be fine.

I would be fine because Wells Ambrose never came to taco nights with our parents.

Wells was here for taco night with our parents. I saw him after I toed off my heeled Mary Jane shoes and my sock-covered feet had taken me into the Ambroses' lavish dining room. I had a bowl of premixed salad in my hands.

I nearly dropped the salad.

That would have sucked because I would have had salad all over my feet in front of Wells, who currently sat at his parents' dining room table. It was a large, oak table with several place settings, and Wells stood the moment I entered the room. He wore a sweater and slacks *and a tie*, like he ever wore a sweater, slacks, and a tie. Wells never wore anything that wasn't the epitome of comfort.

He even moussed his hair.

His platinum-blond locks were slicked back, exposing his dark roots. The dramatic clash in tones gave his formal look an edge that probably wasn't intentional, but what *was* had to be the ice in his eyes the moment he saw me. A frosty set of emerald irises hit me, his eyes narrowing briefly before he smiled up at my parents. He shook my dad's hand and hugged my mom. My parents were like second parents to him and his were the same to Thatcher and me.

Oh, God.

Wells's eyes were on me as he shook my dad's hand that evening, and they were also there when he'd let go to hug my mom. It was like he had something reserved for me, and whatever it was, it was dark.

It was bad.

It was as terrible as what he and Bru caught me doing the other night. I came out of my bedroom knowing what I'd see that night.

I had even hoped for it.

I hadn't heard from Wells after what happened, but Bru texted me this morning.

Bru: We should talk when you get a chance.

Of course, I didn't want to talk. I got caught doing something really invasive. The guys were having a private moment and I…

"Bow," Wells said, striding over to me. The chill in his tone matched his body language. He was rigid, something he let slip only briefly before smiling at me. "Good to see you."

My mouth parted but all four adults in the room smiled, even my dad, who *never* smiled.

Wells's parents were gorgeous. His mom, Cleo, was a lovely brunette who could easily pass for a basketball player since she was so tall. She wasn't much into sports though, but I knew she liked to garden. Wells got his softer features from her but his joking nature from his dad, Jax. Mr. Ambrose was also classically handsome like an old Hollywood movie star, and Wells got that from him.

Wells wasn't joking tonight when he stopped in front of me. I was thrown for a loop when he wrapped one of his lengthy arms around me.

I froze, nothing but a salad bowl between me, this guy, and the obvious heat that rolled off him. Immediately, I was surrounded by his cool scent and it reminded me of the last time I'd seen him. The common room of my dorm had been filled with it. It was ocean breeze, sex, and the deep, crisp smell of Bruno Sloane-Mallick combined with it. Wells and Bru smelled *great* together and my mouth watered just thinking about it.

"You're going to regret coming tonight, you little Peeping-fucking-Tom," Wells ground out in my ear. The words sliced me from my thoughts, and, heart racing, I gripped the salad bowl between us. Wells squeezed my arm. "Let me help you with that salad."

He was taking it in the next breath, and I could breathe when he finally let go. I wavered in my knee-highs, my breaths anxious, rapid, but I was the only one who'd been privy to Wells's threats.

I knew by the state of the room.

The parents, all of them, were staring at Wells and me after the hug and Wells's seemingly kind gesture. My parents looked happy, but Wells's were ecstatic. His dad was nodding to mine, and Cleo had her hand to her mouth. Like what her son did pleased her.

Oh…

It pleased all our parents, and my dad had nothing but a praiseful look for Wells when he passed my parents to put the bowl on the table. He *pleased* my dad, and that wasn't easy to do.

Wells sat down at the table, even taking the time to place his napkin on his lap before facing our parents. He grinned. "I'm ready to eat when everyone else is."

———

Wells sat incredibly close to me that evening. I attempted to sit *across* from him, but he got up and manufactured an excuse to do it. He claimed he could help me with his long reach to get food from across the table.

And our parents ate it up.

Both the Reeds and the Ambroses went without knowledge of whatever it was Wells was doing. He was incredibly accommodating as he got anything I needed while I sat next to him.

He even served me refried beans.

The parents had *loved* that, and Wells showed up with his humor tonight. He took any opportunity he could to joke with our parents, and when he wasn't doing that, he was laughing at funny things that *I* said. He was overly pleasant to me when he little more than acknowledged me before our study sessions together. He was playing some kind of game for our parents. He even thanked me for tutoring him at one point.

"I'm actually starting to get things in my classes now," Wells said, sitting back. He draped his long arm behind my chair, and I sat forward. He smirked. "I can't thank Bow enough for helping me. I think I'll actually do well this semester thanks to her and Bru."

He mentioned Bru's help too but only briefly. Wells had been keeping the focus on me mostly.

Wells grinned wide. "She's even letting me take her to Dorian's draft celebration in thanks."

He was referring to his friend Dorian Prinze. My brother and most of his friends played football for Pembroke, but only Dorian was pursuing going professional. I think he was more passionate about the game than the other guys. He was good and definitely could be one of the greats. He *would* be one of the greats. He worked so hard.

I think we all knew it wasn't *if* Dorian would play for the NFL. He had scouts out for him since high school. It was a matter of which team he'd play for at this point and his parents were already proactively planning a party for him. It was more like a gala, with formal wear and media attention. I planned to be there, but I didn't have an escort.

Apparently, Wells was making himself my escort.

I tried not to shrink in my chair. I tried not *to shake* when Wells's arm brushed my neck. The contact shot a sharp chill through me and I felt like my world was tilting on its axis.

I feel like I'm going to faint.

I held it in, and when I looked at Wells, he was still grinning at our parents. He did with that well-oiled smile, but behind me he had his arm hugging my chair tighter and tighter. He was actually tilting it with the strength of his bicep. His hand squeezed into a white-knuckled fist, but I think I was the only one who noticed it.

My stomach soured. I didn't know what Wells was doing, but whatever he had planned wasn't good for me. He took a drink after his declaration and his mom, Cleo, squeezed his shoulder.

"Oh, honey. That's so nice, and I'm so proud of you," she said.

"We both are." Wells's dad, Jax, put his arm around his wife. The pair were nice, *normal,* and nothing like their son. They didn't play games.

They weren't cruel.

He wasn't always this way.

Swallowing, I faced forward. I couldn't breathe, my lungs squeezing.

"And I have to say, I'm happy this arrangement is working out," Jax said. He gestured between Wells and me with his brandy glass.

"I agree," my dad said, and smiled again. He nodded toward Wells, and, though Wells smiled, the expression didn't quite meet his green eyes. If anything, the smile faltered a little. That was only brief before he beamed at the table, and my dad, again.

"You're going to regret coming tonight, you little Peeping-fuck-ing-Tom."

"Um, I have to go to the bathroom," I said quickly. I got up even quicker and almost dropped my napkin. I laughed a little. "Sorry."

I didn't know what I was apologizing for.

I need to vomit.

My stomach lurching, I didn't get a chance to see the room's reaction to me leaving so suddenly. I just *left* and found the closest bathroom I could.

I ended up dry heaving.

How nothing came up I didn't know, but I stayed by the toilet for a few seconds just to make sure. I was shaking by the time I flushed nothing away. I splashed water on my face, and that was when the door snapped open. A breeze of something cool and masculine filled my nose before I was backed up against the sink.

He threw the potpourri off the counter. The flower petals exploded against the wall like floral fireworks, and I would have screamed but a hand got my jaw. It cut off the sound from my throat when Wells physically closed my mouth.

He honed in.

"I have to lie for you," he said, getting so close, and I was shaking. In fact, the only thing holding me up was my jaw, my face in his grip, his digits literally embedding themselves in my cheeks. Wells tossed *and caught* footballs all the time. He was great at it. Strong. His nostrils flared. "I have to lie *to our parents* for you."

I never told him to lie. I never told him to do anything of that stuff he was doing downstairs. I grabbed his sweater. "Wells—"

The word came out mumbled with my jaw closed, and he shook my hands off him like I was a rag doll. Wells had never physically hurt me before. He'd been angry at me but never once had he ever acted on that anger.

Never once had he looked like he wanted to kill me.

"Please," I gasped out and all that did was make his eyes narrow. He was no longer the clean-cut boy with charisma downstairs. He was now the unhinged dirty blond with a vendetta against his best friend's little sister. He even *looked* unhinged, crazed. His blond hair that had been so meticulously smoothed back was crossing over his eyes. Like he let go of the facade the moment he decided to corner me in the bathroom.

"Did you enjoy what you saw the other night, *Squeak*?" he asked, biting out the nickname. I trembled, and his fingers squeezed harder in my jaw. He growled. "Did you like getting up in *my* motherfucking business?"

I wished I could say I didn't but I'd be lying. I fully knew what I was doing that night. I even liked it, and I knew that didn't make sense. I should be jealous of his connection with Bru. I liked Bru so much… I blinked back a tear. "I'm sorry."

The words weren't a lie, but if I told him the reason I said the words, he would hurt me.

I wasn't sorry for what I did.

I was just sorry he caught me.

Again, *I knew* that didn't make sense, and I closed my eyes as he drew in closer. Another thing that didn't make sense was how that tremble had suddenly moved to my thighs. Nor the *tingle* that pulsed between my legs the harder his hand gripped my cheeks. The cool scent of him glided over my face, my mouth, and it shocked my system with heat as much as the fear that currently immobilized my body against the sink.

"Did your little virgin ass *love* getting off on watching us," he asked, and I swallowed. "Did it get you hot? Get you bothered…"

"I'm not a virgin," I gasped out, again the word mumbled.

Wells let go. I hadn't been expecting it and nearly fell to the floor. I gripped the sink, and when I looked up, he was scanning the tiles of his parents' bathroom.

"What do you *mean* you're not a virgin?" He was on me again in seconds, in my face. His eyes flared. "Who the fuck would touch you?"

My chest rising and falling with rapid breaths, I was still trying to figure out what just happened. "What?"

"I said who *the fuck* would touch you?" His nose was almost touching mine, and I swallowed. He bared his teeth. "Who the fuck would dare?"

I was still so… confused. Did it bother him I was with someone? That couldn't be true. Unless…

I was so dumb. It did bother him. Of course it did. If I was with someone, that meant he hadn't intimidated someone enough to stay away from me. To make me *suffer*.

To keep me alone.

What happened in high school had made me a social pariah, and if someone touched me, that meant someone had gotten through. They beat Wells at his own game, but I never intended to beat Wells. In fact, me losing my virginity had nothing to do with him.

At least, that was what I told myself.

My vision clouding, I refused to think about the moment in question. How I had lost my virginity, and, in the moment, I thought that had given me power. It didn't though. It just made me feel gross, dirty.

"Who, Squeak?" Wells was on me, and though his nose wasn't touching me, his breath was. Heat ghosted over my lips. Especially when he gripped the sink on either side of my hips. "Who was inside you?"

I sucked in a breath, liquid heat pulsing between my legs. I wet my lips, and Wells's green eyes darted to my mouth.

"This turning you on, Squeak? Making you hot?" His chest inched closer.

What is he doing?

I didn't know, but I was frozen when he took a piece of potpourri off the sink. Some of it had landed on the basin, and Wells took a long stick.

He inched my skirt up.

The stick was strong, thick, and it had to be because soon Wells had my twill skirt clear above my knee-highs. He exposed my skin, and I pressed my legs together. "What are you doing?"

He wasn't listening to me, focused as he hiked my skirt up inch by grueling inch. He was right beneath my boy shirts before he stopped. "He or she make you tremble like this?" he asked, and my breath sucked in again.

"A he," I said, and once more, his eyes shot up. Something wild flared his eyes to electric tones. The color didn't actually change, but it seemed like it did, a heat behind them.

"He, then," he stated, the words dark, low. They rolled in his chest before he was taking that stick and moving it *between* my legs.

"Wells—"

He moved my knees apart, pressing the end of the stick hard into both knees. It was thin enough that it stabbed me, and I winced before falling back to the mirror.

Wells was at the space between my legs, and he moved that stick so it was brushing my sex through my underwear. I wriggled. "Wells—"

"Don't *fucking* move," he gritted, the threat keeping me still. Wells's breath was incredibly husky, and my back bowed when he guided that stick between my folds. My underwear was sheer and I felt *everything*. He growled. "How wet did he make you?"

The words followed the movement of the stick. He rubbed, gently at first, but then harder, faster.

"Wells, don't." I said this but my legs were so wide. They'd actually fallen apart and my knees had hit the sink. "Why are you doing this?"

He wasn't listening to me, his eyes *and stick* focused. He looked down, watching them both, and his jaw was so tight I thought the bone would pierce the skin.

"How do you like to get fucked, Squeak?" Wells asked, but he wasn't looking at me. He just kept moving the stick, and, at this point, my hips were rocking against it. I thought to reach out to him, to hold him, but if I did, I'd fall off the sink.

If I did, he might stop.

My toes curling, I wasn't shy about moving my hips. I slammed against him, my ministrations meeting his.

"You like this," he said, his words incredibly dark. "You open your legs this easy for him?"

The words were like an ice bath but that was only part of the reason why I froze on the sink.

Wells had stopped.

He had the stick out between us, the wood damp from the moisture that clearly seeped through my underwear. His expression was deadpan. "Of course, you did."

He tossed the stick at me, and I winced. Right away, I closed my legs, and when I got off the sink, he was already at the door. He had his back to me, his hand on the doorknob. Tears pricked my eyes. "Wells…"

He sounded *and looked* as if he was disgusted by me, and that shouldn't bother me. I shouldn't care that he knew I'd been with someone. It wasn't his business. I shouldn't *care*.

Tell my emotions that when I wiped my tears away. Feeling suddenly naked, I adjusted my skirt and attempted to cover myself as much as I could even though I was fully clothed.

Wells wet his lips. "You tell anybody about what you saw last night and you'll regret it," he said opening the door. He paused. "And you might want to wipe yourself off before coming downstairs. Don't want my parents to know you just got yourself off in their bathroom with a stick."

He could have slapped me in that moment and that would have hurt less.

I supposed that'd been the point.

Wells Ambrose wanted to make me feel dirty for what happened. I hadn't when he'd been doing it, but I did now.

Fighting the sob in my throat, I sat down. I held my knees until I felt like I didn't want to cry anymore, and after, I cleaned up the bathroom. I went downstairs and sat in my parents' car after that.

I told them I was sick.

CHAPTER
EIGHTEEN

Bru

"Bow… Hey, Bow, wait!"

Bow's hands were moving quickly, packing up her stuff on the quad.

She'd started once I called her name.

She'd clearly been studying, but one word from me got her moving. She'd also been ignoring my texts over the past few days. I wanted to talk to her about what she walked in on between Wells and me. I wanted *to talk*, but she'd been avoiding me.

This was confirmed with the way she turned into the Road Runner the moment she heard me call after her. She was on her feet by the time I made it over to her, her book bag slung over her arm. Her face was red, and even though she clearly heard me call her, she gazed down and darted in the opposite direction. She attempted to sprint away in her little skirt, a skirt that swayed and exposed her legs in ways I certainly hadn't noticed before she kissed me in my car.

I did now though. God, *did I know*, and I felt like a perv.

Her brother was my friend, and I definitely hadn't told him the thoughts I had about his little sister lately. I couldn't help it considering the last time I'd seen her. Her hand down her nightshirt...

"Bow." I cut her off, and her eyes flashed. They sparked huge, her cheeks rosy, flushed. I shouldn't have scared her though. She knew I'd been behind her. I posted my hands on my hips. "We need to talk."

About so many things. She'd obviously walked in on Wells and me, but there was also that other thing. She'd been touching herself that night while watching us.

And I definitely wanted to talk about that.

My mind hazed thinking about the way she looked, intrigued and turned the fuck on. She'd been embarrassed, yes, but it hadn't bothered her seeing me with someone else. In fact, her expression matched similar looks women had when Wells and I had threesomes. Sometimes things would get... intense between Wells and me and the women we were with always enjoyed all three of us together.

Bow had sported a similar look, but I wasn't trying to think about those girls. In fact, the very thought about doing what Wells and I did with someone else made my stomach knot. The girl wouldn't have Bow's deep blue eyes, or the sweet flush of her skin. It looked so sweet, smelled sweet...

Bow started to cut around me, my mind going to really fucking inappropriate places. This was *Thatcher's sister*, and there needed to be some respect there. That respect went quadruple for Bow herself. She was my friend and deserved that.

I got in front of her again. "Bow, please—"

"No, Bru." She skittered away, then gazed around for some reason. It was like she was looking for someone. She pushed some of her curls out of her face that had fallen from her normally tight bun. I had her completely frazzled, and I hated that. She huffed. "There's nothing to talk about."

Like hell.

I cut her off again. This time, I folded a hand behind her and guided her behind a tree. We were going to have this discussion whether she wanted to have it or not.

"You've been avoiding me," I said, out of breath and honestly frustrated. I didn't understand why I was fucking out of breath when all I did was jog across the quad to talk to her. I worked out like a lot but my heart was basically charging a million beats a minute right now.

It only picked up its beats when I looked at her.

She had a flush across her chest that matched the one in her cheeks. I was crowding her because I didn't trust her not to leave now that I had her in one place. This meant I essentially had her pinned up against a tree, and though I shouldn't be looking at her chest, *her breasts,* they were right in front of me. The top two buttons of her white blouse were open, which meant I could easily see how ample her chest was, supple. Bow was a tiny girl but the swell could easily fill my hands.

Fuck.

She was noticing me too. Or at least was *aware* of me. She gazed at my chest too, my pecs rising and falling with heavy breaths. I wore a Pembroke sweatshirt but how clearly she excited me could easily be seen.

I closed the distance. "We need to talk about what you saw the other night."

Her lashes flickered. I'd told myself I was going to approach Bow today to make sure she was okay. The situation had been awkward. It was awkward for me because I still didn't know what happened that night between Wells and me. He wasn't talking to me either. I'd sent him several texts.

I just knew Wells had clearly been in his head that night. Something got him riled up and the two of us ended up fucking again. I didn't want to do it. I was tired of that fucker playing with my emotions.

But I wanted him. I wanted his weight on me, *his heat*. I wasn't normally about submitting when it came to sex, but with Wells, that was what I wanted. I didn't want to feel so strong. I wanted my walls broken down. I wanted to be *vulnerable*.

It was different with Bow.

With Bow, *I* wanted to be her force of safety. I wanted to be a safe space *for her* vulnerability, and it was so confusing. I wanted to be both things, and I felt like a selfish asshole because how could I want two very different things with two very different people?

But then I saw Bow that night. I saw her watching us, and something eased inside me. Like it was okay to want both, have both.

Bow's lips parted. "Bru—"

"Wells and I started fucking at parties," I said, getting right into it. Bow's eyes flashed. I nodded. "It started with partners... a woman between us."

I studied her reaction to that. I watched the breath leave her red lips at a rapid pace and the muscle in my chest kicked up more beats.

"Eventually, we forgot about the woman," I continued, getting even closer to her. "It started just being about us. It was a nice release after everything that happened in Europe."

That was how Wells got me to go to sex parties. He knew I was caught up in my head about being kicked out of school.

"So he is the someone else you were talking about," Bow said, and I nodded again. Her face got even redder. "You like him."

"I love him," I said, not beating around the bush. Bow's mouth parted, and I swallowed. "I do, which is why *this* confuses me."

"This?"

I touched her mouth, just a brush of my knuckle, but it was

enough to send a weakness to Bow's knees. I knew because she wavered before pressing herself against the tree, and she gasped when I parted her lips with that same knuckle. "Our kiss, Bow, was just as intense. Just *one kiss* from you was…"

Her mouth opened wide for my finger, spreading, and my cock twitched in my jeans.

My jaw moved. "That one kiss from you in my car was just as intense as what I experienced at those parties, Bow."

Which was *crazy* to me. Wells and I had a lot of hot fucking sex, but one kiss with this girl got me in my head.

One touch.

My hand touched her throat. I couldn't help it. I wanted to feel the column of her throat and how I affected her.

She didn't disappoint. Her swallow was so hard and that got *me* hard, which was so fucked up. This was my best friend's little sister.

And somehow that didn't matter anymore.

"I know you saw us together, Wells and me," I said, my chest brushing hers now, and I was happy that I got her behind this tree. I didn't want anyone else privy to this moment. My thumb touched her throat. "Did that bother you? Seeing me with someone else?"

She kissed me and I assumed that meant she had feelings for me. If so, her seeing me with someone else *should* bother her.

It didn't look like it bothered her. In fact, it very much looked like she'd enjoyed it.

"It didn't," she said, but her voice was so small. She didn't look like she wanted to admit it and maybe even felt some shame. She shouldn't. There was nothing wrong with being into watching two people together, and it was definitely possible to be into more than one person.

My thoughts went back to earlier that night, when the three of us had been dancing. It felt *right*, and I didn't think I was the only one who felt that way. I'd seen how Bow looked at Wells the night he talked her down off that ledge.

It'd been the same way he looked at her.

I didn't get to respond to what Bow said. I was grabbed from behind, and, in the next breath, I was on the ground. A fist came out of nowhere and slammed into my cheek so hard I tasted metal. A second fist hit my head and an amplified ringing hit my ears.

It wasn't as loud as Bow's scream.

Bow

Wells came out of nowhere…

And he was hitting Bru.

Wells shot a direct hit into Bru's jaw. His second punch narrowly missed Bru's eye, and I screamed so hard my throat burned. A crazy look was in Wells Ambrose's eyes as he reared back to hit Bru for a third time. But Bru caught Wells's fist this time and used the momentum to roll both boys. That didn't stop Wells, whose face was ten degrees of red and whose fists were moving so fast he ended up getting Bru in his gut. Bru gasped, the wind clearly knocked out of him, and I screamed again.

"It was you!" Wells shot before throwing an upper cut that caused Bru's jaw to click upon impact. Bru hadn't guarded his face, but this time he did when Wells quickly moved into raining fists down on him. Wells growled. "How could you! How fucking *could you*, dude? She's Thatcher's sister. How could you!"

By now, we were gaining a crowd. People were running behind the tree and pulling out their phones. They were recording, but all the attention was fading into the background for me. I just kept hearing what Wells said. He mentioned *me*.

"What are you talking about!" Bru shouted. He got Wells's fist and flipped them both again. He'd done so with a skill of someone who'd obviously fought before. He'd gotten kicked out of his old university for illegal fighting. He got Wells's arms. "Stop it, man. *Stop!*"

Wells wouldn't stop. It didn't matter that Bru was bigger. Wells shot his knee into Bru's gut, and it caught Bru off guard enough that Wells was able to hit him again. Wells had gotten Bru in his side and both guys tumbled again.

"How could you?" There was an ache this time in Wells's voice, and his face had managed to go even redder. I'd never seen him this way. A pain lassoed across his handsome face as he hit one of his best friends again and again. Bru was a friend who said he loved him, but there was no love coming from Wells. There was just pain anchored across Wells's expression, anguish. At some point, he ripped Bru's sweatshirt. The neck was wide and both guys were dirty from the grass on the quad. Wells cringed. "You're supposed to be *my friend*. You're supposed to be one of my best friends, you asshole!"

Wells hit Bru again, and, for some reason, Bru was taking it. I mean, Bru was guarding himself this time. Wells wasn't getting any good hits in now that Bru was aware he was being attacked. Even still, Bru wasn't trying to physically restrain Wells. He just kept dodging. As if he was trying to listen to the friend who rained fists down on him.

Bru shook Wells's shirt. "What are you talking about, bro?"

"How could you?" Wells said again, his nostrils flaring.

He sounded tired, but he wouldn't stop punching, even though he was clearly getting nowhere now that Bru had his guard up. Wells threw a lazy punch. "How could you? You're my friend, and she's my—"

Wells didn't get to finish. Big hands got underneath his arms. They tugged him away from Bru. Wells kicked. "You fucker!"

I didn't know if he was saying that to Bru or my brother, who was the one who had his hands on Wells. Using his burly arms, Thatcher braced Wells to his chest and shook him. "Stop it, dude. What the fuck are you doing?"

Wells fought my brother as Bru lay on the ground. Bruises had already started to form on Bru's face, and when he touched his mouth, he and I both saw the blood.

Oh, God.

My stomach turned. I immediately headed over to Bru, and the crowd parted as Dorian Prinze entered the circle. Clearly, Thatcher had just gotten here first because here came Dorian, Ares, Fawn, and Sloane.

Everyone's here.

Everyone was here, all my friends. Seeing her brother on the ground, Sloane blinked. She hunkered at my side with Bru and both Ares and Dorian immediately started shoving the crowd of onlookers away.

"Get the fuck out of here, you fucks!" Dorian barked, and it only took seconds for the crowd to disperse. Dorian acted as the leader and voice of reason in my brother's friend group. He was also really intimidating. Dorian growled. "And if you know what's good for you, you'll delete whatever video you guys were taking."

"You'll regret that shit if you don't," Ares added, and the fear that pushed across the dispersing crowd was evident. Ares wasn't called *Wolf* on Pembroke's football field for nothing. Right away, people started pressing buttons on their phones.

Some even lifted them for the guys to see.

The boys had so much power on this campus.

"What the heck happened?" Sloane asked Bru. She started to help him up, but he waved her off. She shook her head. "You and Wells were fighting? Why?"

"People were telling us we needed to come to the quad. We were at the student union," Fawn said. She was a curvy redhead with lots of tattoos. They were mostly covered up today since she wore a jacket.

Her head turned when Wells called out. "Let go of me, you motherfucker!" He was talking to my brother this time. Wells growled. "Let go. I'm cool, dude."

"Like hell you are," Thatcher said, but eventually, he let go when Wells worked his way out of my brother's hold. Maybe Thatcher let go. I didn't know. I just knew that after he did, Wells shot off in the opposite direction of the fight.

He left the aftermath.

He left Bru who was on his feet now but looked worse for wear. Ares put a hand on Bru's arm. "The fuck was this about? Why were y'all fighting?"

Ares had the concern of a brother, and, even though Bru was adopted into Ares's family, that didn't matter. The bond they had went beyond biology. It was that same under-standing of brotherhood all of my brother's friends shared.

"A misunderstanding," Bru said, watching Wells stalk away with Thatcher following him. Aspen had obviously already left town or she'd be here too. Bru huffed. "I just need to talk to him."

"Nah. He needs to cool off," Dorian said. He had his arm around Sloane now. His eyes narrowed. "What was the misunderstanding?"

"I might have an idea, but, like I said, we need to talk," Bru stated. He said the words to Dorian, but his attention passed to me. It was brief and something only I probably noticed.

"You're my friend, and she's my—"

I heard Wells's voice in my head as I thought about Dorian's question. I personally didn't know what happened, or why Wells burst out the way he did.

But I was going to find out.

CHAPTER
TWENTY

I caught the fucker on the couch that night.

And this time, there was no one to save him.

Our friends had all gone out to a movie, so there was no one at Legacy House to keep me from that asshole. He couldn't hide like a *little bitch* behind our friends.

Bru heard me coming this time. He had ice on his cheek for the bruise I left across his stupid-ass face on the quad. He blinked from the couch. "Wells—"

I went for his ass. Bru was bigger than me, but I easily tackled him onto the floor. We both picked up where we left off, and, once again, he shielded his face with his big arms. Once again, he acted like a little bitch ass instead of fighting me back. I socked him in one of his Superman forearms. "Come on, motherfucker, hit me!"

I dared him. I dared him to *try*. I swung at his face and all he did was take the impact in his arms.

"Wells, stop!" he called out, but he didn't hit me back.

Why wouldn't he hit me back? He guarded his face like a fighter. "Bro, stop… Wells, talk to me!"

I hit at his arms harder. At least, I tried. I wasn't his bro. I wasn't even sure I was *his friend* at this point after what he did.

It all made sense.

Bru had been trying to tell me something about Squeak at the ballet. The topic never came up again, and this clearly was it.

And he called himself my friend.

He called himself *more than* my friend and…

"Wells, tell me what this is about!" He grabbed my fists, but I could barely see him. I was driven by a haze I couldn't easily fight out of.

"You fucked her!" I shot out, and Bru's eyes widened. I swung for his pretty-boy face again, but he blocked. I growled. "Hit me, you asshole fuck!"

He was an asshole. He betrayed Thatcher. Thatcher *was our brother.* How dare he do something like this? We were supposed to look out for his sister. We weren't supposed to do this shit. We were supposed to *protect* her. *I* was supposed to…

Bru got me by the arms. He caught me off guard and shoved me off him. He didn't hit me though, and I needed it. I needed the pain.

I needed the reality check.

"Fucked who? Bow?" he asked, blinking. He was out of breath, and I ripped his shirt again. I'd done some damage to his sweatshirt on the quad, but this was worse. In fact, I ripped his t-shirt so bad it was barely a shirt. The neck of the white tee hung forward, his broad chest exposed. He pushed his dark hair out of his face. "You think I fucked Bow, right? You mentioned her on the quad. Why would you think I slept with her?"

I don't know, because he was all over her *on* the quad. I

saw him getting close to her. The fucker had her pinned against a tree, and he'd been about to kiss her or something.

He'd been touching her lips.

I was there long enough to see them tremble, her mouth, and I knew that quiver. She'd done it for me recently. I'd been trying to teach her a lesson about getting in my business at my parents' house, and what a fucking idiot I was. In so many fucking ways. This dude had been fooling around with me *and her* behind my back.

I grabbed Bru's fucked-up shirt, and he let me for some reason. The kid knew how to fight, but he was letting me get the upper hand just like he had on the quad. I didn't know why, but I was going to take advantage.

"She told me she wasn't a fucking virgin, you asshole!" I charged before clocking him in the head again. He was caught off guard I think, because he didn't block me.

A white heat blazed into my fist upon impact, and Bru fell back onto the couch. The burn in my hand felt so fucking good. I needed that shit. In fact, I got off on it, but I couldn't enjoy it long because Bru got his bearings. Getting up, he grabbed my arms, and the next thing I knew, he was hovering above me on the couch.

"What do you mean she's not a virgin? Wells, what do you fucking mean!" He was shaking me and got me out of my head enough where I could see him again. Besides the bruise on his cheek, his lip was bleeding, and his dark eyes were wild as fuck. He shook me again. "What the fuck do you mean?"

Like he didn't know, and like it *wasn't him* to do the act. He did all this behind my back, and again, everything he'd been doing now made sense. I actually thought he crashed my tutoring sessions with Bow to get in *my* head. He was mad at me for fucking him after pushing him away.

I bet he had a good laugh at that. He was trying to get to Bow this whole time. *My* Bow.

I ignored that last thought. I had to. If I didn't, I'd lose the last shred of sanity I had left. It was the only thing keeping me from killing this guy *I thought* was my friend.

But that didn't mean I wouldn't fucking hurt him.

Quickly, I got from under him and was on my feet. *I* had the upper hand now, and I reared back to unleash the same pain blazing inside my body. It was a pain I refused to address and the only relief I could get would be to pound Bruno Sloane-Mallick's face in. I was aware that wouldn't fix shit, but I didn't fucking care.

No, I didn't care.

Bru's eyes flashed as he watched my fist gear up.

"Archer!"

I shot around mid-punch, physically pulled out of my head for the briefest of seconds.

It was enough.

I smelled her before I saw her. It was like the air was filled with the presence of baked goods. She was inches away and then only centimeters before I actually saw her.

By then, it was too late.

TWENTY-ONE

Bow

I kissed Wells to make all the violence stop.

At least, that was what I told myself.

Wells froze against my lips. His mouth went tight, and his eyes were open.

I didn't care.

I grabbed Wells's shirt and put everything into it. A wave of ocean breeze hit me, and I drank it in.

I absorbed it.

I let myself get sucked up in Wells's aura, and it didn't matter that he failed to kiss me back. He wasn't moving, and his body was locked up tight. His heart beat hard against my hands but at least he wasn't punching Bru. He wasn't hurting him anymore, and that was why I kissed him.

My eyes closed as I forgot about my reason, and suddenly, Wells Ambrose wasn't Wells anymore, but Archer. He was *my* Archer.

Wells wasn't kissing me, but he also wasn't stopping me. He was letting it happen, just frozen, and I was taken back to the last time his lips touched mine. It had been when things changed at the pool that summer. It was the day he went from my friend and protector to something else.

It was the day Wells Ambrose became my enemy.

Wells gripped my arms. He was also *shaking*. His big hands dug into my arms so hard I thought he'd cut off the circulation.

Apparently, I didn't care about that, and I might have let the kiss go on longer had I not noticed Bru. I opened my eyes to see him standing off to the side. His head was down, his dark eyes on the floor. He wasn't watching the kiss.

It was like he couldn't.

The seal between my mouth and Wells's broke then. Wells released a breath like he'd been holding it, and I realized I hadn't been breathing either. I stopped breathing when I kissed him. I stopped *thinking*. I just wanted him to stop hurting Bru and did the first thing I could think of.

"What the fuck," Wells started to say, but I couldn't react to that. He'd probably rage out and get angry at me. I was definitely going to pay for what I did, but I tucked that in the back of my mind.

I made myself be brave.

I approached Bru, and he blinked. He had a bruise on his face and a cut lip I felt terrible about. I touched it.

Bru's mouth parted. "Bow—"

I kissed him silent, and his eyes flashed wider than Wells's had. He hadn't expected this. Heck, *I* hadn't expected me to do this.

Why am I doing this?

The why was forgotten as my mouth molded against his, and, where Wells didn't kiss me back, Bru didn't hesitate. In fact, he got a fistful of my skirt and hiked me up his hard body.

He even groaned.

Bru's tongue touched mine, and I dizzied just like I had on

the quad. He approached me about what I'd seen go on between him and Wells. He addressed *what I did*. He saw me touch myself, and it didn't seem like that bothered him. He even asked if what I saw bothered me, like it mattered to him. Like he didn't want me to be bothered.

I didn't know what was happening now. I just knew I didn't like the look Bru had when he saw me kiss Wells. I didn't want him to wonder about us, how I felt about him.

"Dude, what the actual fuck." Wells grabbed Bru, and our mouths broke away from each other. Wells shoved Bru, and Bru let go of me. Bru willingly moved, I think because he was still thrown about our kiss. Bru had a look of bewilderment in his dark eyes, but anger replaced it when he looked at Wells.

Bru shoved Wells back. "Bro, what the hell is your deal?"

"No, fucker. What the hell is *your* deal?" Wells gritted. His green eyes were wild, crazy. He held a similar look when I came into the house, and I'd also seen him with the same expression on the quad. He'd fought Bru twice now and both times sounded like they were about me.

Which didn't make sense.

I heard all the things Wells had been saying to Bru before I intervened. It sounded like Wells believed Bru was the one I lost my virginity to, but it wasn't him.

I wished it was him.

If it was him, things would have been different. If it was him, *I* would be different.

So many things would be different.

I couldn't think about that as I watched Wells approach Bru again, and my stomach flipped. Wells had his fist raised, and I didn't get that. Wells growled. "I knew this shit was true. She's *Thatcher's sister*, bro. The fuck's wrong with you? You call yourself his friend, and you're going behind his back with his little sister? Not to mention kissing her right now. Really?"

"Ambrose, are you fucking demented? Nobody's going

behind anybody's back. Well, not really. Not on purpose anyway," Bru said, then looked at me. He frowned at Wells. "And last I checked, *you* just kissed her too."

It was like the reality of that just resonated with Wells, and his eyes widened in actual horror. Wells did kiss me: even though he didn't kiss me back, he didn't stop it either.

"That's not the same," Wells said, his jaw tight. He stared at the floor, and I felt gut punched; both these guys were talking about me like I wasn't even there. I doubted Bru was doing it on purpose, but I couldn't help feeling invisible in that moment.

I was so tired of feeling invisible.

Invisibility didn't just make you feel small. It made you feel inferior, like you didn't matter. Like *what you wanted* didn't matter. It made you make poor choices.

It made you make mistakes.

I was *so tired* of not having agency in my own life. It felt like that was the case more often than not, and that was all I was thinking when I approached the boys again. I refused to think when I grabbed Wells and pressed my mouth to his *again*.

I just did it.

I wanted to kiss Wells. I wanted that feeling of our mouths together again…

I think I'd wanted it for a long time.

Wells froze again, but, this time, his mouth parted. He let me divide his lips with mine.

He even groaned.

"Squeak, what the fuck are you doing?" he asked me. He lifted his hands. "Stop it."

No, I wasn't stopping. I wanted to kiss him and maybe a part of him wanted to kiss me too. He actually sounded *jealous* that he thought Bru was the one I lost my virginity to. He made it sound like that was about Thatcher, but I wasn't so sure. Wells Ambrose didn't always use to hate me. He used to like me, maybe not romantically, but he hadn't despised me. He used to protect me.

"Archer," I said, seeking out that boy I loved. I wanted him. I wanted him so badly to come back. I pushed my hands in his hair. "I need you."

A noise escaped Wells's chest. It sounded angry, violent, and, when he grabbed me, he pressed me up against the wall. The impact sent the air flying from my lungs, and Wells gazed down at me with a ray of heat I could only explain as madness. He gripped my arms. "I said *fucking no*. Do you understand me? I don't want you. I don't want…"

His voice was strained, heavy.

His chest rose. "I don't fucking want you, Squeak. Not like that. I can't."

Can't?

He shook his head. "Please…"

It sounded almost like a plea, but his hands didn't leave my body. My chest rose up with rapid breaths in response, and Wells followed the movement with his green eyes. He stared *at my breasts* through my top, and I felt a new heat blast through me. No way could Wells Ambrose actually want me.

No way.

My mind had played with the thought before, but I hadn't actually believed it.

I touched his chest.

"Stop, Bow." He called me by my name this time. Not *Squeak* or something equally condescending. He squeezed my arms. "I can't."

I can't wasn't that he didn't want to. It wasn't that he didn't want me.

And that was enough for me.

It was enough for me to be brave again, so I wrapped my arms around him. Immediately, Wells cuffed my wrists and worked them off his neck.

"I won't," he said this time, but, once more, he didn't fight when I pressed my lips to his. He let them settle, and his eyes shut so tight. A noise left his mouth. "You have to stop this. You can't let me do this."

His mouth trembled against mine, and I instantly felt the moment the tide shifted. When his mouth parted with mine and pushed back.

He does want me.

This was confirmed when his lips pinched my own. Wells pulled my lip inside his mouth. He sucked, and my nipples charged to life. I pressed them against his hard chest, and the noise that escaped from his lips was feral.

That was enough.

His response to me was enough for me to push back my own boundaries and take something I realized now that I wanted for years. I didn't want him to hate me. I wanted him to love me.

"Please, Archer," I pleaded again, and, right away, that familiar ache rumbled in his throat. He didn't want to do this, but he was doing it anyway.

"I can't," he said, his voice incredibly strained. He released my mouth. He still had my wrists, and he was now using them to put distance between us.

No.

I tried to go to him, but he was so much stronger than me.

"Squeak," he said, and I never heard a word with such anguish. "I'm sorry."

I'm sorry.

Something was holding him back, and I broke inside. A million insecurities came flooding back, and the tears pricked at my eyes. That I wasn't good enough, worthy enough to love.

"You see what he does to you."

A familiar voice that wasn't my own came into my head. It only confirmed all my thoughts. I was pathetic. I was the little pip*squeak* that wasn't worthy of love.

Wells started to let go, but he sucked in a breath when another set of hands grabbed his. They were big and gripped Wells's hands so hard they went white.

"Let go, dude," Bru said, his voice a honied velvet. His nose touched Wells's ear. "Why are you fighting this?"

Wells's mouth parted, and soon, he was crowding me in. Wells pressed my wrists to the wall, and my chest brushed his again.

We both drew in a breath.

Gripping my wrists, Wells shook his head. "No, dude. I can't."

Wells was pleading with Bru who was, for some reason, egging all this on. He was pushing Wells on me, and I didn't resist it. If anything, I curled into Wells. I let his scent (and Bru's) surround me.

What's happening?

I didn't know, but whatever it was I wasn't fighting it. My eyes closed as I let Bru sandwich Wells between us.

"Give in," I heard Bru say, and, when I opened my eyes, I saw Bru bite Wells's ear. Wells groaned, and his eyes flashed wide. It was like something changed in them and whatever it was had Wells pinning me to the wall all by himself. He craned his big body and bit my mouth so hard I called out.

Wells growled.

"Fuck," he ground out, and, once I had him, I didn't let him go away. I kissed him back, hard, and he started grinding into me.

Bru made him.

Bru's hands were no longer on Wells's. They were on Wells's hips. Bru slammed Wells into me, and I nearly melted into a puddle. My legs widened on their own, and, when I lifted one, I felt a hand lasso around my thigh.

It was Bru. *Bru* was keeping Wells and me together. Bru squeezed my thigh, and at the same time, he gripped Wells's hip. He *was making* Wells thrust into me, and I felt every bit of hardness between my thighs. Wells was hard…

And he was hard because of me.

"Stop," Wells said, his eyes shut tight, his voice *raw*. I thought he was telling Bru to stop, but I noticed Bru's hands were no longer on Wells's hips. Wells was thrusting against me all on his own. Wells pressed his forehead against mine. "Stop this."

But he kept rubbing himself into me. Like he was telling himself to stop, and a noise left my throat as he widened my legs. His fingers bit into my thighs, and he pushed them so hard against the wall. Like he was trying to find the will to stop. But then Bru did the craziest thing.

He unbuckled Wells's pants.

Bru unzipped them too, and Wells actually shook. Dipping his head, Wells shoved his tongue down my throat and kissed me so deeply that I lost my breath. My arms instantly wrapped around Wells's neck just to hold on.

Bru spit into his hand.

Bru made eye contact with me while he slipped his hand into the back of Wells's pants. There was a hazy look in his dark eyes like something carnal took over him. He squeezed Wells's shoulder. "Give in to her, man."

And then Bru's hand was moving, his shoulder working in his t-shirt as he thrust his hand into Wells's pants again and again. The veins in his bicep surged through his tan skin, and Wells's kiss deepened.

"Fucking shit." Wells started devouring my mouth, and his hips moved each time Bru worked his shoulder, his hand. Bru was fucking Wells's ass while Wells fucked me through my skirt.

Oh, God.

I was holding on tight to Wells, my hips moving too. Somehow, all three of us were so in sync, and Bru even closed his eyes. Like this was doing just as much for him as it was for Wells and me.

"Squeak." Wells's voice ached again, and this time, he had his hands on my face. He widened my mouth to take his kiss deeper, his eyes shut so tight. "I'm sorry."

I didn't know what he was apologizing for, and I couldn't focus as I tumbled over the cliff. I came as Bru's hand picked up in Wells's pants.

Wells came in his boxers.

Wells actually let go of me to grab himself, and Bru kissed his neck while Wells shuddered. Bru had a visible hard-on, but he didn't tend to himself. He kissed Wells's neck, but, at the same time, he held my hand. I didn't know when he'd taken it, and I wondered when he did. His thumb rubbed across the top of my hand. He tended to me just as much as Wells.

Something warmed my stomach thinking about that. I squeezed his hand back, and he looked up and smiled at me. He made no moves to get himself off. Like what happened was enough for him.

Wells's head lifted. He'd rested it on my shoulder while he came, and only after the circulation returned to my legs did I realize that Wells had been the only thing that had kept me from hitting the floor. He may have grabbed himself when he'd come, but he also held me. He didn't let me fall.

And he was staring at the floor.

He wasn't moving, but he was breathing. He closed his eyes, and his mouth parted like he was going to say something.

He didn't get the chance.

A door slammed in the house and I was on my own after Wells got me stable. He may have kept me from falling, but he wasn't staying. He dashed out of the room just before Dorian, Sloane, Ares, and Fawn entered.

"Hey, guys. How was the movie?" Bru asked from the couch. He had a hoodie on all of a sudden, and a pillow on his lap. It happened to conveniently cover what I knew to be a hard-on in his jeans.

What happened?

I didn't know, but it was the most erotic thing I'd ever experienced in my whole life. I'd never experienced anything so sexual, and I had had sex.

I'd had sex.

I didn't want to think about that in that moment. It'd soil what just happened.

Another door slammed in the house, and I had to assume that was Wells.

"Movie was good," my brother, Thatcher, said as he came into the room too. He pointed out of the living room. "Where's Wells going? I just passed him. Y'all ain't fighting anymore, right?"

"Still don't know what that was about," Dorian said, frowning. He dropped an arm around Sloane. "You guys have been having this weird tension for a while now."

Everyone looked at Bru, including Ares and Fawn.

Bru started to say something, but he was always saving face. Deciding to save him from that this time, I smiled at the group. "They're not fighting. Actually, I came in on them reconciling."

I never lied, but I did tonight.

That was twice now.

Earlier tonight, I lied when Sloane and the others asked if I wanted to see the movie. I said I didn't want to even though it was a rom-com with some of my favorite actors in it. But I opted out to basically stalk Wells tonight.

I wanted to talk to him.

We ended up doing more than talking, and all Bru did was nod at me before he moved the conversation on to how the movie was again. He lied to them too when he didn't really lie either.

I guess now we were both liars.

CHAPTER
TWENTY-TWO

Wells

I needed to tell Thatcher what happened. He may hate me, but he'd hate me even more if I didn't tell him what happened with his sister.

His sister.

I still couldn't believe I did that. I touched her, and that wasn't allowed. Especially when it came to me.

But she's already been touched.

Somehow Rainbow Reed got one over on me. She knew the rules. The whole fucking world knew they weren't supposed to touch her. She was a pariah, an outcast, and that was well known.

I made it well known.

I didn't know how to fucking deal with that information, and I double didn't know how to deal with the fact that I not only kissed her but *got off*. That fucker Bru was the culprit, and if I wasn't so busy needing to scrub the cum out of my boxers, I would have laid his ass out.

What the fuck?

There was so much wrong with what happened at the house, and Bru egged that shit on. Fuck, he'd been the damn ring leader.

"Give in to her, man."

His rough voice in my ear had done that shit. He'd made me *give in* to it, but this wasn't some girl at a party. This was Thatcher's sister, and it all was so fucked up.

I never told Thatcher.

I told myself I needed to, and even urged myself, but every time I saw my best friend over the next few weeks, I couldn't make my mouth work. I had plenty of opportunities. We shared a couple classes together, and we'd gone to the gym together multiple times. But one of the other guys was always around. There'd be Ares or Dorian.

There'd be Bru.

Bru and I didn't talk about what happened either, but that was because I was ignoring his ass like the plague. He kept giving me this *look*. It bordered between we should talk, fuck, or both, and since I didn't trust myself not to do the fucking part of that, I stayed away.

It was worse when Squeak was around.

Being around her was different now, heavy. She'd swish around in her little twill skirts acting all innocent, like she wasn't the guilty party that started this whole thing. She fucking kissed me not once but twice, and I didn't kiss girls. At least, I tried not to. I kept a barrier up between myself and women. Girls tended to be emotional and needy as shit. Kisses were different with women, which was why I avoided them when I could. Those lips were better for my cock as far as I was concerned.

I avoided Squeak too over the passing weeks because, when I didn't, she also gave me a look. Her cheeks would get all red and her eyes would avert to Bru's. His would get all fiery. Like every time he looked at her, he was imagining shit he had no business imagining. Like he could taste her every time he saw her.

Bow's face would get even more red in response, and then the pair would look at me. They'd both have that same fire, that same heat, like suddenly they were imagining shit *with me*. My cock would twitch, and then, suddenly, *I* was imagining shit. I was imagining filling my best friend's little sister with cock while I kissed my other best friend over her shoulder. I was smelling both feminine and masculine scents, and that feminine one took me over the edge. It made me remember things. It made me remember moments and countless summers. It made me remember stuff before things changed between us.

Shit *had* changed though, and, even if it hadn't, there was no way I was betraying Thatcher.

Even if I already had.

I pulled up to the Reeds' the night of Dorian's draft party in a tuxedo. The formal wear was necessary since Dorian's parents were throwing a gala. He'd been drafted into the NFL.

How time flew.

It was crazy how we'd all gone from teenagers that didn't give a shit to adults that were now about to start our lives. Dorian and Ares would be graduating from Pembroke in a matter of weeks, and Ares already had a job. He'd be running one of his dad's art galleries while he waited for Fawn to graduate. I could imagine they'd be heading off to New York after that. She had aims at becoming a photojournalist at the *New York Times*.

We were all growing up.

I didn't feel that way, despite my fancy attire. My shoes were shined, and my tux was pressed, but I still felt like a fraud.

That went double when I knocked on the Reeds' door that evening. I agreed to take Thatcher's sister to Dorian's gala as a power play. I wanted to show Squeak I was the one in control.

I felt like the punk when my buddy Thatcher opened the door. He wore a tux too, the dude looking like a straight gorilla when he put his hand out for mine.

"Why you knocking like you haven't just let yourself into my house the entire time we've been friends," Thatcher said, snorting, and he was right. I did have a house key. Fuck, he had a key to my house too. We might as well be brothers this dude and I were so close.

My best friend looked *almost* as fly as me tonight when I came into his home. He had his dark hair moussed back but kept his earrings in. He switched them up tonight for the occasion though, with diamond studs. He usually wore crosses.

I laughed as I came in the door. It was a nervous laugh. I guess I hadn't used my key because I needed the extra time on the stoop to calm my fucking nerves.

Relax.

I shook my buddy's hand when he put it out, then snapped after the handshake. I smoothed my hands down my lapels. "I'm trying to be respectful tonight. You know, classy."

In reality, I was trying not to upchuck on my buddy's lawn before I knocked. Tonight, I planned to tell him the truth about everything that happened with Bow. All us Legacy crew would be together tonight, but there'd be plenty of moments were I could take Thatcher off to the side and talk.

I told myself this was the gameplay for weeks. *I told myself* this was why I was waiting to admit the truth that I not only kissed his sister, but came in my pants afterward. The latter had been because Bru had his fucking fingers in my asshole but still.

"You? Classy? That'll be the day," Thatcher said, closing the door behind me. I was surprised his housekeeper didn't answer, and when I asked why she hadn't, he said his parents had given their housekeeper the night off since we all would be at the gala. Thatcher squeezed my shoulder. "And thanks for taking Bow tonight. It'll be nice not to keep an eye on her. Who knows who's going to be at that gala."

He meant I'd be around to keep the guys off her. Thatcher was real protective of his sister, and if I had a little sister, I'd be the same way.

Thatcher smiled. "I'm really glad you put the past behind you. I know it wasn't easy."

I felt gut punched for several reasons. The main one was that, apparently, I was the guy his sister had to stay away from. I mean, I kissed her.

I also hadn't put anything behind me, and his sister was once again putting me in a position to lie.

My hand was knuckling at my side when Thatcher's parents suddenly made an appearance in the foyer. Mrs. Reed wore a white gown that shimmered, and Mr. Reed resembled Thatcher with his own black tux. Thatcher and his pop looked just like each other, but Mr. Reed had zero smiles on the regular. In actuality, it seemed like he only reserved them for his wife and Bow.

Mr. Reed had his hand behind Mrs. Reed as they both came down the grand staircase. It was one of those big ones that made a statement like out of the movie *Titanic*.

"Wells," Mr. Reed said, tipping his chin at me when the pair reached the bottom of the staircase, and, I had to say, I felt gut punched again. There was respect in the nod. It wasn't like Mr. Reed didn't respect me, but he usually acknowledged me like a son. That meant we weren't really equal, but something had changed since that night he had me in the car. I first noticed the change the night the Reeds came to my parents' house for taco night. Thatcher's dad was obviously very happy I put aside the beef I had with his daughter.

I ignored the sour feeling in my stomach as I hugged Mrs. Reed. Thatcher's mom told me I looked handsome as she pulled away. She also touched my hair, the woman a second mom to me. I moussed my hair back like Thatcher tonight. I'd also bought a new tux, wanting to look my best for my buddy's party. It was a classic black and fit my form perfectly.

"Thanks," I told her, but noticed we were absent one. Thatcher's girlfriend, Aspen, was still on tour. She wanted to make the gala but couldn't swing it.

The one we were missing was obviously Thatcher's sister, but she didn't make us all wait long.

Squeak's gown was like her mother's.

The white shimmer glided across her tiny hips, sheer at her thighs but modest everywhere else. The sheerness wasn't a trait of her mother's dress though, nor was the slit at the side. The slit gave a peek of Squeak's thigh every step she took down the grand staircase.

Rainbow Reed didn't look like Thatcher's little sister as she made an appearance in front of us. Her wavy hair was on her shoulders and bumped up at the bottom, like an old Hollywood starlet, and her red lips and flushed cheeks paired with that aesthetic. Squeak normally had flushed cheeks, but tonight, it appeared intentional with just the slightest bit of makeup. She normally didn't wear a whole lot of makeup. She never needed to.

My gut did a twisting thing as I watched her descend the stairs. Her gloved hand guided her way, the sparkly bag on her arm matching her dress. She reminded me of Hermione out of that scene in *Harry Potter*. Completely unassuming until she wasn't.

My gut turned again, and I was distracted from her when Mrs. Reed took her phone out. She snapped a picture. "Oh, honey, you look beautiful."

She did; I had eyes and could admit that. My jaw moved, and I was bumped a little when Thatcher nudged me.

He eyed me. "You going to go get her, dude?"

That was right. I was her escort.

I cleared my throat, then pushed forward toward my obligation. That was all tonight was, *an obligation.*

I took the steps quickly and intercepted Bow two steps from the bottom. With all the room's attention on her, I didn't think she noticed me there at first. She did now, and I didn't miss the way her eyes followed each of my strides to the stairs. Nor how they glided over the fit of my tux before settling somewhere across my chest.

An obligation.

I drummed that into my head. Eventually, Thatcher's little sister made it up to my eyes, and that was when her face managed to get even brighter. It was a natural tint in her cheeks this time when she opened her mouth. "Hi, Wells."

My name was a whisper, and the sound drummed a beat into my chest that I ignored when I put an arm out for her hand. It was the civil thing to do to help her down the stairs, the proper thing. I cleared my throat again. "Hi. My car's outside."

I'd be driving her tonight, and her brother was coming with us. I was happy for that buffer.

Something twitched in Bow's expression when I spoke to her. I didn't know if that was because of my directness or my coldness.

Maybe both.

Regardless, I ignored her response, then, later, the heat of her hand on my arm when she touched me. That warmth pressed through my tux, but that was a physical response. It was a mistake.

And I wasn't going to make anymore.

CHAPTER
TWENTY-THREE

Wells

The Vesperton Hotel was owned by the Costa family. They were some family based out of Chicago that was rumored to have serious ties to the Italian mafia.

No one around here really cared about that though. Especially with all the corruption that came through (and lived) here. Anyway, it was the nicest hotel in town, and the location was where Dorian's parents chose to host his gala. The Prinzes basically shut the place down.

There was even a red carpet.

Thatcher, Squeak, and I had to stand out front for pictures, but I kept my distance from Thatcher's little sister for the most part. I also hadn't talked to her on the drive over, but that wasn't unusual since Thatcher was there too.

Of course, Squeak looked like she wanted to speak to me at some points during the red carpet, but the thing about Thatcher's little sister was that she was shy. She also wouldn't say anything about what happened in front of Thatcher. Maybe she figured I already had.

I hadn't, but I would. I was going to pull Thatcher aside when things were a little quieter anyway. The red carpet wasn't the time, and neither was when we headed off inside.

Dorian's parents filled this place with nothing but the most elite guests. The Vesperton was hoppin', and there was even a charity auction. Dorian's parents were really into giving, and honestly, so were mine. Mom and Dad gave back whenever they could to this town and the same went for my other friends' parents.

"Hey, I'll catch you later," Thatcher said right before our small group was about to enter the ballroom. His parents were probably behind us, but we hadn't seen them at the hotel yet. Thatcher lifted his phone. "It's Aspen. I'm going to chat with her for a while."

My buddy was such a sap now.

Someone might as well be happy.

I shook Thatcher's hand. He was off after that, and I was left with his sister.

Bow chewed one of her painted lips. "Hey, um…"

"We should probably find the others," I said offering my arm again. That was all I could give to her right now.

Squeak's face colored. She once again looked like she wanted to say something, and when she chose not to, something in my chest settled.

We ended up parting in the ballroom.

Squeak had found my parents. Mom looked gorgeous tonight. I'd seen her in her pink dress before I left for the Reeds', and she sparkled under the ballroom lights. Dad looked pretty fly with her, and even though I'd seen him in a tux many times, that wasn't his chosen preference for attire. He liked to be pretty casual like me, and, after hugging them both, I had no problem leaving Thatcher's little sister with them. Mom was speaking to Bow anyway. Squeak had a great relationship with my parents, all the parents, really.

"I'm going to go find the guys," I said to the three of them, and I didn't miss the look Squeak gave me before I left. She still had that longing look. Like she needed something from me when I had nothing to give her.

I need a drink.

Finding my friends was only part of my excuse for leaving. I stole a glass of champagne off a tray from a nearby server, chugging it down before scanning the crowd.

I found Dorian right away. He was in the center of the hoard that was Maywood Heights' socialites. This didn't surprise me since he was the man of the hour. He was taller than nearly everyone in his black-on-black tux. His girlfriend, Sloane, was curiously absent. Ares was with him. He was the only one taller than Dorian, and his fiancée, Fawn, wasn't with him either. I could imagine both their girls were together since they were good friends.

I noticed right away that Bru wasn't in the hoard of guests that were all up on my buddy Dorian, and that was the only reason I felt comfortable pushing my way through the crowd to get to him. I was *not* trying to deal with Bru right now.

"Looking good, my friend," I said to Dorian once I fought through the crowd. His classic black-on-black ensemble made him stand out. This was his party, and he should. He also had his blond hair moussed back like mine.

Look at us all looking like classy guys, men. I shook Dorian's hand. "And I've said it before, but congratulations."

I was so fucking happy for my friend. He was starting this whole new life soon, and I knew playing football was his dream. The rest of us might be good at tossing a ball, but Dorian lived for it. He was so fucking good, and it was his passion.

"Thanks," he said, hugging me after the shake. He grabbed my shoulder. "And you're not looking bad yourself. Almost like a classy fucker."

I jostled him, but I'd been thinking the same thing. Ares smirked watching the two of us, then shook my hand too.

Could this dude not look like a fucking runway model? He wore a regular black-and-white tux, but his curly hair was all out on his shoulders looking like a damn Pantene Pro-V ad. I hugged him after our handshake. "'Sup, my dude?"

"Nothing much, man. Just living," Ares said, and he was doing that shit so well. Ares had a cancer scare not far back, but he was doing so awesome now. He was moving on to the next stage of his life too, and Fawn would be with him.

I asked him about her as well as Sloane. There was never a place these guys went without their girls. I also mentioned Thatcher and Bru at the tail end. I said Thatcher took a call with Aspen. That made the guys roll their eyes which was ironic as fuck considering how they were with their own girls.

It wouldn't have made sense if I didn't ask where Bru was too, so I did but made it sound casual.

"The girls are in the bathroom and Bru hasn't arrived yet. At least, I haven't seen him," Dorian said, and I nodded. Again, I kept it casual. Looking around, I noticed everyone was here but him. I even spotted all of our parents in various parts of the room but no Bru. That wasn't like him to be fashionably late. Maybe he was picking up a date or something.

I didn't care about that. He could date whoever he wanted, and he should.

I found another glass of champagne off a passing waiter's tray. Bru had tried reaching out to me a time or two or *twelve* since that fucked-up shit that happened at the house. I ignored all attempts though. I had just as much to say to him as I did to Squeak. Not talking to him was a feat since we lived in the same house, but I managed.

It only made me that much more grateful that the semester was basically over. I'd move back home like I did every summer and wouldn't have to use an excuse to avoid him.

Dorian glanced around. "Where's Bow? I thought you were escorting her."

"Last I saw her, she was with my parents," I said before downing the rest of my drink.

"That was nice of you, to escort her," Dorian said. He found some champagne off a waiter's tray, and Ares did the same beside him. Dorian laughed. "Though, I'm ninety percent sure that's you still trying to get in good with your dad."

There wasn't much my friends didn't know when it came to me. They knew Bow and I didn't get along. They also knew that I needed her to pass my classes and please my parents, more specifically my father. They knew all that. They knew many things.

Certain things, though, I kept closer to the cuff. Dorian and Ares wouldn't be happy about what happened with Bow either. She was like a sister to them, and they loved her. They protected her for Thatcher just like I had in the past.

I gripped my glass. "Nah, that's over."

I passed my classes. Or at least, I would. I just had to wait for grades to be posted, and I knew those would be fine. I knew the material on my final exams cold.

I had to do a lot of work those final weeks. I stopped sessions with Bow and Bru, so I knew I was on my own. I was, but I managed.

Ares took a sip from his glass. His head cocked. "Any reason why you're escorting her tonight, then?"

I wasn't surprised he was asking me that, but before I could answer, his fiancée, Fawn, and Dorian's girlfriend, Sloane, came over. Both girls were fancied up in ballgowns. Fawn had on a green dress that was sleeveless and highlighted all the colorful tats on her arms, and Sloane wore classic black like Dorian. She probably did that to match him.

Sloane looked pissed. In fact, she'd stalked over to our group with the look of a determined woman, and I didn't understand until I saw the tiny person between her and Fawn.

My eyes lifted. Squeak's arm was in Sloane's hand. She was no longer with my parents, and as soon as Sloane brought her up to our small group, Sloane smacked me up against the head.

"The fuck?" I growled but backed off when Dorian shot me *a look.* I wasn't about to go toe-to-toe with that dude. He got crazy when it came to his girl, but I also wasn't about to let myself get bitch-slapped either. I rubbed my head. "What's the big idea?"

"The big deal is you left Bow when you're supposed to be escorting her tonight," Sloane cut, and Bow shook her.

"Sloane, it's fine," Bow said, and Sloane shook her head.

Sloane pointed at me. "It's not fine. That's not what an escort does."

"She was with my parents. Chill," I said, but I got another look from Dorian. I shrugged. "She was."

"Well, not when I found her." Sloane folded her arms. "Even if she was, you're supposed to be sticking with her."

I wasn't Squeak's fucking keeper.

Saying nothing, I grabbed another champagne glass, and I think I made things worse by choosing to drink instead of engage. I loved Sloane like a sis but she was straight trippin' right now.

My drinking obviously annoyed Sloane. Her eyes blazed, but when she looked like she was going to come at me again, Dorian finally stepped between us. He tried to talk her down in that calming nature only she could bring out in him. He rubbed her arms as he spoke to her, but she clearly wasn't having it.

Sloane's jaw tightened. "No. He thinks he can treat people any way he wants. First Bru. Now this?"

I was alert now and probably reacted too quickly when my head shot up. "The fuck did Bru say?"

Dorian shot a finger at me. "Eh. Check your tone." I got

him defending his girl, but she was being so out of line right now.

"Bru doesn't say anything to me," Sloane said, frowning. "No matter how hard I push he doesn't, but *I know* you did something, Wells. My brother doesn't fight anymore, but suddenly he and you are throwing down?"

"Not to mention avoiding each other. Which you have been for weeks," Ares said, cutting in. His shoulders lifted. "What is the deal? You guys used to be hella close."

I didn't like all this heat on me, the spotlight.

And Squeak was looking at me.

She had that pleading look in her eyes again. Like, once more, she needed something from me, but she didn't. Not really.

She didn't even wait.

The swallow was hard in my throat, and, blinking, I faced away from my friends.

"I'm getting a drink," I mumbled, needing something stronger than fucking champagne. I had zero to give to anyone right now. Not Bru, and especially not Bow. *Never* Bow.

I headed straight for the open bar after leaving my friends. It'd be a miracle if I didn't get drunk tonight.

In fact, I was all but determined.

———

I didn't get wasted because my parents were here, and I was still trying to be on my best behavior for my dad. He hadn't cut me off yet because of school, but that didn't mean he wouldn't.

I also refused to make tonight about me when it was supposed to be about Dorian and his achievements. Because of that, I kept to myself, which was easy to do. The room was filled with influential people and, later, speeches. Dorian's father, Royal, had a really good one around the time dinner was served. He said how proud he was of his son for living out his dreams.

Tonight was about Dorian, but I didn't make myself suffer voluntarily. I avoided my friends when I could, and, at dinner, I opted out, saying I had stomach issues. My mom was hella concerned about that, but she let me go to get some air. I took a *lot* of fucking air and returned just in time for dancing and socialization.

I found Squeak then. She was watching the dancing, and I held out my hand for hers.

"Come. People will expect it," I said, and ignored the heat in my hand when she obligatorily took it. I brought her close then and made sure we were in front of my parents who were also dancing.

Dad smiled at me with a nod before directing my mom's focus over to Squeak and me. Mom smiled too, seriously looking radiant. She and my dad were the perfect pair and complemented each other so well. They found their soulmates in each other.

So many soulmates were on the dance floor now: my parents, Thatcher's, and all my friends' parents. They were all holding each other close during the slow dance.

My friends also had their partners out on the dance floor. Dorian was gazing down at Sloane like she was the only thing he could see, which was probably the case. Those two were ultimately headed down the aisle, just like Ares and Fawn. Ares held Fawn in such a mighty embrace I felt intrusive watching them.

I gazed around for an ally, but all I found was Thatcher. I missed him at dinner, but that was probably because I'd left. He'd obviously joined us in the ballroom at one point. He was currently by the bar but was on his phone again.

He was smiling.

He had that sappy look only adoration could bring out,

love. He was talking to someone who put nothing but joy across his entire being and only one person could do that. Only one girl could do that.

"Wells?"

The sound of my name burned into me. Especially coming from… her.

"Wells, we need to talk… About what happened?"

I spun Squeak instead of responding to her, my jaw tight. When I brought her back to me, I noticed I got another approving nod from my dad and something in my soul told me I got what I wanted. I was in the clear with him, and I didn't have to try anymore. I made him happy just like everyone else was on this dance floor. There were so many happy couples, so much happiness.

"Wells…"

"What do you want from me?" I asked, gritting my teeth. I dared to look down at the small girl who'd spoken in my arms.

I immediately regretted it. I saw those large blue eyes of hers. The ones that constantly stared up at me with hope and adoration. I wasn't an idiot. I knew Squeak had a crush on me when we were younger. She did, like a fool, and *I* was a fool for giving her as much attention as I had over the years. She played me with those blue eyes, that smooth skin…

She touched my arm. "Wells?"

The heat of her hand soldered through my jacket at this point, and I adjusted until she let go. I looked away again. I ignored her, *her voice*, and the fact that it almost always cracked. Especially when she laughed. I used to make her laugh a lot.

I was an idiot fuck, foolish. I shook my head, my gaze on anything in the ballroom but her. "I don't have anything to say to you."

Bru may have egged on what happened between us all, but she'd been the one to start that shit. She had no business kissing me. No. Fucking. Business. Thatcher's little sister or not, I didn't let anyone make a fool of me.

She'd done it more than once.

My brain ignored the fact that I wasn't even thinking about what happened the summer I let that girl drown. *That hadn't been* what my mind had gone to and…

"Well, I have something to say to you," Bow said, and my gaze darted in her direction. She'd never spoken so boldly to me, and her eyes flashed as soon as mine made contact with hers. She didn't back down though, blinking. She nodded. "At Legacy House, we—"

"No," I said, firm. She wouldn't make me relive that day or how it felt. She wouldn't *make me* betray my friend again, even if it was just in my head. My throat worked. "You're making me lie to Thatch."

Lying to my parents was fine. I was their kid. Of course I lied to them on occasion, but Thatcher was different. He was my brother.

Like he knew he was thought about, Thatcher made eye contact with me from the bar. Perhaps he thought it was unusual I was dancing with his sister, or maybe he just didn't care. Maybe *he was happy* I was dancing with her because that meant I truly did forgive her.

On his phone call, Thatcher waved at me with a grin, and my stomach went so fucking tight.

I tipped my chin back at him, forcing a smile I didn't fucking feel or want. I just wanted this goddamn song over so I could hide out again.

I spun Squeak again before bringing her back. She may have wanted to talk, but I noticed Bru was absent tonight. Yes, I'd gone out of my way to avoid him, but I hadn't seen him at all this evening.

There were a lot of people at Dorian's party, and it would be easy to miss him. Especially since I had skipped out on dinner. I could imagine he'd been there…

"I don't want that. For you to lie to Thatcher," Squeak said, pulling me out of my thoughts. That stupid flush had returned to her cheeks, the one that made her look innocent, ethereal. Her red lips turned down. "I don't want that at all."

"What do you want, then?" I asked, forcing my sight away from that delicate flush in her cheeks. This girl wasn't innocent. She wasn't—

"You."

My gaze zoomed down again, my eyes wide. "What?"

Bow's throat worked, and, suddenly, it was her who was finding it hard to keep her gaze on me. Her gloved hand squeezed mine, but soon, she stood tall. "I want you, Wells. Our friendship." Her hand moved in mine again, and that forced me to look at them. How small her hand looked in my palm. She was always so small. "I miss you so much, Archer."

Archer.

How dare she. How *dare* she bring me back to a place *again* where neither of us had been in so long. It was one thing to talk her off a ledge, but it was another to just up and take us to the place we'd both been before the drama, *before the death* and the blood that was on *my hands*. It was a place where I was her protector again, legitimately. I was her archer.

And she was my bow.

I didn't want to go there again. I *couldn't* because, if I did…

"I just want us to be friends again and for you to forgive me," Bow said, pulling me close, and this was so not like Bow. Just like those kisses at Legacy House, this wasn't like her. She was standing up and going for something she wanted. She was going for me, but she couldn't fucking have me. Again, I had nothing to give her. She blinked hard over glassy eyes. "What do I have to do for you to forgive me?"

Something inside me broke when she fucking said that. *It shattered* like when she said she screwed some fucking dude. I thought it'd been Bru, but I wasn't so sure now after his reaction when I approached him. In fact, he'd looked just as shocked as I felt the day she told me.

That day…

It was the day in my parents' bathroom where *I* first touched *her*. Stick or not, I'd put hands on my buddy's sister.

She didn't wait…

Why do you care?

I didn't care who Bow had been with. All I cared about was that she made a fool out of me. No one was allowed to touch her, but she figured out a way.

The thoughts were something all my sanity had to believe in. Anything else would make me face reality. I couldn't forgive Rainbow Reed for what happened in the past, not really.

Because, if I did, I'd have to forgive myself.

"Everything okay?"

My throat worked at the sound of his voice. Bru's deep baritone was behind me, the proximity intimate, close.

Bow's reaction to Bru was similar to how it'd been to me when she saw me at the bottom of the stairs. Her face went up a million degrees of red. He put color in her cheeks, which was normally something *I* did.

The growl was low in my chest, and I said nothing to Bru before forming a territorial hand on Bow's hip. Again, no one was allowed to touch her, but this fucker had before.

You both did.

I refused to think about that shit, and the same went for turning around and looking at Bru. That dude constantly got me in my fucking head, and that wasn't happening. I gripped Bow's hand. "What do you want?"

"I wasn't talking to you," Bru said, and, not standing for that shit, I did turn around, which was a big fucking mistake. Bru filled out the entirety of his tux with his Superman body, the smooth black tapered in tight at his waist. He had a hand in his pocket and his sight was very much not on me. His eyes narrowed at Bow. "Are you all right?"

I didn't like the way he was looking at her, like *he* was her protector. I also didn't like the way *I* was looking at *him*. I was noticing shit like how he may have looked like Superman in his tux but gave off just as much farm-boy energy as Clark Kent. He looked like him too, his dark hair slightly messy, tousled. Like he'd just been through a round in the sheets, and I *didn't* like that. I didn't want him having a date. I didn't want anyone having their hands on him.

Either of them.

I had territorial feelings about both of them, and I couldn't have any of that shit. It was too fucked up. *I* was too fucked up.

"I'm fine," Bow said, and she let go of me before I could let go of her. I felt the draft between us immediately. She pushed back her wavy hair. It was still flawless even after all the dancing. She pointed toward the exit. "I'm just going to go to the bathroom. Freshen up a little."

I noticed how I never answered her question about forgiving her, but she didn't wait for me to give it. She just left, and the urge to follow her was instant.

Don't.

I didn't in the end, but that didn't stop Bru. Of course, him and his Superman hero shit went after her.

"I'll go with you. Well, escort you," Bru said. He had her hand, and I heard him because we were in between songs. I also heard what she said to him in response.

"I'm okay. Enjoy the gala," Bow said, and Bru truly looked conflicted as he stared at her gloved hand. My instinct was to go push them apart. That shit was incredibly bold in front of all our friends and family, in front of *Thatcher*, but thoughts drifted as I watched Bru touch Bow. Bru *made me* touch her at Legacy House, and it hadn't been so bad when we both were. I'd come so hard between them both. The thoughts made me ill, but not because I didn't like what happened that night, and that was so fucked up.

When Bru let go of Bow, I could breathe again. It was like I'd been holding my breath, just like I had earlier that night when shit went down between all three of us. Bru and I had been showing Squeak how to dance, and it hadn't been a bad thing, our hands on her, his hands on her.

I put away the messed-up thoughts and stared at Bru and Bow longer than I should have. Standing there, Bru watched her cut through the crowd and ultimately through the door. There was so much longing in his eyes.

I needed to find Thatcher. Bru and I both had to stop this shit. It was only physical, and if I told myself that enough, I'd start to believe it. I *would* believe it. I had no fucking choice.

I turned away as the music started again. I needed to find Thatcher and tell him the truth about everything, but someone got my arm from behind before I could move.

"Ambrose," Bru said, and, though I could have fought when he brought me toward him, I didn't. I let him grip my arm and turn me around.

Bru pulled me into a dance.

I straightened immediately, my body stiff, tight. Bru attempted to get me against him. He had one hand at my waist and the other in mine, and when I tried to let go, he shook me.

"Stop, Ambrose," he said, getting in my head again. He focused his dark eyes on me, and I was pinned in place. He was never so direct with me, commanding. His mouth parted. "Dance with me."

I didn't want to. I couldn't…

But I was.

For some reason, I allowed him to bring me closer to him by the waist. He swayed, and I was letting him lead.

Why?

I found myself moving too, for a second. Until I realized

we weren't the only two on the dance floor. Back in my head again, I looked around. I found eyes on us, but they were only from the people that mattered. I caught my mom and dad looking at Bru and me as well as Bru's parents, Ramses and Brielle.

I saw our friends looking at us too.

Dorian and Ares were still on the dance floor with their girls. They were slow dancing just like Bru and me. The guys whispered something to the girls, and soon, Sloane and Fawn were looking at Bru and me too. Right away, Fawn smiled, and Sloane, though she blinked, smiled too. It was slow, like she just realized something.

Dorian and Ares did the same. Their smiles slow as well, they exchanged a glance with each other. Like they were both let in on some secret that they didn't know the answer to until this very moment.

My mouth parted after their focus went back to their girls. I noticed Thatcher after that. He was no longer at the bar, but he was still on his phone. Well, kinda. The phone was kind of hovering away from his face as he stared at Bru and me. He did a little maneuver where his dark eyebrows flicked up, but then, he was raising his drink to me. He also had that same clarity our friends had on their faces before smiling wide and going back to his call.

The parents had a similar reaction with their smiles. It was like everyone knew something I didn't.

"I see you're looking for a reason, Ambrose, but you're not going to find one," Bru said, pulling my attention back to him, and he smelled so fucking good, looked good. He frowned. "You're not going to find one with our family and friends. A reason to deny this…"

He moved just briefly, and my cock twitched when his hand dug into my back. He got my jacket in a tight fist before he moved his breath to my ear.

"So why are you denying this? *Me*," he growled, before

his lips did brush my ear. His nose brushed too. "Why are you denying Bow and me?"

My eyes flashed open. It was like I repelled from him, *his words*. I tried to work myself away, but his grip was too strong. I gripped his shirt. "Don't you *dare*. You fuck—"

"I love her too," he said, the words stopping me, sobering me. He placed a hand on my chest. "I. Love. Her. Too."

He tapped my chest with every word, and my heart slammed against my ribs just the same. He didn't just say he loved her. He insinuated *we* loved her.

"I've seen the way you look at her," Bru said, scanning my eyes, and he *had* to feel my heart. How much it raced. His throat worked. "You look at her like she's everything. You look how I feel."

How he feels.

"I know you, Ambrose." He had a hand behind my neck now, and I forgot about everyone who was probably looking at us right now. I needed to pull away. I... He wet his lips. "You're fighting her like you're fighting me."

My friend did know me, but he didn't know shit about this. It wasn't possible for me to love him like that, and I especially couldn't love *her* like that. One couldn't give love when there was so much hate in their heart, hate for themselves...

I did hate myself. In fact, I fucking loathed myself, and it was so easy to pretend to be the opposite. When a guy was the life of the party, no one questioned it.

I supposed that was the point.

Bru started to get even closer, like he was about to do something on this dance floor, and rather than deal with it, I pulled his fingers off my neck.

He shook his head. "Ambrose..."

I left him standing there when I did what I did best. I *ran*, and couldn't get away from him fast enough.

If only I could escape myself.

TWENTY-FOUR

Bow

I felt nauseous.

In fact, I'd felt this way for weeks.

Anytime I even thought about approaching Wells (or Bru) about what happened between all three of us, it brought on violent illness. I thought there was something seriously wrong with me. I'd even *thrown up* a time or two, and could barely eat.

I hugged my knees, staring at the pool in the Vesperton. I was the only one here because everyone was at Dorian's party.

I laid my head on my knees. Tears burned at my eyes just thinking about Wells's reaction to what I said. I thought the answer to my illness, my sickness, was just to put myself out there. I wanted to be brave and just go for what I wanted for once. I did miss Wells, but not just his friendship. I wanted *him,* my old best friend. I wanted Bruno too, and even though that was confusing, it'd just felt *right,* all three of us.

"What do you want from me?"

Wells let me know he didn't want me, and what was worse was that Bru had seen the rejection too. I was completely mortified when he'd come over. He automatically tried to be there for me and that almost made things worse. I felt so pathetic.

Sniffling, I wiped my eyes before the tears could fall. Before I knew it, I did something crazy.

I took off my dress, shoes, and gloves.

I still had my bra and underwear on, but I wasn't thinking at all as I exposed them. If I was thinking, I'd go back to Dorian's party and pretend I never talked to Wells. I never told him I missed him and begged him for his forgiveness. I hadn't sounded *pathetic*.

The water hit me in a rush. This was totally crazy, but I didn't care.

I didn't care.

I felt like I *actually* wanted to drown when I sank down. The pain hit me like an avalanche, but I waved my arms to keep me afloat.

"You see what he does to you? How he hurts you."

A deep voice was in my head. I blocked his number, but he kept getting ways around it. The voice had made me feel special for a time, how much he cared…

I stopped waving my arms. I just fell, and I glanced up at the ceiling. I could see the light from the pool room beneath the water. It was blurry, but I could see it.

"He doesn't care about you. None of them do. If they did, they wouldn't have let him hurt you. I care, Bow. You're so beautiful."

It was funny. I felt beautiful when those words were first spoken to me. They were beautiful when they were just words.

They were beautiful until he touched me.

Starting to choke, I waved my arms. I used my legs to kick, and soon, I was above the water. My lungs gasping for air, I let them take it in. I breathed.

I closed my eyes, my hair around me as I started to swim. I was a good swimmer actually, and used to love swimming. I loved it until I didn't.

I glided through the water, not caring about my makeup or my hair. I didn't care about what people would ask me once I got out of the pool. I didn't care about anything, and that was so unlike me.

I was doing a lot of things that weren't like me recently. The latest was trying to get Wells to forgive me, even though he shouldn't.

I wanted to drown again. I felt like that day I had on the balcony at the party. I'd wanted to fall, but Wells hadn't let me.

They hadn't let me.

Bru had saved me too that night, even though I hadn't wanted to be. I'd wanted to drown, just like I did now. My humiliation because of Wells's rejection and Bru watching it was too much. I didn't want Bru to be there for me out of pity.

"They don't care about you."

I could hear that voice again, the one that told me I was nothing and no one wanted me. It was that same voice that made me ignore Bru after what happened between all three of us at the boys' house. Bru had reached out several times. I told him I hadn't wanted to talk. For weeks, I did to him what Wells did to me tonight.

And all because of that voice.

"They don't care about you."

I was about to let myself go limp again. Maybe this time my body would hit the pool's floor.

Maybe this time I would drown.

I closed my eyes, but I opened them when I heard a sound behind me. I immediately turned around.

My eyes flashed.

His didn't though, his green eyes harsh, narrowed. Wells

Ambrose had a way of pinning me in place every time, but this time, I was in a pool in a very vulnerable position.

I was basically naked.

Completely aware I was in nothing but my bra and panties, I lowered below the water. In fact, the only thing I had above the water was my eyes, and that was enough to see Wells circulate the pool. He strode along it in his fitted tux and black shoes, his hands in his pockets. He stopped at the pool's stairs and stared at me in a way that completely made me shrink.

As well as tighten my nipples.

I felt like an idiot for that and immediately hugged myself below the water as if he could see. I started to back away, but the mere shock of what Wells did next froze me in place.

He took off his jacket. In fact, he tugged it off, aggressive about it. He exposed the white button-up shirt beneath that was tailored perfectly to his broad shoulders. Then he took off his vest and tossed them both on a pile of clothes.

My pile of clothes.

I shrunk again as Wells went for his cuff links. His face was red as he undid one, then the other. The next thing I knew, he was working the shirt off and exposing a white tank. I didn't know what he was doing. Then, that went too, his tank. He worked it off, revealing his tanned abs with an anger on his face I didn't understand.

If I could have physically gone beneath the water, I would have. I was frozen. After kicking away his shoes and pulling his socks off, he stripped his pants down to his boxers, then dove into the pool swimmer-style. He glided across the top like the expert swimmer I knew he was. I mean, he was a life-guard in the past for a reason.

White-hot panic had me quickly swimming toward the nearest pool exit. I had no idea what Wells was doing, but it didn't feel like a good thing.

He knew I wasn't drowning, right?

This time, I'd been above the water when he spotted me, but I had considered letting myself sink to the bottom.

Dread hit me that maybe Wells did think I'd been drowning, and, when my back hit the pool wall near the stairs, I just stayed there. I watched Wells swim toward me, his broad figure beneath the water now. He looked like a shark before he breached the surface with a snap of his platinum-blond hair. He pushed his hair back, his eyes open, narrowed. He swam long strides toward me, and I hugged the wall.

My mouth parted as he came up on me, and again, I was very aware of my lack of clothing beneath the water. I was aware of *his* lack of clothing too, and how beautiful he looked in the pool's glowing lights. His blond hair back, his dark roots were exposed, the water dripping down his chiseled jaw to the solid build of his shoulders. Wells was a work of art and always had been.

"What are you," I started to say, but then his strong jaw clenched. It was like my voice made him angry for some reason, and I didn't understand why. I shook my head, water dripping from my chin to chest. I sucked in a breath. "I wasn't drowning."

There would be no other reason for him to come into the pool, and I wondered why he'd bother saving me at all. He obviously hated me and hated what happened between us. He hated what happened between *all three of us* because I'd seen him avoid Bru too. Not just me.

The fact made my chest sink, but I remained standing tall in front of him. I didn't know how I had, but I managed.

Wells said nothing. His green eyes analyzed me, the water dripping down to my chest. His nostrils flared, and I hugged the wall again when he crowded me. He pressed one palm on either side of me. He had a long reach, but that still placed him a foot in front of my face.

I swallowed. "What are you doing?"

And how good he smelled. He smelled like him, Wells,

and that had been one of my favorite parts that night at Legacy House. I loved how familiar Wells smelled to me. Between Bru and him, I'd been in euphoria.

I wished for that ally now, Bru. Especially when Wells managed to get closer to me. His jaw tightened. "I want to know something."

Again, I didn't understand.

"Who touched you, Squeak?" he asked, analyzing my body again. He followed the tremble in my chest, the race in my heart. His eyes flicked up. "Who did you let between your legs?"

What. The. Fuck.

That was my instinctual thought, even though I went out of my way not to curse if I could help it. I even tried not to in my thoughts. "Why would you ask me that?"

He had no right to. That wasn't his business.

My answer displeased him, clearly, and I blinked when that foot between us turned into inches. A heat rolled off him I physically felt, and it manifested as a deep red across his sharp jaw. He gripped the pool's ledge. "You're Thatcher's little sister. Because of that, it's my fucking business to know who touched you."

I couldn't believe what I was hearing, and the wild anger that surfaced…

My life, *my body* was not any of his business, and the fact that he brought Thatcher up? It was like he socked me in the freaking chest. My jaw clenched. "It's not my brother's business, so it's definitely not yours."

He blinked like I hit him.

I didn't care.

I was so *tired* of Wells throwing his weight around when it came to me. I felt bad for what happened all those years ago. In fact, it ate me up so badly inside I doubt he ever had to punish me for all these years with public alienation. I punished myself enough for the both of us.

"He doesn't care about you."

I let the wrong person in because of him. I made mistakes, and, at the time, I believed I'd been empowered. I finally did something for me, what I wanted.

I hadn't wanted it.

I hadn't *at all*, and that was what all Wells's hate did to me. I shook my head. "It's not your business. It never was and you can stop punishing me now, Wells," I said, blinking down tears. "I'm already broken because of what happened. You *broke me,* so if that's what you wanted, you've already—"

His hands were on my shoulders.

He was shaking.

I felt the tremor in his hands, and it felt like he was using me just to stay upright. "Wells..."

He flinched when I put my hand on him, but I didn't stop until I made it to his shoulder. I squeezed, and he winced.

"Don't, Squeak," he gritted through his teeth, but he forgot that he touched me first. He was *still* touching me, and when I placed my hand on his flushed jaw, his face screwed up. "Please."

The plea sounded desperate, but I couldn't tell whether it was for me to stop or keep going. He was still shaking, and he shook even more when I pushed my fingers into his wet hair. A sigh left his lips and goose bumps lined my skin.

"Please stop. *Please,*" he ground out, and it was just like what happened at Legacy House. He was saying to stop but his body language, *his body* was saying something else. His eyes were closed as I got closer, but he gripped my wrist before I could put my other hand in his hair. He shook his head. "I don't want to break you."

The words froze me in place. My fingers curled. "What?"

He didn't say anything at first. He just cringed, and the next thing I knew, he had my face in his hands. I gasped, and I gasped again when he stared right at me. His expression was so serious, so pained it was like I felt it myself. "Wells?"

Again, he said nothing. He just shook his head again. He kept shaking his head. "I don't want to break you, Squeak. Punish you? I don't even hate you."

My heart beat rapidly inside my chest.

"I'm sure you think I do but I..." His nostrils flared, and when he winced again, my heart only kicked up its beats. He looked me straight in the eyes again, and I'd never seen such anguish in his. His jaw clenched tight. "Squeak, I hate my-fucking-self."

CHAPTER
TWENTY-FIVE

Wells

Every day I saw that tragic fucking summer. Every day, I saw the girl I let drown. Her name was Megan. I didn't know Megan. In fact, that day at the pool was the first day I'd seen her. She flirted with me, and I flirted back. I always flirted. I was shameless about it, even if it didn't mean anything. If a girl or guy didn't mean anything. That day, it had been Megan.

That day it had been Megan.

The memories of what happened that summer flooded my entire being on the regular, but not in the ways they should. I allowed Megan to drown that day, but what was worse was why she'd drowned.

"Wells?" Bow had her hands on my wrists. She studied me with these deep blue eyes that should remind me of her brother. Fuck, that should be all I saw when I looked at her. I should see my best friend's little sister.

Not the girl I'd been aware of for so long.

I hated myself for that. I *hated* my-fucking-self.

"Wells?" Bow was able to squeeze my wrists because my hands were still on her face. Why was I still touching her? She scanned my eyes. "Archer?"

She could see me again, her Archer. I wasn't bothering to hide him. Why couldn't I hide him?

"I don't hate you, Bow," I admitted, and I wished so hard I could. *I tried.* I tried so hard for so long. "I hate me. I hate what I did."

Her blue eyes got so sad. Her mouth turned down, and even though her lips were painted red, I knew they'd be flushing right now. They always flushed.

Stop.

I couldn't help myself. I touched her full lips, and they trembled. Her mouth moved at a mere touch from my finger, and that shot so much awareness into my being, my cock…

Stop.

I couldn't. I wanted to, but I couldn't fucking fight.

Why can't I fight?

"What do you mean you hate what you did?" she asked me, so innocent.

She *was* innocent. Rainbow Reed couldn't hurt a fucking cockroach. I knew because I saw her interact with one once when we'd been cleaning out her parents' garage. Thatcher made me help. His dad said we couldn't hang out until it was done, so I helped.

Anyway, a roach ran right across Bow's feet. It rightly scared the shit out of her, but after that initial reaction, she got a mason jar and a piece of paper from the kitchen. She scooped the thing up and set it free out in the wild because *that* was the type of person she was. She was, no matter how much I tried to convince myself she wasn't.

"It was my fault. It was my fault. It was my…" I started, and I couldn't fucking *breathe*. My jaw was so fucking tight, locked. "It's my fault that girl died, Bow. Not yours. Never yours."

It couldn't be. Rainbow Reed was kind. She was *innocent.* She was perfect.

"What?" Her voice was a whisper, and I barely heard it.

I squeezed her arms. "It was me, Bow. This whole fucking time it was me. What happened that summer?" I shook my head. "And I wish I could blame you for my fuckup. I tried. I tried for so long."

"I don't understand." Her whole body was trembling now, and I saw it well. She had very little clothing on right now, and even though she was mostly beneath the water, that didn't matter. I saw her ease her trim hips into the pool up to the point of her breasts. I saw her pert nipples pierce through her lace bra before she glided the rest of the way into the water. *I saw her.*

Because I watched her.

I watched this girl so many times when she didn't know. I was aware of where she was at virtually all times, and the same went for that summer I allowed an innocent girl to drown. I wasn't watching Megan. In fact, I was barely watching anyone else at the pool that day even though I was a lifeguard. My attention had been divided because it was always, *always* on one thing, on one... person.

Bow's mouth parted. "Wells—"

"It wasn't your fault." I heard the ache in my voice. It was the same ache I was forced to live every fucking day. It was the death of an innocent girl, yes, but it was also knowing what I knew about my best friend's little sister. It was knowing how my insides felt every time I was forced to be around her and act like I was fine.

I wasn't fine.

It fucking *ached* to be around Rainbow Reed. It ate at me every fucking day, and it was easier to make her suffer. If I was suffering...

She touched my hair again, and it felt like she gave me life. She did for a time. Every day seeing her at Thatcher's house growing up was like light. She was the sunshine to the darkness of all our problems, my friends and I. My best friends had some really fucked-up shit happen to them over the years. They all had their own dark constants. I didn't know suffering like my friends but Bow... little Rainbow Reed was always glowing. She brought color to our dark world.

And all she had to be was herself.

It was like how *couldn't* I watch her, protect her? Something that pure needed to be protected. It was delicate, beautiful.

"I was watching you," I said, my fingers on her shoulder now. Her soft fucking skin. Her soft, *perfect* fucking skin, and she trembled. I squeezed. "I was watching you, Bow. I was watching you, and I took my eyes off the water."

I still remembered that day. It was so fucking vivid. Bow and her little friends were talking. They were having a good time, laughing.

Until they weren't.

"You took your eyes off the water because of me," she said, shaking, and I let her believe that. I did because I was weak and so fucking selfish. A little lie let me not face reality. It let me drown in denial and not see the fucking truth. *My* truth. She bit her lip. "You thought I was drowning, and you tried to save me."

I had thought she'd been drowning. I'd been *terrified*, and that was on me too. I'd just been so distracted. I'd just been...

"Wells?"

"I'd been watching you, Bow." My voice was so raw, stripped. I closed my eyes. "I'm always watching you."

This was an understatement. I saw her everywhere, even in my dreams. I saw *her* drowning sometimes, and I felt like an asshole. I was relieved each and every time I woke up and that wasn't the case. I was relieved that someone else had died that summer.

Because that person wasn't her.

I was aware those thoughts, at best, made me a terrible person. I mean, what kind of person did that? Thought like that…

"You watch me?" Bow brought me out of my dark thoughts. She looked so little in front of me, so small and petite. When we were kids, she was just Thatch's little sis. She was the pipsqueak that got in our business and chased us around. Now, she was a woman in a pool with a glow still around her. A woman with flushed skin and a mouth I'd tasted. She blinked. "Wells, I don't understand."

She wouldn't, would she? I was so good at bullshit, *lying*. The only person I lied to more than her was myself.

"I watch you, Bow," I said into the humid air. The pool wasn't in operation tonight due to Dorian's gala. His parents shut this whole hotel down and the only light in the room was from the pool itself. Even still, I found Bow, *the light* found her. Her skin… I swallowed. "I was looking at you before I thought you were drowning. *I was looking at you*, and I wasn't paying any fucking attention to the pool."

I let someone drown because I was watching my best friend's little sister. I told myself for a long time that was my responsibility. I was looking out for her, but only for Thatcher.

"Wells—"

"Don't you get it!" I was angry now, but not at her. Bracing her arms, I brought Bow close to me, and her eyes widened in surprise and maybe even a little fear. I used to get off on intimidating her. It made me feel better about myself. If I could control her, she wasn't controlling me.

I cringed. "I was watching you so fucking hard that I wasn't watching anyone else. I was watching my *best friend's little sister* because I'm sick. Because I'm an asshole and because I…"

I couldn't pull the words out. If I did, I'd have to hear them. I would have to admit to myself what I was actually doing that day at the pool. I wasn't watching Rainbow Reed because I was worried she'd get herself into trouble.

I was watching her because I couldn't *not* watch her.

"Because I love you," I whispered, and a burst of air left Bow's lips. It brushed my chest, and when I brought her closer, I could taste her. Her wonderful fucking scent engulfed my senses and how good she fucking tasted, felt. I cringed again. "I love you because you're good and you're kind and you're so much better than me."

She was. She'd never let her parents down and squander their money. She'd never even kill a fucking roach. Bow didn't have a selfish bone in her body *and that* was why I loved her.

It was why I always had.

I was shaking, way more than she was. Her fists curled. "You love me?"

Hearing her say the words hit something hard inside me. It made my reality real and showed what an asshole I truly was. I was the guy who fell in love with my buddy's sister. *I lied* for years and also had someone's death on my hands because of it. Because *of my obsession* with her and her goodness.

I squeezed her arms. "I'm the reason someone drowned all those years ago. I'm the reason *a girl died* because I was obsessed with my best friend's sister like an asshole."

I was a terrible person, and I had no right to love anyone, least of all her.

The same went for Bru.

He asked me time and time again why I was resisting. He asked me why I couldn't let go and just be with him. And her.

I had nothing to give either one of them. I had nothing because I wasn't worthy of either of them. Bru was such a good guy too, and, if they were smart, they'd be together. They were perfect for each other.

The thought of that broke something inside me. Bru and

Bow deserved each other and that didn't include me. It didn't include the pain or the burden of me.

"You don't hate me?" Bow's lips quivered, the words gasping from her mouth. She was so fucking innocent, *too* fucking innocent.

"Hating you meant I didn't have to admit the truth to myself," I said, and the sadness in her eyes nearly broke me. They were ringed with a despair that burrowed its way inside and carved me from the inside out. This girl would feel bad for me like I didn't literally treat her like shit for years. People actually started alienating her for the shit that happened over that summer. They felt bad for me, and that was laughable. My throat worked. "Punishing you meant I could go on with the lie."

"Lie?"

"That I wasn't completely and hopelessly in love with you."

Her mouth parted and she looked in awe of me, *in awe* like what I said to her wasn't a complete betrayal of her brother. Like I had any fucking right to love this girl.

I lifted her closer in the water. She needed to fucking hear what I had to say, and it was such a mistake bringing her to me. She felt so good, her breasts perfect and quivering. She was inches away from my chest and I had to physically fight to keep her there.

Let her go.

I was. After this moment, this touch, I would no longer be her burden. I was going to go tell Thatcher the truth, and, after that, I didn't know what happened. I could lose one of my best friends and the ache of that nearly shattered me into smaller pieces than I was already broken into.

Because I knew what I had to do next.

"I can't love you, Bow," I said and couldn't even look at her. I was looking behind her, at the wall like some weak fucker. My jaw clenched tight. "I don't have a right to love you."

I whispered the words, but I think she heard them. She touched my face, turning it toward her so I had to look at her. She was looking at me like I wasn't the sinner, the monster who let a girl die, then punished her for it for years. She was staring at me, with all the goodness in her heart, like I was good.

And I almost believed her.

Bow had a pureness about her that made a guy see himself differently and, for a time, I thought I could be different. When we were kids, I willingly became her archer. I denied my truth. I was never this girl's hero.

I was the devil in human skin.

Bow said nothing. She merely guided my head down. She pushed her fingers back into my hair and I was weak again. I didn't stop her, but I did grab her wrist. I clenched it. "I'm the asshole who falls for my best friend's sister, then lies about it. I punished her *for years* after I let a girl drown because of that lie."

She winced in front of me but she didn't recoil. If anything, she brought me closer and used her other hand to do it, putting it on my chest. It burned into me so hot I thought I'd lose myself.

Stop her.

I was such a weak fuck, and *I* was wincing now. I knew I had to let her go, but I couldn't find the will. I was letting her touch me, letting her look at me like she felt sorry for me, when all I did was ruin her life. I also stole someone else's. Didn't she see that?

"I'm not worthy of you, Bow," I said, and she winced again. There was sympathy in her blue eyes, maybe even empathy. This girl was too kind for her own good. My jaw moved. "You and Bru can do so much better."

She stopped then. She stopped getting closer, and I hoped

that reality finally hit her. She knew I was right. She and Bru were good people. *They* should be together.

"You should be with him," I said. If she was to choose someone, it should be him. He was good enough for her, and she was great for him. He'd been dealt a shitty hand in the past, and, though he'd overcome it, I knew Bow could be that missing piece. She could give him so much love.

Her hand on me ached at this point, envisioning her and him together. It was right, though. It made sense.

I looked away, but I came back when she touched my jaw. I squeezed her wrist. "You shouldn't touch me. You should go be with him. You guys would be great together."

They would be great, amazing.

I shut my eyes. "I don't deserve either one of you guys."

"You're right. You don't."

My eyes flashed open. Little Bow was standing in front of me, and she was completely serious. She also still had her hands on me and used them to angle my head down to look at her. Her mouth parted. "But the thing is, you don't get a choice. *I* get to choose. And he gets to choose too, Wells Ambrose."

I didn't understand. Didn't she hear what I said? Anything I said? I wet my lips. "I made people hate you. Alienate you because I couldn't admit the truth to myself. I couldn't admit my mistakes and how I—"

Her mouth touched mine and stopped all thoughts. The kiss was soft, sweet, and distinctly Bow.

It was beautifully Bow.

It was filled with everything Bow was. It was my light just as much as my undoing. It brought me completeness I could only say I felt with one other person. It was her and it was him.

It was them.

I fell into the kiss more than I should have. I let Bow direct it and take me to a place I couldn't go. I bit her lip. "I can't,

Bow. I was a piece of shit to you, and I hate myself for it. I was shit to both of you guys and I—"

"I forgive you," she said, and I tasted salty wetness in our kiss as she sucked my lip into her mouth. A burn charged itself inside me. Especially when she deepened our kiss.

She forgives me.

She couldn't. I shook my head. "You can't. I don't deserve it."

I wanted it though. I *desperately* wanted her forgiveness. I wanted *her*, and I didn't fight it when she pushed her fingers in my hair again. Her touch was heavenly. It was euphoric.

"I forgive you, Wells Ambrose," she repeated against my mouth, and it unfurled something inside me I didn't know I needed. She unleashed something, a breath, a weight. Her nose brushed mine. "Now forgive yourself, Wells. *Love* yourself like I always have."

I stopped kissing her, blinking.

"I love you, Wells," she said, and her face was so cherry red. Her mouth pressed to mine. "I love you."

She... loves me.

She undid me with the words, and I pressed my mouth so hard against hers.

She loves me.

It was like I was enough for her. I knew the truth of that, of course. I could never be like Rainbow. I could never be as good or as kind.

She loves me.

But I'd try. I'd try so fucking hard for her, and I knew that was selfish. And I definitely knew I'd never *ever* be worthy of her.

Or him.

I didn't know what was happening right now. How I could be kissing her and thinking about him. The same happened when I kissed him.

Bru was right about what happened at Legacy House. I

fucked him because I was so messed up *about her*. It was like they both had a piece of me, and I knew they both liked each other too.

"You're fighting her like you're fighting me."

Bru was right about that as well. I was fighting him and her.

Because I loved them both.

I didn't know how it worked. But I knew how it felt.

"Why are you denying Bow and me?"

Bru's voice was in my head as I kissed Bow deeper. As I let myself… have her. It was like he was egging me on, making me brave.

"I love you." I pushed into Bow's mouth, and she gasped so hard. She trembled, and I shook my head. "I know I have no right, but I fucking love you, Bow."

I did, so fucking much.

I didn't know what that meant for Bru and me, but something inside me told me he wanted this for me just as much as I wanted this, needed this. Something told me he'd already given me permission for this. To have this, her.

"I love her too."

His love for her didn't feel like a threat. If anything, it made me feel good that she could have him too. Rainbow Reed deserved as much love as could possibly be given and I knew that didn't make sense. I should want to kill Bru for admitting how he felt about her.

But I didn't.

I didn't want to kill him, and, in this moment, I wanted to just have what I'd desperately wanted. I wanted to be inside Bow Reed.

I wanted to have her.

"Archer…" Bow's lips parted as I tasted her neck, as I sucked and pressed her up against the pool. I thrusted into her through my boxers, and she shook so hard I thought she'd fall apart. "I love you."

It pained me to hear it just as much as it livened me. I felt so unworthy of her love, her care. My tongue swept hers. "I love you."

Admitting it again nearly made me wince. I did love her, but, at the same time, I was betraying Thatcher with that love.

She loves me.

I parted Bow's legs, the only thought in my mind her heat. The thought of touching her made me blind, and I eased her panties away. My fingers found their way inside her and…

Fuck.

Bow's mouth fell open as my digits pumped, her greedy sex devouring my fingers. She grabbed my biceps just to hold on, and I growled when she dragged her fingernails down my skin. She instantly left welts, and I forgot myself. I forgot who she was and the consequences that would befall us both after this moment. I forgot the consequences that would befall me as I took my cock in my hand and stroked it through my boxers. I wanted to be inside her. I wanted to *fuck* her.

I wanted to make love to her.

I knew nothing about love. If I did, I wouldn't have shown it for years as hate. I wouldn't have treated someone so innocent so poorly.

My growls became something different as I pumped my cock. At the same time, I fucked her with my fingers. I couldn't go there. I refused. I couldn't *let go*, and it took everything I had to keep distance between us. Bow looked so beautiful as she fucked my hand. There was a glow to her skin I wanted to taste, just like her nipples. They were beaded hard through her bra, and I pressed my chest against hers.

She called out again, and I did too. I pumped my dick, and she came hard over my hand. Jolting, her slick body slid against mine, and I engulfed myself in the warmth. My cock surged, and soon, I was coming in my boxers just like I did at Legacy House. I came like a fucking teenager *again*.

Because of her.

I kissed Bow, her mouth open as she laid her head back to the pool's ledge. Her dark hair spread out like she was a damn mermaid, a siren sent to tempt me.

This girl did prove to be my undoing in the end, and, as my lips moved against hers, I found that kissing her, tasting her, was the only thing that kept my thoughts at bay. I felt the influx of betrayal and regret threatening to crash though this moment. I couldn't pass off that I made my best friend's little sister come *again*, but Thatcher wasn't the only one in my mind. I thought about Bru too.

I thought about how he wasn't here this time.

TWENTY-SIX

Wells

Me: Something happened between Bow and me.
    Bru: I know.
    Me: You do?
    Bru: Yeah.
    Me: How?
    Bru: I followed you to the pool.
    Bru: I wanted to make sure you were okay, and when I saw her, I wanted to make sure she was okay with you being there.
    Bru: I left when things… got intense.
    Me: Are you angry?
    Me: At me?
    Bru: I think you know the answer to that.
    Bru: I already knew how you felt about her. I was just waiting for you to admit it to yourself, which you did. I'm glad. Like I said, I feel the same way.
    Bru: So my question now is what happens next?

Me: I don't know, but I'm not lying to Thatcher about all this.

Bru: I agree you shouldn't, but maybe you should figure out what all this is with her first.

Bru: Maybe we both should.

CHAPTER
TWENTY-SEVEN

Bow

I got a text from Wells that said he wanted to talk.

I didn't know what to think.

After what happened at the pool, he was pretty quiet, and helped me dress.

"We should get back out there," he said, then proceeded to take me back to Dorian's gala.

He took me home after the evening wrapped, and he was mostly silent on the drive home. I was sure that had to do with the fact that my brother was in the car talking his ear off about Bru.

Apparently, the guys had danced together, and my brother wanted to know if that was a declaration about their relationship. "It all makes sense now," Thatcher said, appearing more than thrilled. "Things have been so tense between you two. The fight even makes sense now." Thatcher squeezed Wells's arm. "I'm glad. You two deserve to be happy."

I felt gut punched. That I'd somehow been left out of

something, but the text that came from Wells after I got inside my house later that night was followed up quickly.

Wells: Bru's going to be there.

That was when I realized someone else was in the group chat with Wells and me.

And I swallowed upon seeing the message.

Bru: We both want to talk to you. Let us know when's a good time.

I didn't know what was happening between us. I just knew something was and whatever it was made my heart race.

"I don't deserve either one of you guys," Wells had said. Like there was an us, and it went beyond just Wells and me. I'd never experienced something like this. I just knew I'd loved Wells for a really long time.

But I also loved Bru.

It was crazy to admit that. To have feelings for two guys at the same time.

Me: Sure. Anytime.

Me: At my parents' summer house just off campus?

Were the guys really going to address what happened between the three of us?

It was weird to think about there being a *three of us.* I mean, I was still trying to wrap my head around what happened with Wells and me in the pool.

"I don't hate you, Bow. I hate me. I hate what I did."

The fact that Wells hated himself made me sad, but it made sense. He'd been channeling all that aggression toward me when, the whole time, he actually held guilt. He held guilt because he'd been watching me that day at the pool, and even though I had a crush on him for longer than I remembered back then, I never thought in any reality that'd been recip-rocated.

And then there was Bru.

My heart surged thinking about being with either one of them, let alone both of them.

The three of us decided to meet up the following weekend at one of my parents' cabins. My parents had several around the country since my dad was in real estate amongst other things. Things with school had basically wrapped but there was still a lot of traffic around campus with people moving out and everything. Normally, I'd be focusing on my move-out too.

I'd be focusing on that or something else.

The frequent calls to my phone had stopped. The texts too. It was like things had started over in my life just in time for something else to happen. I never anticipated what Wells had told me. I'd always wanted his forgiveness, and it was a crazy spin that he needed mine. It was like he needed my love too, and to wrap my head around that...

My friends and I spent many summers and even a few holidays at the cabin with our families. The dads would take the sons fishing while the moms and daughters would bake or go shopping. It was just a fun time with family and friends.

I wanted some time to myself at the cabin. I just needed *to breathe* and think about whatever was going to happen, so I told the guys I'd meet them up there. I gave them the code to get in, but I didn't think that would be necessary in the end since I planned to get there early. Again, I'd just wanted to think.

Apparently, the guys had the same idea.

Bru's Audi was already there, and I wondered if they arrived together since I didn't see Wells's car.

I decided to take my breaths in the ride share I pulled up in. Bru had texted me several times on my way up. He'd wanted to drive me himself, but I made up some excuses about needing to do a few things on campus. In reality, I'd just wanted the time alone and I'd also felt sick again that morning. I'd more so felt nauseous. I'd never had a strong stomach when it came to my nerves.

And I was *nervous*.

I'd never had anything like this happen to me before. In fact, being alone had been my religion for so long that I'd just kind of gotten used to it.

You weren't always alone.

I supposed I wasn't, but my stomach turned if I thought about that. When I'd helped one of my professors last year, it was supposed to be for extra credit. I hadn't needed the extra credit but burying myself in schoolwork was just what I did. It was how I dealt with my loneliness.

"Come back to me, Bow. It'll be different this time."

This time, it would be different. This time, it wasn't my loneliness that was guiding my actions. I was doing something because I wanted something. There was no desperation, and that was what settled my stomach when I ultimately got out of the ride share.

Bru was waiting for me at the door. He had a smile on, his hands in the pockets of his well-worn jeans. Those were my favorite jeans on him, and I didn't know I liked jeans like that until, well, him.

"Hey." He brought his long wingspan around me at the door, and I sucked in a breath. I sucked in the smell of him, the essence of him. His masculine scent was like being surrounded by a warm breeze in nature, when the sun peeks through the canopy of large trees and makes you feel good, safe.

I always felt safe with Bru, and maybe that was why kissing him in his car had felt natural. He noticed I had a bag with me but didn't say anything about it when he took it.

Again, I didn't know what this was.

I didn't know if it was presumptuous of me, but I packed, um, stuff. I was prepared to stay the weekend, stay with them.

Wells sat in my dad's armchair.

He had on jeans too, the ones that hugged his long legs, but he had holes in his whereas Bru never wore jeans like that. Bru was like the boy next door, and Wells was always the local bad boy.

Wells's head lifted when I came in, and he smiled. Wells got up, but he didn't hug me.

If anything, he kept his distance.

"Hey, Squeak," Wells said. His green eyes were warm, but his expression was tight, serious. I didn't know what that meant. Things were so different at the pool. Until it was over. It was like reality had hit him with the way he helped me put on my clothes, then later took me home.

Maybe Wells was going to tell me what happened between us at the pool had been a mistake. Maybe he didn't like me, let alone love me like he said.

"Hi," I said, feeling ashamed that I wore makeup. I even pulled out a dress. It showed off my legs and made me feel sexy, pretty.

My face hot, I fought myself from tugging at the hem. I suddenly felt exposed and foolish.

I also noticed what Wells had called me. I was still *squeak*. I was the little sister who had a crush on her brother's best friends.

Wells gestured toward the couch. He wanted me to sit, so I did, but he made sure to return to my dad's armchair. Bru sat on the couch with me, but he kept his own distance and stayed on the opposite side.

Anxiety unfurled in my chest like an intricate forest of spiny pricker bushes. I wriggled in my seat. Especially when I noticed Wells suddenly *not* making eye contact with me.

"What's going on?" I asked, scared, terrified. I'd been scared recently, but this was a different kind of fear. This wasn't fear for my physical self.

Bru's hands came together. He still wore his smile, but it

wasn't like one of his normal Bru smiles. This one felt put on. Like he was trying to keep me calm, but I didn't feel calm. I felt tense, worried. Bru leaned forward. "Wells and I wanted to talk to you about something."

Like Wells was his right-hand man, Bru looked at him. Wells returned the look and I found the shift of power weird. Wells Ambrose never let anyone in his life take the wheel on anything unless it was Dorian. Dorian was like their leader, but Dorian wasn't here.

I swallowed. "Okay."

Bru didn't speak right away. He just kept looking at Wells. Bru wet his lips. "Wells told me what happened between you two at the pool. I actually saw some of it. I followed you guys, but left when things got intense. I didn't want to intrude on you guys."

I didn't know what to say, my face a furnace now. "Bru…"

His smile changed then, but it didn't falter. It actually warmed as he stared at me, but it didn't feel put on. It also didn't feel like a reaction of anger or jealousy. He had told me he shared women with Wells before at parties.

My lungs tight, I didn't know what to say.

"I also heard why Wells came to you initially, and, though I don't feel like any of that is my business, Wells shared some concerns." Bru's gaze clashed with Wells before Wells's attention shifted to the floor. Wells's expression was tight, terse, and that confused me. Bru faced me. "And I do too after we talked about it for a minute."

I didn't understand what he was talking about.

Bru leaned in. "I'm aware of the history between you and Wells, Bow. I know what he did to you." He said this, and Wells cringed. Bru sighed. "He made it hard for you to have any type of relationships outside of Legacy *for years*, and that included intimate relationships."

Intimate relationships.

"And like I said, your personal life is none of my business.

As far as I'm concerned, you have a right to be with anyone you please, but from what I understand, that would have been difficult considering what Wells did to you."

I really didn't understand now, sitting back. "What are you trying to say?"

Bru shifted a little at this point, and Wells was no longer studying the area rug.

"I blackballed you, Squeak. Point-blank," Wells said, and I winced. It wasn't what he did, but what he called me. It was like he used that nickname to disconnect himself from me and that hurt, more than hurt. Wells sighed. "The fact of the matter is there aren't many people who would have over-looked something like that, and I'm kind of worried you might have gotten yourself wrapped up in something."

Something...

My heart raced.

"It takes the right kind of fucker to overlook something I would have put out there like that. People don't fuck with me. They don't fuck with *Legacy*." Wells's eyes narrowed. "And I know you're aware of that."

Heat flashed me. In fact, I felt like I was drowning in it. My heart beat faster, but it wasn't because of shame or embarrassment. It was anger. White-*hot* anger, and it infuriated me just like it had in the past. It was a time when I made mistakes.

It was a time when I messed up.

"Or in this case, it's the *wrong* kind of fucker," Wells continued, my anger surging, blazing. Wells opened his mouth, I assumed to say something else, but Bru raised his hand. Again, the shift of power was foreign to me. Bru obviously had Wells's respect.

"I guess we're worried someone might have taken advantage of you," Bru said, his jaw moving. He shook his head. "Again, I personally feel you should be with whoever you want to be—"

"You're right," I gritted, honestly done with this conversation. I couldn't believe I came all the way out here for this, and it was worse than rejection. I thought the worst thing Wells Ambrose could have done was keep people away from me. To hate me *for years* and make me hate myself.

I had hated myself. I did for so long that I did get wrapped up with the wrong person.

"You see how toxic he and your other friends are?"

I blocked out the voice, borderline in tears. I sniffed them back. "My personal life is none of your business."

"Bow." Bru stood up because I did. He reached for me, but I backed up like he had the plague.

Wells stood up. Two large, all-encompassing men surrounded me, and I actually thought they wanted me. That they brought me out here to talk, talk about us.

I was an idiot, a fool in so many ways, but when I moved toward the door, both guys came with me. They only had to take a few steps since my strides were small. I knuckled my hands. "Move."

Wells was in front of the door, but Bru wasn't far away. In fact, Bru was by my side like Wells's backup. All this was more of Wells's manipulation, his control.

"You see how toxic he and your other friends are?"

I attempted to blink back tears, but I couldn't help them spilling over. Wells moved closer, but he stopped when I winced.

He shook his head. "Squeak—"

"Stop it. Just stop!" My voice radiated through the room, a squeak in it, a tremor. My jaw clenched. "Just stop, Wells. Please stop…"

He made me hate myself. He did, and I did the wrong thing. I was angry. Betrayed by someone I cared about.

Someone I loved.

Wells used to protect me, but in *one* moment, that protection was gone. I hadn't meant to distract him, but he let go of me when I needed him most. I also had that girl's death on my hands, and I had to deal with that alone.

He left me.

Wells Ambrose was my friend. He was my first love. He was…

"I wanted to feel like I had some power," I admitted, cringing. I wiped my eyes. "I wanted to have power over my own life."

I was so tired of the loneliness. So I made a friend, and I thought that was all he was. Heck, I even thought I wanted it when things went deeper.

I didn't.

I was crying. I was freaking crying in front of two guys I actually wanted.

My shoulders were shaking, my body quivering. I felt like I was going to collapse into a puddle of my own shame, and I wanted to. I actually felt my knees buckle.

He caught me.

Ocean air surrounded me, and it was deep, potent. The feel of muscular arms followed closely behind the scent, as well as a broad chest when I was pressed up against it.

"Squeak." The nickname no longer felt like a disconnect from Wells when he hugged me tight. He embraced me so hard against his firm body. "Bow, tell me what happened."

My tongue felt too big for my mouth, so much shame there.

I buried my face in Wells's chest. I felt so at home there. So cared about, so safe. I gasped. "I wanted to control something for once. It was my body, and I wanted control over it. I wanted control over my life."

It was my life, and though the decision to lose my virginity had been my own, it hadn't felt like it.

"Come back to me, Bow. It'll be different this time."

I'd been manipulated, and that was where my shame

came from. I did what I did to have control over my own life, but that wasn't how I felt after it'd been over.

"It's my life," I whispered into Wells's chest. His heart beat quickly, rapid like mine. I hugged him close. "I wanted control over something. Power."

"You do have power. So much power, Bow," Wells said and the words surged through my body. He pushed his face into my hair. "You have no idea how much control you have over me."

I shook, my entire body unstable. I thought I'd fall even though Wells held me, but then a hand came to touch me from behind.

Bru's touch was soft, gentle. He rested a hand on my waist, but it was steadfast.

"And me," Bru said, the words burning through me. Especially when I felt his other hand come up to tangle with Wells's. Wells's hand was still in my hair, and their fingers intermingled.

"What do you need, Bow?" Bru said from behind me. His hand squeezed my waist. "Tell me what you want from me. Tell me what you *need.*"

"Tell us," Wells stated, his voice rough, heavy. He reached around me to brace Bru's arm. He ended up gripping Bru's hand on my waist, and Bru growled from behind me. A deep sound left Wells's lips in response, and the heat of it brushed my hair. "What do we need to do to make you feel powerful? Tell me what *I* need to do. Please..."

Please...

"Please tell me, Squeak. I'm begging you." Wells's hand gripped my hair, and Bru's did too. Wells's mouth warmed the top of my head. "I need you to tell me what you want. I need you."

He needed me.

I needed him too. I needed *both* of them.

"Make love to me," I said, and both guys sucked in a

breath. I reached for Wells's neck, seeking his mouth. "Make me feel loved."

The words barely left my lips before Wells closed the distance. His mouth sealed with mine, and he tasted my lips like a man consumed with hunger. Like he waited so long to taste me again.

Like he waited so long to have me.

Wells's mouth devoured mine, and Bru hiked me up to meet it. Bru pressed me into Wells, and when Bru ground his cock into me, I gasped.

"Tell me if this is too much," Bru gritted out. His hold on me was firm but shaky. Like he was attempting to hold himself back but failing.

Reaching back, I rubbed Bru's dick. I stroked him through his jeans, letting him know he was okay, and the noise that he released behind me was feral.

"I want this," Wells said and wrapped an arm around both Bru and me. Grabbing Bru's waist, he forced Bru into me. Bru and I both called out, and Wells bit my lip. "I want you both so bad. I shouldn't, but I fucking want it."

I understood. Both guys seemed to have been at war with not just what was happening between the three of us, but each other. I'd seen them be intimate before, but there seemed to be some resistance there.

"Let us love you, Wells," I said to him, and instantly, he started shaking beneath my mouth. I kissed his neck, his chest, and I felt his heart beat into my lips. His heart was going at a rapid-fire pace. Especially when I pushed my hand under his shirt.

Bru ended up reaching around me and taking off Wells's shirt. His golden chest was hard and perfect in front of me, and I touched it. In fact, I started licking my way down it, and Wells growled before reaching up and grabbing Bru. I was sandwiched between both guys when Wells bit Bru's mouth. Bru groaned, and his tongue started flicking Wells's.

They did this while *grinding into me*, and a charged moan left my lips.

"I shouldn't want this," Wells gasped, his tongue dueling with Bru's. "I shouldn't want you, bro. I'm an asshole. I treated you like shit."

"It's a good thing I don't break easy, then, Ambrose," Bru returned before grabbing Wells's neck and forcing his tongue down Wells's throat. Bru deepened the kiss, and Wells let him. Bru moaned. "I told you before. I fucking love you, and I meant it."

He meant it.

I wasn't sure if I should be a part of this moment between them, but I didn't feel weird about it. In fact, I felt almost closer to Bru that he felt comfortable enough to say something like that to Wells in front of me. Bru obviously trusted me to be a part of the moment, and I didn't feel jealous. In actuality, I loved that he loved Wells. It was so weird and confusing, but I did.

"You shouldn't love me," Wells said, an ache touched his voice that I recognized. He sounded the same way at the pool with me. Wells grabbed my hip. "Neither one of you should."

The thing about love was that sometimes you couldn't choose who received it. Sometimes it couldn't be helped.

Sometimes it just happened.

I couldn't anticipate falling in love with two of my brother's best friends let alone at the same time. The fact that they already had feelings for each other just made things make more sense. We all felt so strongly about each other.

"You don't get a choice, Ambrose," Bru said, and kissed Wells harder. "My love isn't conditional. It isn't for either one of you."

A wild heat blazed inside me as Bru lifted my dress from behind. He also stopped kissing Wells and pressed his mouth into my neck.

Bru loved me too.

Bru loved both of us, and he pressed me against Wells again. Wells was so hard through his jeans, and his eyes were wild as Bru lifted my dress.

Wells helped him.

Together, both guys pulled my dress off, and I forced a confidence I didn't naturally have when they removed it. It pooled into a heap at my side when the guys dropped it, and I was left standing there, braless in front of them. The black dress I'd worn hadn't needed it.

"Fuck." Wells's green eyes appeared luminous as he stood in front of me. My chest rose up and down with rapid breaths, and I sucked in a breath when Bru squeezed my shoulders from behind.

"She has such perfect nipples," Bru said, and nearly sounded enamored when he put his hands on my sides. His hands were warm and rough as he massaged my skin. "I want to taste them."

I wanted him to taste them. "Please."

He didn't hesitate when he filled his hands with my breasts. He drew his fingers over my tight nipples.

"Me first." Wells was on his knees, but, with his height, he was basically at my shoulders. He appeared crazed before he leaned forward and sucked my dark nipple into his mouth. I moaned. Wells Ambrose was on his knees for me.

And Bru quickly joined him.

"Fucking stunning," Bru said before he, too, sucked in a nipple. My eyes rolled back and his did too before he sucked harder. Bru growled. "I knew you'd taste good, Bow. So sweet…"

"Too fucking sweet." Wells was biting me now and what a sight to have both of them like this. I had two amazingly powerful, intimidating guys on their knees for me. I didn't know what to do with that and my moan intensified when Wells reached between my legs. He pushed his fingers into my lace underwear, and I was basically on my tiptoes in front of them.

"Taste this," Wells said, then put those same fingers to Bru's lips. Right away, Bru opened his mouth, and both guys' eyes were on each other as Wells made Bru taste me.

Oh my fuck.

I was shaking watching the euphoria on Bru's face as he sucked Wells's fingers. Bru's nostrils flared and a deep sound reverberated low in his chest.

"Heaven," Bru said, and I watched as he took off his shirt. His muscled chest reminded me of Superman without the spandex. He was perfectly shaped from his sculpted shoulders to his hard pecs. He tossed his shirt before looking at me. "You're heaven, you know."

He was making me feel that way, and I was surprised by the sudden wetness in my eyes. *This* was how it was supposed to feel.

"Come back to me…"

I pushed out the voice in my head, his voice. I wouldn't let my past mistakes ruin this. *I wasn't* going to feel shame about wanting this.

I wasn't going to feel ashamed about wanting them.

I realized that, just like Wells, I had issues with feeling worthy. I hadn't felt like I deserved love, and I let someone convince me that the only way I could receive it was giving a part of myself away to someone. But Bru was right. Love wasn't supposed to be conditional.

Bru's forehead touched my stomach. He didn't do anything else, and I played with his hair. He smelled so good, warm. He moved his head. "Tell me what you want from me, Bow. I'll do anything to make this special for you."

I knew he would, and I had a feeling they *both* would. These guys were literally on their knees for me, and I pushed my hand into Bru's hair. I yanked his head back, and he growled. I did the same with Wells's electric blond hair, and the pull of his roots made his eyes ignite again. My sudden forcefulness was turning him on. It was turning them both on, judging by the current state of Bru's charged irises, and I was right there with them.

This wasn't like me, to be so direct, and I really did feel so powerful in this moment. I felt in charge, and being in charge could be anything that I wanted it to be. It meant I got to choose, and, as I pulled both guys' heads back, I knew what I wanted.

"Don't hold back," I said, exposing the columns of their powerful necks. I wet my lips. "Do what you normally do when you share."

I didn't want them to treat me like some delicate flower. I wanted to feel like a woman, and I wanted them to treat me as such.

My words did something to them both, and I saw that the instant I exposed their throats. Both their chests rose with huge breaths, and soon, they were rising above me like two colossal mountains. They were like two mighty forces I honestly wasn't sure I would be able to control.

But I didn't want to control them. I wanted them in their element.

I wanted them unhinged.

Wells's hand braced my throat. Not tightly, but hard enough to make me gasp. He used it to make me look at him, then smashed his mouth up against mine in an angry kiss.

Yes.

It was angry, heated, like he was pushing so much into my mouth. Like he was forcing history and a well of emotions he had bottled up for who knew how long down my throat. All the while he held my neck, and, as he squeezed, I felt my air supply cut off. It was all so intense, and my eyes started to roll back from lack of air.

"You'll tell us if this is too much," Wells stated, and it almost sounded like a threat. Like he dared me to back off, say no. His tongue flicked mine. "I won't stop unless you do."

"Just tell him to stop, and he will, Bow," Bru said. He held my hips. He was holding me while Wells's tongue danced with mine. Bru squeezed my hips. "I'll stop too, but it'll be hard."

I had no intention of telling either one of them to stop, and I cut Wells's kiss off when I reached back and grabbed Bru's hair again. Bru sucked in a breath before I smashed my lips against his, but I barely got a taste before Wells pulled us away from each other. Wells had *my* hair in his hands, and he had Bru's too.

"Did I say you could kiss each other?" Wells asked, his eyes ignited and were oh so intense. He let go of Bru, but then, he strengthened the hold he had on my hair. I had my hair up, but that didn't lessen the tug on my scalp. Tears pricked my eyes, but not in a bad way. He grabbed my throat again. "Did I say you could kiss him?"

I'd never seen him this way. I mean, I'd seen him angry. I'd seen his hate directed at me, but I'd never seen him, well, *hot* like this. He was commanding, and the wanton look in his eyes let me know he was turned on.

I was too. I actually rubbed my legs together as he braced my scalp.

Wells wet his lips. "Don't do that again. Not unless I tell you to."

I didn't know what to say and was *so* frickin' turned on it was crazy.

Wells squeezed my throat. "Acknowledge what I said."

"Yes, sir," I said, and that was the first word that came to my mind. I didn't know what he wanted to be called, but I think I chose right.

Wells's eyes ignited again. He kissed me long, kissed me full, before pushing me to my knees. The hardwood dug into my kneecaps, but I didn't allow myself to react to the discomfort. Wells let go of me. "Go upstairs to your room," he said, then looked at Bru. "Take her."

Take her.

Bru listened. Like Wells was his master, and seeing the power dynamic between the two of them only made more moisture pool between my legs. I was so hot it wasn't even funny.

Bru didn't ask for permission before picking me up, damsel-style. He wasn't his normal polite self. That wasn't the game we were playing right now. He just picked me up in his strong arms, and I was surrounded by his woodsy scent as he took me upstairs. He knew where my room was in the cabin, both of them did.

"Where do you want her?" Bru asked Wells, again like his submissive. Bru stood with me in his arms in the center of a bedroom I suddenly wished wasn't so juvenile. Like I said, I'd come here a lot when I was younger, so I still had boy bands on the walls from when I was in middle school.

I tried not to think about those, and neither guy was paying much attention to them anyway. Wells drew the curtains and then started a fire. He did it slowly, and my heart beat fast. He just had Bru and me stand there waiting for his direction, for so long.

"On the floor," Wells finally said, and instantly, Bru placed me down. Wells eyed the area rug. "On her knees."

I didn't know if he was telling me to do that, but before I could make the maneuver, Bru had his hands on my shoulders.

Oh.

Bru forced me to the rug with a firm hold. It wasn't with intent to hurt me, but it was enough to show me his power. He, like Wells, could definitely make me do anything he wanted, and that turned me on even more. That Bru could be just as unhinged as I knew Wells could be.

"You too," Wells told Bru, and Bru's big chest rose. Bru

joined me on his knees, the both of us there as Wells did something else slowly.

He removed clothes. His shirt was already off, but he removed his socks and shoes. He placed the shoes nicely near the fireplace and even took the time to fold and roll his socks. He put one sock in each shoe before finally coming over to Bru and me.

What's he going to do?

My mind was a flurry of thoughts as Wells stood in front of me. He grabbed my hair again, and I yipped in a way that made him smirk. He studied my arched throat. "I want your mouth on me, Squeak," he said, the burn charging between my legs. He let go of my hair. "Bru will show you how."

Bru didn't hesitate, but I noticed his hands were clenching a bit as he went for Wells's pants. Maybe because he was nervous or anxious. It honestly might have been a little of both, and my mouth watered watching Bru remove Wells's belt before undoing Wells's jeans. I'd never *tasted* someone before and definitely didn't know how.

Bru showed me. He pushed down Wells's jeans and boxers like this was all second nature, and Wells was already hard when Bru exposed him.

Oh my gosh.

Wells was so big. It sounded cliché, but he was probably the biggest guy I'd ever seen. I supposed I hadn't seen many. Only one...

No.

I wouldn't think about that. I wasn't going to ruin this moment. This moment, right here, was on my terms, and I lifted on my knees as Bru opened his mouth for Wells. Wells pushed Bru on his cock before Bru could take the action himself.

Bru's eyes expanded. Right away, he gagged, but relaxed into the blowjob as Wells pushed his fingers through Bru's hair.

I was so wet.

I couldn't help it watching the two of them. As Bru sucked, he hugged himself against Wells like this was the greatest gift. Like Wells was giving Bru something that Bru truly wanted. Bru groaned, and, though Wells did too, I noticed Wells's eyes were on me. Wells was watching me while he slowly thrust into Bru's mouth. Like it was *my mouth* Wells was fucking.

I wanted to taste him myself. I didn't know how, but I wanted to try.

"Let her try," Wells said as if he heard my thoughts. He pulled Bru's mouth off him with a pop, and Bru had a haze in his eyes I recognized as lust.

"Can I taste her while she tastes you?" Bru asked, looking so needy, so hot. The fire from the fireplace gleamed off his massive chest, and his throat worked before he faced me. "I want to taste her again, please."

I seriously thought I was going to come. I was going to and nothing had even happened yet.

All Wells said was "we'll see" before stepping in front of me. His dick was slick from Bru's saliva and probably precum. Wells stroked himself. "She tastes me first."

She tastes me first.

I moved quickly on my knees to do so. I grabbed Wells's hips, but he held me back by my throat again.

"What do you say," Wells stated, but the look in his eyes was so hungry, wanton. Like it was taking everything in him to pace this, pace himself. "What do you say since I'm giving this to you?"

He really was talking about himself as if he was a gift, and I never role-played before, but I found I liked it.

"Please," I said, and Wells nodded before letting me hover over his cock. I opened my mouth. "Thank you, daddy."

I didn't get his reaction to what I said before I drew the length of him into my mouth. It was so much, too much, and I might have overdone it when he hit the back of my throat right away.

"Fucking… *fuck.*" Wells grabbed my head. He gripped into my scalp, and I felt the burn through my entire body. He sucked in a breath, and, right away, he started rolling his hips. He growled. "You're going to make me come in two seconds like a fucking teenager saying shit like that to me. Fuck."

He was angry that I played with him, teased him, but he was paying me back when he didn't ease into fucking my throat. He treated me like his little doll, his whore that he wasn't going to pace himself with. I honestly loved it, and the heat between my legs made me think that I was the one who'd come early.

"Edge her," Wells said, and I was too distracted by the taste of him to know what that meant. I was also too busy gagging. I couldn't breathe, but the suffocating feeling of all of him in my mouth just made me want more. Wells gripped my hair. "Let him between your legs."

Let him between my…

I felt my legs being nudged apart. It must have been Bru, and I had no warning before he was sliding his fingers between my thighs. He stroked the thin material lining my sex with intension, with precision, and my bud buzzed like a light bulb. I attempted to push back against Bru's hand, feel *more*, but Wells grabbed my throat. I gagged again over his cock, and his green irises heated above me.

"Don't make me take him from you," he said before pushing me hard on his cock, in and out, in and out. Wells sucked in a breath. "Go for it, Bru."

Bru's fingers eased into my underwear. He parted my pussy lips, and soon, he was stroking my clit. I moaned on Wells's cock, but I didn't stop sucking him. I'd *die* if Bru stopped.

"Faster," Wells said, and, at first, I thought he was talking to me, but then, Bru's fingers moved quicker behind me. Bru stroked me faster, firmer, and the next thing I knew, *his tongue* had replaced his fingers. He was lying down beneath me.

Oh God.

Bru drew his tongue down my clit to the point where I thought he might push his tongue inside me. He didn't though. He just kept going back and forth, long strokes up and down.

"Bow, baby. You taste amazing," Bru said, pushing his face against me. I shook, the tremors rolling through me. Bru braced my hips. "Can I tongue-fuck her, Wells?"

I was going to go over the cliff if he did, and Wells must have said something because Bru's tongue did push inside me. He sucked, his tongue moving in and out with force, and I felt myself stop sucking Wells. I couldn't help it.

It felt so good.

I pushed my hand between my legs, squeezing my sex as Bru took me to the point of no return. My legs started shaking, on the brink before I heard Wells's voice again.

"She's had enough," Wells said, and Bru groaned. Bru pulled away, and I thought I would die. He left me hanging, right on the edge…

"That's what you get for your little nickname," Wells said, pulling me off his cock. He hunkered down, getting right in my face. "You don't get to come, sweet girl. Not yet."

Not… yet.

It almost felt cruel what he did, but I believed that was the intention. He wanted me to pay for teasing him. My jaw tightened. "Are you serious?"

He showed me he was, his finger stroking my face before he reached down. Wells took my nipple between two fingers, and I called out when he pinched.

Bru was between my legs again. His tongue picked up right where he left off when he licked, then pushed his tongue inside me. He tongue-fucked me again, taking me to the point where I was going to come.

"She's had enough," Wells said again, and once more, Bru stopped. This was a game. Wells was intentionally taking me toward the edge before denying me.

"Edge her."

I was hearing Wells's voice in my head as he reached behind and grabbed Bru. He got Bru by the neck before forcing their mouths together. Wells tasted Bru's tongue. Wells tasted *me*, and while he kissed Bru, Wells looked at me. He was playing a game, a cruel one.

"You want us?" Wells asked me, still flicking his tongue with Bru's.

Bru sucked in a breath. "Bro, don't play with her. She's had enough—"

"She said she wanted us to do what we do when we share, when *I* share," Wells said, giving Bru's tongue one final taste before letting go of him. Bru's expression was hard, but he didn't say anything. Wells grinned at me. "What are you going to do to have us, Squeak?"

This was a power play, and it was something I knew because I knew Wells Ambrose. Wells had bullied me long enough that I knew what it was like to be within his crazed web, to be woven within his insanity, but I also knew what would take him over the edge.

I'd just never done it.

I said nothing when I sat back on my haunches, but both guys' looks were curious when I lifted one leg, then the other beneath me. I did it to remove my underwear.

I fucked myself.

I didn't need these boys to take me over the edge. I didn't need *anyone*. I could take myself there.

I was good enough.

I felt that way as my fingers strummed my clit, then I pushed down on my *own* hand. I finger-fucked myself right in front of both of them. Bru's mouth parted, and Wells started gripping his own hands so tight they went white.

"Stop it," Wells said, but all I did was push down on my hand more. He got in my face. "Stop it."

I kissed him instead. I kissed him while I screwed myself, and I laughed when he pulled my hand from between my legs. I broke Wells Ambrose and how did I know?

Because he tasted me.

He pushed my fingers into his mouth and sucked so hard I thought he'd swallow my fingers. He shivered while the taste exploded across his senses, and I did too, seeing the effect I had on him. He looked drunk, his eyes hazy, when all he did was *taste* me.

I did really have the power here, the control. We were in the middle of a game, and I managed to break him.

"Punishing you meant I could go on with the lie. That I wasn't completely and hopelessly in love with you."

I felt that love as Wells's sucks turned into licks, then gentle kisses. He was being so soothing with me, my fingers, and my attention went to Bru, who was behind Wells.

Bru was smiling.

It was like Bru saw it too. No one could beat Wells Ambrose. Wells Ambrose couldn't be beaten, but I managed to do it.

"You're perfect for me," Wells said before taking my mouth, and I dropped the game when I let him. Wells smiled against my lips. "So fucking perfect."

Perfect.

He was perfect for me, and I kissed him back so hard. I wrapped my arms around his neck, and Wells fell to his back.

"I want inside you, Bow," Wells said, slowly grinding against me. He closed his eyes. "But once I do, that's it."

He didn't finish, just kissed me harder, fuller.

"It means you're mine," Wells said and sounded angry again. He shook his head. "I can't let go. I won't."

I didn't want him to.

"You both will be," Wells stated, and glanced at Bru when

Bru started kissing Wells's forearm. Bru bit Wells's arm, and Wells cursed. Wells looked at Bru. "I won't be able to let either of you go."

The pair looked at each other for a long time before Bru looked at me. Bru's forehead touched mine. "What do you want, Bow?"

I think he knew what I wanted. I think they *both* did.

"I want you guys," I said, kissing Bru and tasting his tongue. It was so different than kissing Wells, but it was a good different, a great different. I pushed my hands into Bru's hair. "I love you. Both of you."

Bru made a noise during our kiss, like something inside him released with the words. He folded a hand behind my neck, kissing me hard and deep before pushing me on my back.

"I love you." Bru's nose brushed mine, his smile so big. He pressed his mouth against mine. "I love you so fucking much, Bow. Both of you."

"Yeah, we all love each other," Wells jostled, his eyebrows dancing. Going serious, he pushed a hand behind my neck, then Bru's. Holding us both, Wells touched all three of our foreheads together. "We love each other."

We did somehow. The odds of all that felt crazy. Especially since Bru and Wells were my brother's best friends.

I was sure Wells didn't love that fact, but he was pushing past it when he forced a kiss between the three of us. Bru didn't fight, and I definitely didn't fight it.

God.

Kissing two guys at once was different. Wells coaxed my lips apart, and, as soon as he did, Bru pushed his tongue inside my mouth. I moaned, then panted when I felt Wells's tongue slide against mine too. Wells sucked, his mouth charging heat into mine, and I felt the boys' tongues dueling over each other. Like they were fighting for purchase. Like they were fighting *for me.*

They didn't have to fight. I was both of theirs and showed them that when I took their hands and forced them to palm my breasts. Instantly, the charge between my legs went in overdrive and both Bru and Wells let out a sound so feral in my mouth I thought I'd come right there. We all ended up in my bed in the end.

We all ended up naked there.

Wrapped up in my sheets, we were a fury of tongues, mouths, and hands for a while. Both large guys and I didn't quite fit on my queen bed, but we made it work. We made out for I didn't even know how long with me on top of Bru, and then Wells on top of me while Bru watched. All three of us managed to hold back sex while we were naked, but I didn't know how.

"Can I have you first?" Wells eventually asked. He was on top of me again, his palms on either side of my head while he kissed me hard into my sheets. Bru was watching again.

Bru had his hand on one of Wells's shoulders while he played with my breasts. Bru kept pinching my nipple between two fingers, and I had to rub my thighs together not to come.

Wells was holding his weight above me while Bru played. Wells rubbed his cock against my stomach. "Let me inside you."

I opened my legs without question, pushing his hair away and his eyes closed when I did. Like I was giving *him* a gift. Growling, Wells bit my wrist before reaching for something. That something turned out to be his discarded jeans, but Bru already had them. Bru also had the condom that was in Wells's wallet. Right away, Bru started to hand the condom to Wells, but I grabbed Bru's wrist.

"I want you to have each other too," I said, feeling shy right away when I said it. My face heated. "I want to feel connected to both of you. I mean, if that's okay…"

I didn't know who I was right now, being so forthright,

but when both guys smiled, I knew us all being together wouldn't be a problem.

"I have no problem putting Ambrose beneath me," Bru said, and Wells flipped him off before grabbing Bru's neck.

"Don't get used to it, asshole," Wells said. He bit Bru's lip, and Bru sucked in a breath. Wells grinned. "You know you like me in your ass."

Bru bit Wells back, and the two jostled each other a little before their kiss turned different, passionate. It slowed, and the heat between them filled me up with so much love. It was crazy that a connection between two other people felt as if it were my own. They were my guys.

I was theirs too, and my eyes closed when they both moved their attention toward me. They both began kissing my neck, and I pushed my fingers into their hair. My back lifted off the bed, and that was at the same time I felt Wells move between my legs. He worked the condom on, then put one of my legs over his shoulder.

He didn't hesitate.

The invasion wasn't slow or even delicate, and I didn't want it to be. That wouldn't be Wells. He was all intensity. He was all raw passion and heat. He was madness, and he showed me that when he went balls deep inside me.

I called out, the pain ripping through me in ways I hadn't anticipated. I'd only done this one other time, but even regular use of my vibrator couldn't prepare me for Wells Ambrose inside me. He got so deep my back lifted. My mouth opened, and I knew I'd feel him for a long time. Even after this was over, he'd still be there with me.

Good.

He felt so good, untamed. Wells's abs worked while he labored, and his hand gripped my ankle so hard I thought he'd break me.

"I knew you'd feel so fucking good, Squeak," he said, sweat on his brow and moisture beading his chest. He was glistening as his hair swayed with every thrust he made. His eyes closed. "My own personal heaven."

He was mine too, and I lost my breath when he let go of my ankle and pressed his chest against mine. His slick pecs charged activity into my sensitive nipples.

"Fuck, you guys look so good like this," Bru said from somewhere, but I definitely saw him when he kissed me.

They both kissed me.

We were dueling tongues again, all three of us, and when I opened my eyes, I noticed Bru's hand. It was on his cock. He was pumping himself while he tasted Wells and me.

I didn't know how I found myself to be in this moment, to have both of them. I closed my eyes and called out when Wells bit my mouth. He nearly drew blood, and I understood when I realized Bru was no longer a part of our kiss. He was behind Wells.

Bru spit into his hand.

That was all he did before forcing himself into Wells so hard that the bed moved. Wells growled, and Bru picked up right away. Bru's hips slapped against Wells's ass, and the momentum caused Wells to bury himself deeper inside me.

Oh my God.

I'd never felt anything like it. I was connected to them both in such an intense, intimate way. I held on to Wells, and at the same time, he held on to me. Wells kissed me, and from behind, Bru kissed Wells's back. Bru also had his palms on the bed. Like he was shielding both Wells and me.

Like he was protecting all of us.

All three of us were in our own universe, a barrier of love and protection.

Perfection.

I'd never felt so connected to two people before, and like Wells said, I wouldn't be able to let go either.

"I'm going to come," Bru said, grunting. He grabbed my hand. "Can I come on you?"

He wanted to come on… me.

I nodded. I didn't know exactly where he was going to come, but when he pulled out, Wells made room for Bru to get closer to me. It was like the two were so in sync that Wells just knew what Bru wanted to do.

Bru came on my breasts.

Thick ropes of cum surged out of his dick over my chest, and at the same time, Bru pinched my nipple. That sent me over the edge, my back lifting, and that was when Wells called out.

"Fucking fuck, you two," Wells said, stiffening. His cock twitched inside me, and his face went beet red as he came too. Wells was holding my hips, but he collapsed when he finished. He caught himself though, but when he saw the cum on my breasts…

Wells's tongue dragged across one of my nipples. He *tasted Bru's cum,* and the look in his eyes was wild. Like it was the best thing he'd ever tasted. Like *Bru and I* were the best thing he'd ever tasted. Watching him brought out a heat in Bru's eyes. Bru squeezed Wells's shoulder before Bru pressed lips to mine. Bru connected all three of us again. We were connected.

We were bound.

Bru

"Dude, what the fuck!"

My eyes flashed open. A scream sounded, Bow's voice…

She was naked between Wells and me.

At some point, the three of us fell asleep in Bow's bed. We'd fucked, but *fucking* definitely wasn't the term for it.

Love. It was pure and unquestionable. I was in love with not one but two people, and they were in love with me.

It was crazy.

It was crazy and amazing and exciting. I hadn't been thinking. I dropped all the bullshit. I dropped all the logic, and Wells certainly had. He'd obviously been fighting his desire for not just Bow but me as well.

He hadn't done that last night. Honestly, I wasn't even sure if it was last night or morning. Time seemed to exist in a vacuum, but it sped up when Thatcher Reed shouted in Bow's bedroom. He'd been the one to wake me up initially, made Bow scream, and now, he was reaching for Wells with a fire in his eyes.

Shit.

Bow did what she could to cover herself. She was obviously naked, and that hadn't been the objective when Wells and I asked to meet her. We'd just wanted to talk to her.

When I texted Wells about figuring things out with Bow, a lot had come up before we wrapped up the thread. One of those things was how Wells had shared his concerns about Bow losing her virginity, and after listening, I felt the same. I didn't know who she lost her virginity to, but that was none of my business. I was concerned though after Wells had explained how he'd gone out of his way to blackball her for years. All of that made sense now after I overheard what was said at the Vesperton between them. It was shitty, but at least I understood where his head had been for all those years. Wells obviously had deep feelings for Bow, and after overhearing how much he hated himself, I knew why he hurt her.

I also knew why he denied me.

Wells Ambrose didn't feel like he was worthy of being loved and last night had been all of us breaking down our walls. It'd been emotional, but it all felt like it was long overdue. The three of us loved each other, and we definitely hadn't been thinking about anyone else. We definitely hadn't been thinking about *Thatcher*, and though I definitely didn't regret making love to his sister, Wells and I had snuck around with her.

Bow was covered beneath the comforter, but I let her have what was covering me to make sure. Regardless, Thatcher wasn't paying attention to either of us. He had his sight set on Wells. I assumed Wells had also been woken up. His hair was all over the place, and Bow had been sleeping on him. He had his arm around her and his other hand had been in mine. I'd been holding her too. I'd been holding both of them, but that connection obviously severed when Thatcher shoved Wells to the floor. Naked, Wells clipped an end table on the way and a decorative vase fell off and shattered on the floor.

That made Bow scream again, her face red as she shouted at Thatcher to stop. Her brother had his fist drawn, but Wells was quick.

"Thatch, wait!" Wells called, his hand up, but he wasn't about to let Thatcher get a piece of him. Swift, Wells evaded a right hook, and coming from Thatcher Reed, that would have sent a dude fucking flying. Wells grabbed a pillow. This allowed him to cover himself, but he still kept a hand up. "Bro—"

"You're not my fucking *bro*. You're not..." Thatcher eyed his sister who was covered, but still naked on the bed. He had his coat and shoes on like he'd just come from outside, his face beet red.

I was sure my presence with his sister didn't help.

Bow held on to me. I had an arm around her but was outside of the bed. In the fray, I'd managed to get my boxers on but was still basically naked.

I had my hand up. I was holding Bow, but I'd also intercepted myself between Thatcher and Wells who was still on the floor. I was pretty sure Ambrose could handle himself, but I wasn't going to let Thatcher put hands on him again. I wouldn't come at Thatcher, but he *wasn't* hitting Ambrose. Not unless he got through me.

I think Bow shared that sentiment because the next thing I knew she was scooting herself out of the bed. She wrapped the bedding around herself, then stepped between her brother and me. She was shielding both Ambrose and me with her little body. She put a hand up too. "Thatcher."

Thatcher panned between his sister, Wells, and me. Wells had his mouth parted, but I think that was because he was just as shocked as me to see Bow step in the middle of this whole thing. The shock didn't stay for long because soon Ambrose was getting in front of Bow and me. I didn't like that shit, and Thatcher definitely didn't like that shit. The heat in Thatcher's eyes shifted to molten lava.

"You're not my brother," Thatcher said to Wells, and Wells cringed. Thatcher looked at me. "And you aren't either."

My heart thudded, and I winced when Thatcher left the room. The door slammed behind him with a snap, and we jumped.

I reached for my pants. I was going to talk to Thatcher, but Wells grabbed my arm.

"It has to be me," he said, and, though it probably should, I didn't want him to go alone. I ignored him until he suddenly kissed me, calmed me.

His mouth felt so good. It was warm like him, and I knew why he'd done it. He wanted me to know he had this, *he had me* and her.

Her.

Bow was between us during the kiss, and I squeezed her shoulder while I received it.

"I'm going to fix this," Wells said against my lips, but I didn't think his words were just for me. They were equally for Bow, and he showed her that when he kissed her next. He did so openly and unashamed.

A heat flashed within me watching them. It was the same one that burrowed inside me just like it had when the three of us finally got together hours ago. The feeling was right. *It was perfect*, and I pushed Bow against Wells while he kissed her.

"I am going to fix this, Squeak. I promise," he said, then pressed his lips against her ear. "I love you."

He loves her.

I think that was what she needed to hear, and she nodded when he pulled away. Wells could have easily denied all this between us for Thatcher's sake, but he wasn't. He was standing by this.

He was standing by us.

"I love you too," Bow said to Wells, then looked at me.

She didn't have to say it though I was grateful when she did. On her tiptoes, she wrapped her arms around my neck.

She kissed me, those words pressed against *my* lips. She loved me too.

She loved us.

CHAPTER
TWENTY-NINE

Thatcher was sitting on the couch when I came downstairs, and I was surprised. I thought I'd have to go after him.

I was aware what I was about to walk into. My best friend was furious on the couch, rubbing his hands.

Thatcher lifted his head. "Pop said the alarm had gone off at the cabin," he said, his eyes narrowed. He faced me. "I came out to check things out."

Well, that made sense now, why he was here.

Damn.

Thatcher's jaw moved, his spiked earrings dangling and his dark hair unruly. A lot of fucked-up shit had just happened upstairs. It wasn't the first time my friend and I had gotten into a fight but never over something like this.

Thatcher's eyes heated. "I hoped it was a dumbass animal or something. Guess I wasn't far off."

He could have said worse, and I would have deserved it.

I came around the couch. I rushed, so I only had my pants,

shoes, and a jacket on. I was very much not wearing a shirt, and Thatcher noticed that right away.

It made him wince.

He said nothing, and, not testing things, I took the chair across from him. I could have said something first, come right in on things, but I didn't. I wanted to wait. I needed to wait for my friend.

There was a reason why he stayed.

I knew Thatcher Reed. Normally, he probably would have left. All of us guys were rageful fucks. We reacted, so the fact Thatcher was still here meant something. He could have left, but he stayed, waited.

I waited too, no matter how nervous the silence made me. I knew exactly what would happen the moment I let go in regards to his sister. Actions had consequences.

Thatcher stared at the area rug. "How long's this been going on?"

"Not long," I said, refusing to make him wait. Since he was ready, I spoke, and was grateful to break the silence. I gripped my hands. "I tried to fight it, Thatch."

I did for so fucking long, and my head lifted when Thatcher's did.

We weren't alone.

"Both of us did," Bru said. He was on the stairs but came down into the light. I didn't know what time it was, but it was dark through the windows. There was barely any light in the room, just the lights from the end tables, but there was enough for me to see Bru had gotten on at least a shirt with his jeans, his feet bare and hair mussed.

Facing away, I sighed. "I told you I'd handle this."

"You shouldn't have to. Not alone," Bru said, and the next thing I knew, he was coming over to me. He sat down on the arm of the chair, smelling distinctly like Bru, and when he grabbed my hand, something stirred inside me. I looked at him, seeing so much love there in his dark eyes. I tried to deny that too, but he didn't let me.

Neither of them had. Rainbow Reed had broken me down *for years* before Bru came in and swept me over the edge. I fully believe he was the reason I finally allowed myself to go there. *To have her* and him.

To be… happy.

"This is serious," Thatcher said, and Bru and I cut away from each other. We didn't let go, but we did face Thatcher. Thatcher's head tilted. "Hindsight really is crazy. It really does make sense with you guys." He rubbed his hands. "I just didn't know my sister was a part of it."

I didn't even know his sister was a part of it. Bow Reed snuck up on me and made me admit something to myself. Both Bru and her had.

"I really tried to fight it, Thatch. With Bru and especially with Bow," I said, and Thatcher glanced away. I released a breath. "I did, Thatcher. I did for so fucking long. You're my brother, man, and you know I'd never want to hurt you. Not on purpose, I…"

I stopped. I closed my fucking mouth, but not because I had to.

It was because I wanted to.

I wanted this, a relationship with Bru *and* his sister, and I was tired of the shame surrounding it. The fear and self-loathing I had…

"Forgive yourself."

Bow's beautiful voice was in my head, her kind voice. She really was so much better than me, and even though I may not deserve her or Bruno's love, I needed it. I craved it. It healed me and made me better, stronger.

I bet Bru had to fight through his teeth to keep Bow from coming down here. She was a spitfire, and I would never forget what she just did upstairs. She stood in front of Bru and me, like she could actually keep her brother away from us, but she was going to try, and that was why I loved her. She was selfless, so good.

She was perfect.

"You know what? I'm not fucking sorry," I said, and I stood. I was pumped full of adrenaline. I pointed upstairs. "I love your sister, man. I do, and I think I have for a really long fucking time."

I'd been in love with Bow Reed before I knew what love was. It hit me like a bus, and that was why I'd been watching her that day at the pool.

I always had.

That love caused me to make mistakes, but that wasn't her fault. What happened to that girl at the pool had been an accident. It was.

"Forgive yourself."

Her love did make me stronger. It made me see things differently, and now, I was telling my best friend the truth. He was a best friend I did love like a brother, and, though I needed him in my life, I needed her too.

"So I can't be sorry about that," I said, and felt Bru squeeze my hand. He was still sitting on the arm of the chair, and I glanced down only to see him smile at me. He was giving me support right now, and I squeezed his hand right back. I faced Thatcher. "Now, if you want to kick my ass because of that, I'd understand. But I'm not going to deny how I feel. It will kill me to deny it. It has been. *For years.*"

I'd been dying a slow death since I pushed Bow out of my life. It'd been a life of fuck buddies and one-night stands, but, no matter how much I fucked my way through campus (and high school), I felt nothing. I felt hollow with every conquest.

Because they weren't her.

I hadn't even touched Bow and had more love for her than I'd felt for anyone I fucked in the past. That physical love had been temporary, a high. It was an itch I couldn't scratch no matter how many people I had in the sheets. It wasn't until

Bru came along that I started to feel something again. Being with him reminded me of what truly being with someone you cared about could feel like. I got drunk off the feeling, and when we were finally with Bow, everything felt complete. It was like she was the missing piece in my life.

She was the missing piece.

Bru and I had fucked so many people together, as well as each other, but it wasn't the same without Bow. We loved her.

I may not be worthy of either one of them, but I was going to have them. That may have made me a selfish prick, but I didn't care.

Beside me, Bru stood. He continued to hold my hand, stand with me in front of our best friend. Thatcher didn't say anything, just watching us.

"I just might kick your ass," he said, and my stomach dropped. I was prepared for this, to lose him as my buddy, my brother but... His lips went tight. "Because it honestly took you a hell of a long time to fucking admit it."

My mouth parted, and Bru's eyebrows jumped. We both looked at each other before Thatcher rose from the couch.

"I had a feeling you were into my sister, Wells," he said, and I blinked. Thatcher's head tilted. "You're my brother, man. I've known you for a long time."

Yeah, but how did he know when I didn't even know? I denied that shit for years. I rubbed my neck. "How did you know?"

Thatcher shrugged. "I mean, I wasn't certain, but there were signs. You've always looked out for her and you guys were hella close before, well... everything that summer."

That summer.

A lot of stuff changed. My whole entire fucking life. I made a ton of mistakes, so many.

Thatcher pocketed his hands. "I guess I kind of always knew, but it was easier for me to deny it." His lips went tight. "She's my sister, man."

She was, which made me feel like shit. I grabbed my arms. "I can't say I'm sorry."

"I don't want you to," he said, and shock flashed across Bru's face again. It was the same shock I felt. Thatcher pushed back his hair. "Honestly, if I admit it to myself, I know there's no one better for her," he said, then tipped his chin at Bru. "Both of you."

Both of us.

Thatcher raised his hands. "Don't get me wrong. This shit is still fucking weird and seeing y'all like that with her I *fucking can't,* which was why I reacted the way I did initially. It was shocking to say the fucking least, bro."

I could imagine, and if things were the other way around, I was sure I'd act that way too. Honestly, I wasn't sure I'd have been able to stop myself. I supposed that was what made my brother better than myself. His love for his girl-friend also changed him. He was a different person now than he'd been even a year ago.

Thatcher shook his head. "But you guys are all adults, and, like I said, I know there's no one better for my sister. You guys will look out for her. Protect her."

I didn't know what to say, and, when I didn't, Bru stepped forward.

"You mean you're okay with this?" Bru asked, and Thatcher lifted his hands again.

"'Okay' is a hella strong word. I *accept* your relationship, yes, and being in one myself now, I know how that shit can take a hold of you." He smiled a little. "Being with Aspen put a chokehold over me, bro. I can imagine it was the same for you guys. Especially you, Wells."

I glanced up.

He nodded. "Bow must have broken you down something crazy, because you'd jump in front of a bus before you'd let shit go bad between you and me."

I would. I nodded too. "For that, I am sorry. I'd never want to hurt you."

"I know that, and I'm sorry too. For what I said upstairs? I didn't mean that. Any of it," he said. He looked at Bru. "And I'm sorry to you too. Things just got crazy in the moment."

"I get it," Bru said, and we all just stood there for a moment. I didn't think any of us knew what to say.

It turned out we didn't need to speak.

Thatcher's hand coming out did all the talking. He was waiting for mine, and when I shook, Thatcher turned it into a hug. He *hugged me*, and there was so much relief there. I hadn't lost him.

"Just be good to her or I will kick your ass, Wells," Thatcher said, squeezing me hard. "No fucks given."

I laughed, hugging him back. Thatcher Reed's hugs were no joke. He was a big fucking dude and put a lot into it.

I did too.

"You know I will," I said, and he nodded at me when he let go. He reached for Bru too, and Bru received the hug/handshake just as effortlessly.

"She'll always be safe with me. With both of us. I promise," Bru said, and Thatcher didn't let go of him right away.

"I know." Eventually, Thatcher did let go. He put a hand on my shoulder, then Bru's. "You guys are good with me. It's my dad you're going to have to worry about, so you probably should be thinking about what you're going to say to him about all this."

Holy fuck, I didn't even think about that.

Thatcher laughed. "Anyway, send my sister down. I want to apologize to her for going all caveman."

Thatcher may have gone caveman, but his dad would go Godzilla on my ass. I couldn't say it wouldn't be worth it though. I'd die a thousand deaths before I ever let Rainbow Reed go again. I wasn't letting go again.

Not this time.

CHAPTER
THIRTY

Bow

"I still can't believe it," Sloane said, gazing off onto Pembroke University's football field. We were sitting on the bleachers with Fawn and Aspen. Aspen had a break during her tour and was hanging out with us today on the empty bleachers. Sloane smiled at the field. "You, *Wells*, and my brother."

I glanced away to that same field. The guys were out there, my brother and his friends. The men known as Legacy were tossing a football on an empty field when most of Pembroke University's student body was packing their stuff into moving boxes. These were some of the final days people actually may be on campus with graduation around the corner.

The guys weren't packing. They were having fun. This was probably the last time they'd be doing something like this for a while. We were all growing up. We were all *grown* up. Dorian had accepted an offer to play football with a team near Boston. Sloane would obviously be going with him after graduation. Ares was graduating too, but he'd be sticking close to home until Fawn graduated. She was a junior like Thatcher, Wells, and Bru.

Lacing my fingers, I leaned forward. Bru and Wells were on the same team out on the empty field, but one wouldn't know it with the way they tackled each other. Laughing, Wells took Bru down after he intercepted a pass from Dorian to Ares. Obviously, Wells hadn't *meant* to run into Bru while catching the ball, but Bru was really big. He happened to take up a lot of surface area, so Wells clipped him when he intercepted the pass.

Both guys hit the ground in a fit of laughter and chuckles. Bru shoved Wells before helping him up, their faces red as they clasped their hands together.

They were also shirtless.

Their slick, beautiful bodies gleamed in the setting sun, and their clasped hands turned into a hug before another shove. The moment of shared affection was quick before they got back into the game, and I saw the other guys on the field noticed as well. Dorian and Ares exchanged a glance, their smiles subtle on Wells and Bru before they all started tossing the ball again. Thatcher took a second to get back into the game, his burly arms folded. Thatcher's smile was big on Wells and Bru which made Wells in particular roll his eyes. Thatcher gripped his arm around Wells's neck. Thatcher was in the midst of giving Wells a noogie until Wells socked Thatcher in his gut. It made Thatcher laugh instead of angry. He really was supportive of his friends being together.

Thatcher even apologized to me.

My thoughts went back to that day at the cabin. It wasn't long ago, but it felt like eons with everything that had happened since. I'd been on the stairs with Bru when Thatcher was talking to Wells. Initially, I was going to go down and talk to my brother, but Bru talked me out of it.

"Let us handle it," Bru said to me, but my brother had no right to get involved with something that had nothing to do with him. I was going to tell him that, but it turned out that I didn't have to. Again, Thatcher *apologized* to me, and he was even there when Wells and Bru ultimately told our parents about, well, the three of us. Surprisingly, it had been Wells's idea to tell our parents right away, to tell my dad. Wells had been adamant about wanting to do that for some reason.

I wouldn't lie. That night was… awkward. It was a weird situation, but I understood Wells wanting to do that. Our parents were really close, and my dad ended up taking Wells and Bru into a separate room after the initial discussion. The guys invited all our families over to Legacy House for dinner, and the parents had definitely been surprised. They'd been very supportive though, just like all our friends were. We'd told all our friends about everything the night before.

Again, that'd been Wells's idea.

He wanted no secrets, and he didn't apologize to our friends or families for wanting to be with Bru and me.

He loved us.

I still couldn't believe that, how wonderful and crazy that was. I also couldn't believe what happened the night Wells and Bru told our parents about our relationship. Again, my dad had taken Wells and Bru off to the side. I didn't know what that meant.

I'd been holding my breath the whole time Dad talked to Bru and Wells even though my mom and Bru's and Wells's moms told me things would be okay. Wells's mom, Cleo, hugged me after the news. She'd always seen me as her daughter. She was also a second mom to me just like Bru's mom, Brielle. Things ended up being okay when my dad returned to the room with both guys. I noticed right away neither Bru nor Wells was dead, so that was good. They also didn't appear to have any bodily harm.

"Your dad said he's okay as long as you are," Wells said to me later that night. He'd made love to me again after the house cleared out, and, this time, the three of us had been in

Wells's room. That was the second time we'd all been together intimately, and it was wonderful. It was more than wonderful.

I felt so loved.

Being with both of them was like two forces that somehow worked and created magic, harmony. They didn't move until I moved and vice versa. We just worked.

We loved.

I did love both of them, but I was aware it wasn't *just* the three of us in our world. We all had families, but we also had friends and *my friend*, Sloane, was Bru's sister.

"Is that weird?" I asked her, referring to what she said about me being with her brother. I meant weird beyond the whole trio thing, and it wasn't lost on me that I never told her I had feelings for her brother. I hadn't told her I kissed him multiple times.

Out of nowhere, Sloane brought her arms around me. She never used to be a hugger, but she gave me the biggest one after finding out about my, well, relationship. She squeezed me. "Girl, no. I'm so happy. It's different, but that's not bad. In fact, I think it's great."

I held her waist. "You're not mad I didn't tell you about what was going on?"

After everything came out, I told her about that initial kiss in Bru's car. She'd been surprised but, again, supportive.

Sloane let go of me. She smelled like flowers, and her hair was up in a messy bun. She was wearing one of Dorian's football hoodies. It was actually from his new team. I was going to miss her when she went away, but I couldn't be happier for her. She and Bru had such a rough life growing up, and it was nice she was finally getting her happy ending. As far as I knew, Dorian hadn't proposed to her yet, but we all knew that was happening. He loved her so much, and they were perfect for each other. Sloane smiled. "You know I'm not, sis."

Sis.

She was my sister, and I hugged her so hard. Holding her hand, I noticed something metal on her finger, her *ring* finger.

Sloane noticed *I noticed* and slid her hand back into the sleeve of Dorian's hoodie. My mouth parted, shocked, and Sloane pressed a finger to her lips.

Slowly, she showed me the ring on her hand. It was a diamond nearly the size of a baseball. Well, not really, but it was freaking huge.

Sloane pressed her finger to her mouth again before hiding her hand in her sleeve once more. She smiled. "He asked the night of his draft party."

Oh… my…

"We're telling everyone soon," she said, hugging me again, and I had to fight from squealing since Aspen and Fawn were with us on the bleachers. The two were watching the boys play football too but were distracted as they chatted about Aspen's tour.

I hugged my sister back. I expected a story soon about her engagement.

"God, I love when they do this," Aspen said, and Sloane and I faced the field. Thatcher was taking his shirt off. He tossed it before getting back into the game, and Ares and Dorian did the same.

That got Fawn and Sloane's attention, the two of them sighing. Aspen did too which made me laugh, but I stopped when my eyes locked on to Wells and Bru. They'd been shirtless from the jump, beautiful, but now, they had their attention on me. Bru waved, and Wells winked. Wells even gave me a set of heart hands before playing again, which was crazy.

It was crazy wonderful.

———

"You okay?" Sloane asked me. We were taking a cooler of drinks to my brother's car. The guys finished playing football, and Sloane, Aspen, Fawn, and I were helping load up the stuff we brought. The girls had packed a picnic earlier in the day, and we all ate on the field before the guys started their game.

It'd been nice, but I got killer heartburn after eating one of the sandwiches. That'd subsided, but now, I was feeling a little nauseous for some reason. I had bouts of nausea lately, but I figured it'd been all the stress I'd been going through. I'd never had a strong stomach.

"I just have a little stomachache," I told Sloane. We'd had to slow to a stop with the cooler after the world kind of tilted, and my stomach flipped. I released a breath. "I'm okay."

"You sure?" she asked, looking concerned, but I was. We picked up the pace and met Thatcher and Aspen at his car. The trunk of his SUV was open, and it was no surprise the two were basically making out under the open trunk.

Sloane made a gagging noise when she and I came around, and I was sure I looked like I'd sucked a lemon. It wasn't the first time I'd come across my brother all over a girl. I loved Aspen of course, but he was basically mauling her.

Looking embarrassed, Aspen attempted to let go of my brother, but he wasn't having it. He pretty much strengthened his hold around her and flipped Sloane off which made her laugh. My brother was lucky Dorian wasn't around. He was really protective of Sloane and probably would have hit him. Dorian was still on the field gathering stuff with our other friends.

My brother did drop his arms from around Aspen when he saw what Sloane and I had though, a cooler. Immediately, he took it.

"Why are you guys carrying this thing? It's heavy as fuck," he said but didn't look fazed picking it up himself. I wasn't surprised since he probably bench-pressed something twice that size if not more daily.

"Um, we may be girls, but we're perfectly capable," Sloane said, which was the same argument she actually gave her boyfriend before we took the cooler. Bru and Wells had headed off to the restroom which was probably the only reason why I hadn't been in the same argument. They probably wouldn't have let me take the cooler either, but I wanted to help.

Sloane was like me in that regard, and Dorian definitely argued with her about the cooler. When it came to an argument though, Sloane was a spitfire. She easily won, and Dorian gave up. He said we could take one of the lighter coolers while he and Ares got the other two. Fawn was getting some of the lighter things from our picnic and said she'd catch up with Sloane and me.

My brother frowned. "I'm aware you're capable, but you don't have to do shit like that. You got us guys."

Sloane lifted her eyes. "Yeah, okay."

Thatcher looked like he wanted to say something else, but Aspen patted his big chest. She calmed him down like Black Widow and the Hulk, and it was so funny to see. My brother was so in love.

He wasn't the only one, and the need to see my guys suddenly hit me. I hadn't gotten to spend nearly enough time with them today. We'd been with our friends, and really, the last time we'd been *alone* was after the dinner the other night with our parents. We did have plans for the three of us to get together tonight though.

The guys said they wanted to date me.

I didn't know how this would work, me and the two of them. Whatever was going to happen, I was open to things. Especially sexually.

A surge pulsed between my thighs thinking about that. I quickly got distracted by the thoughts, and Sloane actually had to get my attention. I passed my dirty thoughts off by asking to see her ring again. We'd left Thatcher and Aspen. They were basically mauling each other again beneath the open trunk, so Sloane and I stepped away from the SUV a bit while we waited for our other friends.

I admired Sloane's ring again while we waited. I couldn't believe another one of my friends was engaged. Ares and Fawn were engaged too.

"It's so beautiful, Sloane," I said to her, studying the sparkling ring.

Sloane sighed. "He did pretty good, didn't he? He said it was one of his grandmothers'."

It was lovely, and we were both fawning over it when we heard shouting.

"Watch out!" a girl screamed, and jumped from in front of a green SUV. It nearly clipped the girl, the car speeding up in a pretty empty parking lot. I mean, most people were packing up to leave school.

Most people.

It took me a second to realize what was happening. The SUV drew closer and closer. I knew that SUV... Then I saw the driver's face. He wore glasses, his hair dark and messy as he gripped the wheel.

Sloane screamed, the vehicle charging at us at full speed, and I was frozen. I was a literal deer in headlights as I made eye contact with the man behind the wheel. He bared his teeth at me, hatred in his eyes as if he hated me.

He probably did.

My screams matched Sloane's, the SUV on the cusp of hitting both of us. It was too fast.

We were going to die.

These were my only thoughts as I got hold of my friend. I pushed and Sloane fell. She rolled out of the way so it was only me in the line of fire. Sloane would survive. This wasn't her fault.

She did nothing wrong.

Sloane screamed for me in the distance, and I closed my eyes. I waited for the impact I knew would ultimately come.

It didn't.

I was grabbed, gathered within two burly arms. Tucked into a firm chest, I rolled with someone's arms around me. The breath left me as I impacted the ground and whoever still had their arms around me.

They hadn't let go.

The screech of tires was what caused me to open my eyes. The green SUV passed, missing me.

Missing us.

The car sped away into the distance and, above me, Bru's handsome face materialized. He was calling out my name, panicked as he looked at me, and his sister, Sloane, was beside him. She was calling out my name too. She was okay.

"Bow?" Bru had my face, looking at me. A fierce terror ringed his dark eyes, his arms shaking. His body was doing the same, and his arms were scraped up.

He saved me.

Of course he had, and the cuts on his arms were bleeding. It didn't look bad, but he was *bleeding*. He looked at me with wild eyes. He touched my forehead, and I winced.

I was bleeding too, I saw when something wet clumped my eyelashes. It wasn't tears. It was blood, lots of blood.

Oh, God.

There was an ache in my ribs too, a dull ache, and I wasn't sure what else was hurt.

I wasn't concerned about me. I was looking at Bru, his arms. I touched one. "You're bleeding."

"I don't give a shit about me." He pulled his shirt off, and he used it to touch my forehead.

I sucked in a breath, the pain radiated through my skull.

"I'm going to call 911," I heard Sloane say before the world started to go hazy, dark. I heard shouting in the distance, and I recognized one voice above all else. It was Wells, and I smelled him as the world faded away. Wells had come for me too, but Bru obviously had gotten there first. They both came for me, and I was happy in that moment.

I remembered so much happiness as I ultimately drifted away.

CHAPTER
THIRTY-ONE

Bru

I was at the campus hospital with my family and friends, Wells beside me, rocking. Our parents were on the way to campus from Maywood Heights. The drive was long, and it'd take them a couple hours.

Bow's parents were on their way too.

Shit happened so quickly. I'd seen a green SUV zooming toward my sister and Bow.

I didn't think.

Bow had pushed Sloane out of the way by the time I got there, but I'd been able to grab Bow in time. I'd gotten scraped up a bit in the process, but I didn't care.

Bow.

She'd blacked out, which had been scary as fuck, her head seeping blood. The blackout had been brief though, and she'd woken up by the time the paramedics arrived. My sister had called them. Thank *fuck* for my sister since I hadn't been thinking clearly with everything happening.

"Why the fuck aren't they telling us anything!" Wells shot

off his chair, his hands in his hair. We'd both been coming back from the bathroom when everything with Bow went down. We'd both seen the SUV coming, but I got there faster. Wells came in shortly behind me as well as Thatcher and Aspen. Our focus had all been on Bow, so no one had paid attention after the SUV went by. Nobody had seen who was behind the wheel or even a plate number. The driver had gotten away, and here we were with the aftermath.

The aftermath was Wells who, when he wasn't sitting, was pacing the hospital's waiting room. Both Dorian *and* Thatcher had started to get up, I assumed to talk to Wells and calm him down.

The guys' help wasn't needed though. I lifted a hand to them, and they nodded, going back to their girlfriends. Dorian was needed more with Sloane, who was rocking too. She'd gotten checked out like me. She was fine with just a few scrapes and thank God for that.

Returning to his seat, Dorian put his big arms around my sister, and she hugged him back. She buried her face into his chest, and I think the only reason Thatcher was able to be a semblance of calm was because of Aspen. She'd gotten up and put her arms around his waist. She was supporting him. We *all* had support, and Ares and Fawn were here too of course. They'd gone off to get coffee and bottles of water for everyone.

"Eh!" Wells rushed up to the reception desk, getting the attention of the entire ER's waiting room. He slammed his hands on the desk, which made the lady behind the glass jump. He growled. "I need an update on Rainbow Reed. I needed one like *fucking* yesterday and—"

I got an arm around his chest. I pulled him away, and it wasn't without effort. He punched at everything, and that included me when I brought another arm around his chest. Wells growled. "Let go, Bru. I swear to fucking God."

I didn't let go.

My arms were covered in bandages, my own wounds raw, but I used all my strength to hold him back. I wanted to punch something too. I wanted to go to old habits and fight, but I had to be strong here. I had to be strong for him and her.

"I swear to God, Bru," Wells croaked, but he stopped fighting when I held him close. Getting a good hold of him, I guided him out of the ER. Some of the guys started to follow us, but I shook my head. Wells and I didn't need them.

We needed each other.

"I swear, if she's not okay." Wells paused like he couldn't even continue the thought. Once we were outside, I let go of him, and he squeezed his eyes shut. His whole face was red, his hair messy. He laced his fingers on top of his head. "Bru, what will I do?"

What would *we* do. *We.* The three of us had just figured this all out, and, even though we were all still coming to terms with our relationship, we'd solidified it. We were together. All three of us.

"She's going to be okay," I told him, and not just for him. I needed the words just as badly. I hooked my arms around Wells's waist, and he brought one around my neck. He took me into a tight hold. We hugged that shit out. We engulfed ourselves in the moment and the emotion of it. We had to release this shit so we could be strong.

"She's going to be okay," Wells whispered to me, and I nodded. He pressed his face into my hair for long moments before he pulled back.

I held his face.

"She's going to be okay," I said before pressing our mouths together. We took the final seconds to release this shit. We felt it in the moment so we could let it go and deal with whatever was about to happen. I think we needed the moment, this moment.

So that's what we did.

———

Wells and I returned to the ER as a unit, our hands together. It wasn't lost on me that my family, *this family of tight friends* seemed to always be in the fucking hospital. It was like the grim reaper followed us on the regular, but he wasn't going to win this day. He wouldn't. He wasn't.

Our friends' eyes were on Wells and me when we arrived. Ares and Fawn were there, so everyone had either a coffee or a bottle of water.

I sat by my sister, and Wells took my other side. Sloane gave me a warm smile that had to have taken energy. Her face was just as red as Wells's had been.

I squeezed her shoulder, but our attention drifted when a doctor approached our small group. She was a woman who appeared to be our parents' age. She introduced herself as Dr. Miller.

"Are you the family of Rainbow Reed?" she asked, and Thatcher immediately stood up.

"I'm her brother," he said, but the rest of us stood up too. Thatcher waved to all of us. "We're all her family."

I could tell Wells was fighting beside me. He was squeezing my hand, and I'd bet he was screaming on the inside. I certainly was for something, *anything* of an update.

Dr. Miller smiled. "Rainbow is fine. She has a mild concussion and a few bruised ribs, but she's okay. We're going to keep her overnight for observation, but she should be good to go home tomorrow."

It was like a weight in the room lifted. Like someone had let the air in when we all collectively breathed.

She's okay.

I faced Wells, hugging him. He hugged me back, and I heard Dorian say he was going to text our parents.

"Thank God," Sloane breathed out. She had tears in her eyes as she hugged Dorian, then Thatcher. Thatcher, too, had looked pretty rough. He was definitely considered the pretty boy in our group, but he was completely disheveled with the weight of a thousand thoughts playing all over his face.

He hugged Aspen, squeezing her so hard.

"I told you she'd be fine," Aspen whispered to Thatcher, but I was more focused on Wells. Wells had never hugged me so hard. Hell, I was usually the one giving the firm hugs.

He wouldn't let go of me, and he didn't have to. I smiled. "She's cool, bro."

"Yeah," Wells said, and when he pulled away, he kept my hand. I didn't mind at all. Wells released a breath. "When can we see her?"

"You can now, but I'd go in groups of two or three," the doctor said. "The room is on the smaller side. But, before you do, I need to know who Wells Ambrose and Bru Sloane-Mallick are."

"That's us," I said before Wells could. I touched my chest. "I'm Bru, and he's Wells."

Wells nodded.

The doctor smiled again, but this time, it didn't quite reach her eyes. She nodded. "Rainbow requested to see you both first if that's all right."

It was more than all right, but Wells and I exchanged a glance with Thatcher. I think we didn't want to encroach on Thatch. Bow was his sister after all.

"Go on," Thatcher said, obviously reading our look. Thatcher nodded. "I should call my mom and dad anyway. Tell them exactly what the doc said."

That was so good of him, letting us see her. I knew this whole thing was driving him crazy as well.

"Squeak." Wells entered Bow's room before I did. There was just enough room for Bow's bed and all her monitors.

I'd sort that out for her, get her a bigger room. Wells and I would.

Bow sat on her bed in a hospital gown, her hands in her lap. She looked up when Wells called out to her, though.

"Wells," she said, a small smile on her face, but it was so faint. Gingerly, she lifted her arms, and the bandages on them matched the one on her forehead. Her hair was down, but her curls only covered some of it.

Her head had been bleeding so much in the parking lot, and I'd been terrified. Why had I not grabbed her differently? Protected her better?

The guilt weighed heavily on me, and I stayed back when Wells rushed in and wrapped his long wingspan around her. He brought her to him gently, and her small body disappeared in his embrace.

"Fucking hell, Squeak," Wells gasped, his eyes shut tight. I'd never seen Wells the way I had in the past few hours. He'd gone from hopeless wreck to this very hug giving him air, giving him life.

I felt whole inside, watching them. Especially when she hugged him back so tightly.

"Wells…" She was shaking a little, and I saw that in her limbs, her petite and *scraped*-up limbs. She didn't just have bandages on her arms but bruises as well.

It was illogical as fuck, but I felt her condition was my fault. Obviously, there'd been that asshole in the SUV, but I didn't have to grab her so hard, hurt her.

I was still frozen at the door, wanting so much to go in there and hug them both. I wanted to *love* them both.

Swallowing, I couldn't move, and it was like something otherworldly happened. Both Wells and Bow broke away from each other slowly, then their attention was on me.

"Bru." Bow blinked down a tear. She had tears in her eyes. She lifted a hand. "Bru."

Her voice sounded stripped, raw, and I saw something equally emotional in Wells's eyes. There was a plea there, like he needed me to be a part of this moment.

I didn't fight anymore. I came over and immediately cradled Bow. I did as softly as I could. She was so delicate.

"Bru," Bow sighed as she hugged me back, and she did so hard. Well, as hard as she could considering the circumstances. She pressed her face into my chest. "Bru."

I heard a sob escape her.

When she pulled away, there were tears falling from her red eyes, and I felt kicked. Like the SUV actually hit me today, and my insides were tossed, battered. I shook my head. "I'm so sorry, Bow. I shouldn't have grabbed you so hard. I—"

She cut me off with a kiss, which dulled my panic instantly.

I pushed back her hair, drinking in the moment. She sighed against my mouth, and that was when I felt Wells. He had his arms around us, holding us. Bow's bed was high up, so it was easy for him to do so.

This felt so fucking right, all of us. I'd never known a love like this before. This was so right. This was home.

There was a cough, and we separated to see the doctor standing in the doorway.

"Hi, Rainbow. How are you feeling?" Dr. Miller asked. She closed the door, and I felt Bow's hand find mine.

She found Wells's too. In fact, she held on to us both as the doctor took a seat on a stool at the foot of Bow's bed.

"All right," Bow said, staring at the bed.

Dr. Miller's head tilted. She just stared at Bow, and, again, Bow didn't make eye contact. Bow must have been aware the doctor was looking at her though, because she nodded slightly.

I didn't know what the nod meant, but Wells noticed it too, glancing at me before staring down at Bow. He sat beside her on her bed. "You should be going home soon, Squeak. The doctor said you're all right."

Bow nodded again, still not looking up. Something kicked at my chest then. Especially when Bow squeezed my hand.

She also winced.

"Bow asked me to explain to you both exactly what's going on," Dr. Miller said, glancing between Wells and me. She smiled. "She said you're both very special to her."

I also took a seat on Bow's bed. There wasn't much room with Wells already there, but I found a little.

"What's going on?" Wells asked, and, even though the doctor had spoken, he looked at Bow. He touched her face. "Squeak?"

Bow winced again like Wells's touch hurt her, but that was unlikely. He'd touched her so gently.

"Rainbow was pregnant, Mr. Ambrose," Dr. Miller said, and Wells's eyes flashed. His attention shot to the doctor and mine did too.

"I don't understand," Wells said before I could. "Pregnant?"

"She *was?*" I cut in, then stared at Bow. Her head was still down, and she gripped my hand like she was holding on for dear life.

Bow shook her head, her gaze lost on the white sheet covering her legs. "The baby wasn't yours."

The words were a whisper, so soft.

"The baby wasn't yours."

My brain couldn't compute what she said. It didn't make sense. The confusion only resumed as the doctor continued on for Bow. She talked about how Bow was pregnant, and it wasn't either of ours. It wasn't Wells's *or* mine, and that Bow had lost it. She lost it because of the fall she had in the parking lot. The fall *I* caused.

"The baby wasn't yours."

Bow couldn't have been pregnant because that didn't make sense. The three of us had *just* had sex, and we used protection.

"I'll let you have your time," the doctor said as if she hadn't just dropped a bomb on the room. Dr. Miller stood.

"Rainbow, let me know if you need anything. Just use your call button, and I'll come."

Bow nodded, but just barely.

She'd also let go of our hands. She held herself, rocking.

"Bow," I started to say, but Wells lifted his hand. He shook his head, and he put his arms around Bow. He held her in silence.

It was like he knew what she needed.

Bow lost it there in Wells's chest, sobbing, and Wells held on to her like he was trying to fuse himself to her, both of them rocking together. Like he also needed her in order to continue on in that moment.

"It's okay," Wells said, the words tight. He was restraining his emotion, his face red. He kissed the top of her head. "It's okay."

It's okay.

Wells looked at me, and our eyes connected. We shared a brief moment of something before I brought my arms around Bow too.

"It's okay, Bow." I was shaking, and Wells's hold was the same as mine.

"I have to tell you something," Bow gasped between us. She was *so small*, so fucking fragile. She shook her head. "I have to tell you about him."

Him.

Wells and I glanced at each other. Right now, Bow needed us. She needed our love. She needed our support, and that was enough to keep both our monsters at bay, I think. Someone didn't just touch her. They did something else, and I could fucking feel that in my soul. Someone hurt her.

And that was all I needed to know.

Wells

He was her professor.

He'd even had dinner with our parents.

I sat in horror as Bow told Bru and me about him. The guy had stalked Bow all semester and only *kinda* stopped after she spent more time with me. He was why she wanted people to see me with her.

I was silent while Bow spoke, dangerously silent. I was sure I appeared calm, but inside a war raged within me only one person related to. He was sitting on her other side.

Bru also remained silent while Bow spoke. He held her, one arm around her waist while his other hand was on my shoulder. Bow couldn't see that hand, the one that gripped into my flesh with a fucking viselike grip. She didn't see Bru's face, his complexion the color of a thousand suns, red. His jaw clenched.

Bow sniffed back tears while she told her story. Bow was lying between us and gripped my shirt. "I'm so stupid. He told me so many things. Made me feel things…"

I held on to Bow to keep from fuming, shaking.

She shook her head. "I was just so lonely."

She was lonely because of me. It was because of something *I* did. I blackballed her. Hell, she couldn't even have *friends* unless they were a part of our crew. That was something *I* did, me.

The grip on my shoulder loosened a bit, and I think that was because Bru transferred his attention to Bow. She started crying, and he hugged her into him. He swept back her hair. "Baby," he murmured.

She was our baby, and I knew I had no right to think of her that way. It was because of me this fucker had access to her. She was *vulnerable* because of me.

She held Bru's hand, squeezed it. "I didn't even want to have sex. I thought I did. He made me think I did." She sniffed. "I asked to stop at first. I didn't want it, but he got in my head."

Something happened to Bow she neither wanted or liked, and that was assault. Point-blank.

Eventually, Bow stopped crying. Eventually, she closed her eyes, and even after she grew quiet, Bru and I didn't say anything. We just held her. We were doing what she needed in the moment. We stayed present *for her.*

We'd do anything for her.

———

The three of us remained like that for a long time, in Bow's hospital bed. We only let go when her parents came into the room. Mrs. Reed immediately went to Bow, and Bru and I gave them both that space. Mr. Reed was right behind her, as well as the rest of the Legacy families. That tiny-ass room didn't stay tiny for long after our parents made some calls. They got Bow the space she both needed and deserved, and the parents only added to the comfort.

Before they arrived, Bow had asked us to stay silent about the pregnancy to our folks. She wasn't ready to tell them, and we understood. Bru and I let her be surrounded by love that night, and eventually, all our friends came in to visit her too. Bow had a lot of love. She had a lot of family.

"I lost the baby. I lost her, him."

Those were the last words Bow said to Bru and me before the parents arrived as she clutched her stomach. She'd been pregnant, but she wasn't now.

She wasn't now.

Bru and I looked at each other, a silent exchange shared between us. We had so many silent exchanges, but we kept that shit on lock.

We had to.

Bru and I texted Bow in our group chat before we left the hospital that night. She was physically safe with her family, our families. She was alive, but she wasn't okay. She might not ever be. She might not be for a long time.

"I lost the baby."

Bru and I kept our texts with Bow simple. We told her we were going out for a little bit, but we'd come running if she needed us. She was good with our families, safe, but, before we actually left the hospital, we asked if it was okay to tell the Legacies about the pregnancy. We'd only tell our friends.

Bow: Yeah, it's okay.

It's okay.

Bow: I love you both.

She was our everything which was why we were going to bat for her when she physically couldn't at the moment. Bru and I were going to take care of the girl we loved.

We *all* were going to take care of her.

THIRTY-THREE

Wells

Honestly, it didn't take long to find Bow's professor. Again, he had dinner with our parents, so I knew about him. He was a man of influence and only taught because he was a scholar. He was a man dedicated to a life of research, and because of that, he had a lot of clout. He also had a lot of money and came from a long line of scholars which was why he knew our parents. They all often attended benefits together, and my parents even donated to some of the grants that funded this fucker's research.

All our parents had.

Which meant that I knew how to find him.

This guy had access to Bow. He did in so many fucking ways, and Bow hadn't been the fool. She'd been her trusting and kind self.

He let us right in.

Well, his maid had, and my friends and I found this fucker in front of his fireplace. He was a brunette with perfectly coiffed hair. He had a bottle of vodka beside him, no glass.

Like he'd been drinking something away, his fears maybe. Maybe he knew my friends and I would ultimately come for him.

He didn't even fight.

We stood in front of him now, all my buddies and I. We dragged this guy in his velvet robe and matching slippers into the woods behind his house. He lived on the outskirts of Pembroke's campus. The woods known as Grimwood Hollow were known for being a labyrinthine. In fact, hikers got lost out there all the time, and even attacked by coyotes and mountain lions.

There were five animals here now, but only one monster.

Bow told us she recognized him from the parking lot when no one else had. Shit, no one had even caught a plate on the person who almost ran her and Sloane over. My friends and I had asked around. We were also well connected to the university, so we knew the school was conducting an investigation. Our intel let us know even the authorities had no leads on the person yet though. The driver had gotten away, went ghost.

But even ghosts could be found.

They could be found by the grim reaper, and I watched as Thatcher threw this guy into the leaves. His name was Patrick Donovan, and the fucker squirmed when he stumbled to the ground. He was obviously drunk off his ass, but he didn't bother running.

My friends and I surrounded Donovan. It was Dorian who squatted in front of the man. My friend D had no problem getting a little blood on his hands.

None of us did.

Someone else had messed with Bow once in high school. It'd been one of her teachers, and I'd taken care of that shit then. I had the scars to prove it. That fucker had lived, but that was only because he'd been fortunate that I took care of his ass before he could hurt Bow.

Donovan wasn't fortunate.

Dorian's expression was deadpan. "He has to die."

I knew he meant it. I knew for a fact he hadn't killed anyone before, but he'd come close a time or two.

Even still, I knew Dorian would have no problem taking a life. All my friends and I had been through some dark shit. It was like a blanket of bullshit had surrounded us from birth. We all had various reasons why and mine surrounded Bow.

Something happened to me the moment I allowed that girl at the pool to drown. It changed something in me and I hurt the one person who never *ever* should have received the fallout from it.

I'd spend my life trying to make it up to the woman I loved, and, even though I wasn't worthy of her, I'd damn well try to do right by her.

Donovan was on his back in front of Dorian.

He came from a long line of scholars and his family had almost as many buildings named after him on campus as my friends and I had.

Almost.

I knew it would have taken the right kind of fucker to mess with Bow. It'd take *an arrogant* fucker to mess with what was mine.

Ours.

Bru squeezed my arm, looking at the filth on the ground, and Donovan's eyes widened after what Dorian said. Dorian had some stake in this too even if this guy hadn't messed with Bow. Donovan almost ran Dorian's fiancée over too.

My boy Dorian was engaged; he told us about it at the football stadium earlier that day. That was probably the last time we all got to be kids before the next leg of our lives took over. My friends and I were brothers through and through.

Donovan lifted his hands, trembling. He may have known something would happen after messing with Bow, but he obviously was still coming to terms with things. Donovan gripped the leaves. "You don't mean that."

He thought Dorian was bluffing.

Donovan's throat jumped. "Now, come on, boys. All of you can stop this right now. I will make sure no words about what you've done so far will be spoken. Nothing will come from—"

Slap.

That was right. Thatcher, a huge-ass dude who could tackle a motherfucker, had slapped this guy.

Like a bitch.

Donovan was lucky it hadn't been a punch, and he was so shocked by the slap he rubbed his face.

"You don't talk," Thatcher said, shaking. I knew it was taking everything in him not to do something more. Bru and I had told him everything surrounding Donovan's coercion as well as the stalking that occurred after. That Bow offered to tutor me in hopes the guy wouldn't come around anymore.

Thatcher also knew about the baby. All my friends did, once Bow had given us permission to tell them, which was why my buddies had no problem coming to get this guy.

Thatcher inched toward Donovan, but Dorian held him back. Dorian was normally the voice of reason and the leader to all of us, but even he said this guy had to die.

"He does have to die," Thatcher said, and Donovan's eyes widened again. Thatcher's jaw clenched. "For my sister."

"And mine," Ares said. He was holding Thatcher back by the other arm. Whatever Dorian did, Ares "Wolf" Mallick followed. We all did. Even still, Wolf was holding back too. He braced his fist. Donovan had almost killed Sloane too in all this, and Ares had just as much rage lacing his already wolfish features. Ares's eyes narrowed. "This fucker sealed his fate."

It was an understanding between all of us. Especially for Bru and me. Oddly enough, I was the one holding Bru back.

I'd never seen the kid so charged up. Bru, ironically enough, had been introduced to violence more than all of us. Despite that, he was just as kind and good as Rainbow Reed. Unfortunately, life had kicked Bru in the teeth more. I knew for a fact Bru Sloane-Mallick could take a life.

Because he had before.

I saw that rage in his eyes too, that capability. Bru wet his lips. "It's up to her," he said, then faced me. He nodded.

I did too.

Bru and I had come to an agreement after we left the hospital. The idea had been proposed by me, but he quickly agreed. He did because he loved me, and I knew I'd never be deserving of that love. I wouldn't, but I was taking it. I needed his love.

I needed it just like I needed Bow's.

Her love made both of us better, and it made me stronger.

"She'll decide," I told my friends. Swallowing, I placed my hand on Bru's neck. "She'll decide."

I spent years dictating things in Rainbow Reed's life. I played with her like a little puppet, just like Donovan had. I manipulated her.

"I'm so sorry, Wells," she'd said to me at the hospital between fits of fallen tears. She cried so much. So damn much because of things I'd allowed to happen to her. She looked up at me. "He made me hate you. He said I let you bully me. I let you use me and I needed to take something for myself."

That was how Donovan had ultimately gotten to her. He made her stand up for herself, take something back, but it hadn't been for her. It'd been for him.

"It's up to Bow," I clarified but not for my friends. They all knew why we were here today. We were here for Bow, and no one would speak on Donovan's fate but her. She would get to decide something for herself.

I'd make sure.

THIRTY-FOUR

Bow

The call came while I was in bed, my eyes itchy, red. I didn't even need to see them to know they were.

I'd been crying so much, and I wanted my boyfriends. I wanted Bru and Wells and their arms around me.

I wanted something else too, and I didn't know that until I realized how long I'd been hugging myself. I had no idea I'd been pregnant, but, in hindsight, there'd been signs. I'd been nauseous a lot. Food hadn't tasted the best lately, but I hadn't thought much of that.

I just hadn't thought.

I'd been so stupid, and it was a relief seeing Wells's face on my phone screen. His FaceTime call came in the wee hours of the night at the hospital.

The call woke my parents up from where they'd been sleeping on the couch.

"We'll give you some time, honey," Mom said, taking my dad with her. "We'll get some coffee."

I knew they were the reason why Bru and Wells hadn't

come back yet. The guys wanted me to have time with my parents. My mom and dad had been freaking out when they got here. My parents didn't know about the pregnancy. They just knew I was alive and okay.

I wasn't okay.

I knew that right away, because as soon as my parents left and I stared into Wells's lovely face on my phone screen, I burst into tears. His hair was swept back, messy, and Bru was beside him.

They were both so handsome.

They were like lights in my darkness. Wells Ambrose had somehow become my light again. I had my archer back as well as my rock in the storm, Bru.

"Baby," Wells said, and my heart moved, stirred. He obviously saw my tears. He winced like something hurt him, and I glanced away.

"Look at me, Bow."

I came back with Wells's words. I swallowed. "Where are you?"

I wanted them here and wherever they were at it was dark like they were outside. Had they left the hospital?

"Not far away," Wells said, and Bru nodded.

Bru edged more into the phone screen. "We're about to do something, but we want your guidance."

"What happens will ultimately be up to you," Wells stated, and when he faced Bru, Bru nodded again. Wells's expression was tense, serious. "You deserve to have a say."

A say about what?

Wells's nostrils flared. "We have Patrick Donovan."

My heart thudded.

It stopped.

No sooner had it ceased its beat than it revved up again at jackrabbit speed. Sloane called me that, little rabbit, because I moved at a mile a minute sometimes.

Sloane had been at the hospital earlier too. In fact, all my friends and family had been here at one point before they ultimately left so that I could have time with my parents.

Sloane held me when she finally saw me though, and I cried. I was so happy she was okay. She barely even had to be looked at by hospital staff. She had not one bump or bruise from the accident.

I saved her from him.

Wells's breathing picked up. His big chest rose and fell rapidly, and when Bru's jaw clenched, I knew it was because of me, my reaction. What Wells had said froze me where I sat.

Bru looked at Wells. "This is too much. Maybe we should have waited."

They were trying to protect me, both of them, and I had a feeling my brother and his friends were there too. Wells had asked if it was okay to tell them about the pregnancy, and there was nothing any of the guys did without each other.

Bru's expression went serious. "We shouldn't have surprised her with this—"

"I want to see him," I said, and both guys' eyes darted toward me.

"You deserve a say."

Wells's words were clear for me now. He and Bru had Professor Donovan, and I had a say on what ultimately happened from there. I had a choice.

They gave me a choice.

I realized now that I didn't have one back then. Professor Donovan had convinced me that he was my friend, and our relationship started innocently enough. I went to him for extra credit, and he expressed interest in my work. He gave me care.

He gave me attention.

Soon our meetings weren't just about the work. He started talking to me as a friend and one thing led to another. Soon, we weren't just meeting at his office but his house. He convinced me he was my friend, and I told him too many things. I told him *everything* about my life and my pain. I told him about Wells, and Professor Donovan already knew a bit about the manipulation because everyone knew what happened in the world of Legacy. I actually thought he was my friend, and he convinced me that I wanted to have sex.

I hadn't wanted to have sex.

I knew that as soon as it was over, and he held me. I felt so dirty, used, but I didn't want to believe he did things to me that I didn't want. I didn't want to feel *weak* and lied to myself for a while after the fact. I convinced myself what happened was on my terms and what I wanted.

But it hadn't been.

"I want to see him," I said again, and, even though my voice threatened to shake, I steadied it.

The guys nodded and the camera view passed Thatcher, Ares, and Dorian before it ultimately found Professor Donovan. He was on the ground in a robe like he'd left from his house quickly.

I swallowed. He was older than my parents, but I hadn't thought about that when he'd been kind to me. Hindsight told me now he only let me know what I wanted to hear. He used me. And he tried to kill me.

"Come back to me, Bow. It'll be different this time."

Some of Professor Donovan's final texts had been after we had sex. They slowed down significantly after I started being seen with Wells more. I hung out with Wells in public places I knew Professor Donovan frequented.

"Just let go."

Professor Donovan had kept saying that during sex. He saw how painful it was for me, awkward. As soon as we started, I wanted to stop, but he convinced me to keep going. *He didn't stop* even though I clearly hadn't wanted to continue.

They had Professor Donovan gagged, and, when he saw me, he tried to speak around the fabric in his mouth. He was trying to use his voice, which I realized now was his most powerful weapon. The gift of persuasion he used to make me do things I didn't want with him.

I clutched my stomach again. I felt empty, hollow. My lips pressed together. "We were pregnant. You and me… *We were pregnant*, and I lost it."

Professor Donovan stopped trying to talk around his gag. In fact, he bit down on it, and his eyes widened. His head shook, and I realized I was happy now for the gag. He'd done all the talking now up to this point, the manipulation, but he wasn't now.

My voice was a powerful weapon too.

"I *lost it* because of you. You tried to kill me," I said, and he winced. I nodded. "You tried to kill me and my friend and you *murdered* our baby."

The camera tilted then to Wells, who looked broken. His jaw was clenched tight, and Bru was still beside him. Bru's expression was just as tense. His nostrils flared, but when I mouthed to both guys that I was okay, the camera tilted back.

I sat up in my bed. I held my waist for strength. I was giving my child a voice too. Theirs was also taken, stolen. I swallowed. "I want you to hunt him down. I want you to chase him and *break him down* like he did me."

Again, hindsight was something else. Professor Donovan's manipulation came so easily to him. It was so *easy* for him to get to me, find me. He knew how to find weak and vulnerable girls.

But I wasn't weak anymore. He hadn't *broken* me, but he would break.

He would break.

Right away, Professor Donovan started pleading through his gag. His voice was muffled, strained, and I was so happy I wouldn't have to hear it again. The camera left him, and I was happy for that too.

"We love you," Bru said before the call ended abruptly.

I didn't wonder why he said that on behalf of both him and Wells because I saw what Wells was doing in the background. Wells's attention had been on Professor Donovan. Wells had gathered my professor to his feet and even took the gag off him. He unbound his arms too, and I heard Wells say one word to my professor before the call cut off.

He told him to run.

CHAPTER
THIRTY-FIVE

Jax

"Dorian Prinze."

Knight's son, Thatcher, and my son, Wells, stood up as their friend Dorian took the stage. They'd done the same for Ramses's son, Ares. Three of our kids were graduating college today. Dorian was Royal's son, and Sloane, Ramses's daughter, had already walked the graduation stage.

Royal, Knight, Ramses, and I stood up too, as well as LJ, who'd flown out for this. He was god-dad to my kid and all my friends' kids. He and his wife, Billie, never had biological children of their own. They had ours though, and we were all so fucking proud of our children.

Dorian saluted all of us from the stage, and in the distance, I noticed Ares standing up too. That was probably frowned upon, one of the graduates getting up from their seat, but he wasn't alone when his twin sister, Sloane, stood as well. That was her boyfriend up there, her fiancé.

None of us parents were surprised to see those two getting

engaged so close to graduation; I think we were all blown away they hadn't done so sooner.

It was crazy how our kids were grown and moving on in life. I still had a year until Wells graduated, but he'd be moving on too, growing up.

I watched him applauding Dorian with a strong clap. Honestly, I think his was only drowned out because of how loud Thatcher's—Knight's son—was. Thatcher had the loudest applause, but he was a huge fucking kid like his father.

Knight stared at Thatcher with pride. He was proud of the man Thatcher had become. Thatcher's girlfriend, Aspen, was by his side and clapping too. She was a celebrated cellist if one could imagine, and Knight bragged all the time about that. My friends and I did all we could to one-up each other over the years.

There was no point in running a tally. All our children were badasses, and they took after their moms. They were all here too of course: Greer, Knight's wife, Brielle, and December. They were Ramses's and Royal's wives respectively, and, of course, my Cleo was here beside me. Between all us parents and kids we nearly took up an entire row of Pembroke University's Memorial Stadium. Well, not quite, but we did take up a lot of fucking seats.

"Yeah, go D!" Wells yelled. He even stood up on his seat like the joker he was. Like father like son. He cupped his mouth. "You earned that shit, bro!"

A healthy part of the crowd heard him and laughed. Dorian heard him too and shook his head before receiving his diploma. My son almost fell off his chair in all his excitement. He would have if not for his boyfriend, Bru. The guy grabbed him down, which was a feat with their girlfriend between them. Bow Reed, Knight's daughter, flushed with all the attention they had garnered from my crazy kid. I assumed that was why she'd flushed, anyway. She tended to do that a lot.

After all the excitement (and my son returned to the floor), Wells put his arm around Bow. She had a bandage on her forehead, and Wells checked it before kissing her forehead. I liked to say I was surprised to see them together, but I wasn't. Wells had always been fond of Bow, even if he hadn't acted like it. He clearly had feelings for her, considering how protective he'd always been of her. That went double when they both were kids.

I *was* surprised when the three of them got together. The trio thing was different, but I had no problem with it. I just wanted to be sure Knight's daughter was taken care of, but I didn't have to think about that long when I saw the three of them together. The boys loved Bow, and I knew they were good guys, good men. The boys had bent over backward to be there for her after her accident.

Yeah, her accident.

All us parents had been terrified. Thankfully, Bow and Sloane were okay. Of course, right away Knight went into protector mode. He wanted vengeance for whatever fucker decided to almost hit two of our children, then run.

All us parents felt the same way. We all wanted justice, but, even with Knight's tech skills, no one knew who had driven that green SUV. There was no camera footage, and no one even caught a plate it'd all happened so fast.

I knew Knight was still at war with that. He might be hunting that ghost for the rest of our lives, and, though my friends and I would help him look, karma was a bitch, and that shit always caught up. That'd given me some peace, and I hope Knight got some, too. That and the fact that our kids were happy, healthy.

Cleo nudged me when our kids all returned to their seats, and I noticed a small smile tug at Knight's lips. I tapped his shoulder in acknowledgement of him accepting his daughter's relationships; I knew he struggled with his daughter having two boyfriends.

But he saw our children sitting together, *happy*. Wells still had his arm around Bow, and around Bru. He had a hand gripping Bru's neck while Bru's hand had Bow's in the center. The three of them had found serenity, and, in the end, that was all I wanted for our children. That was all I wanted for *my* kid.

I was proud of him too.

———

"Come in."

I opened the door and came in to see my son fiddling with a tie. With as many events as I made my kid go to, he still couldn't manage it. It was undone, and he had a suit jacket on his bed. It matched his dark pants that had a similar check pattern.

He was getting dressed rather formally for a graduation after-party, but I wouldn't question it. Any time I could get my kid in something that didn't have a barbecue stain on it, I celebrated the fact. He grew up around the food service industry since I owned a bunch of fast-food chains. Needless to say, he was always getting into something.

Laughing at him and his tie issues, I closed the door of his childhood bedroom. "Here. Let me help."

"Thank God," Wells breathed out.

This wasn't what he'd worn to Ares, Dorian, and Sloane's semi-formal graduation party.

I mentioned that to Wells as I fixed his tie, and he froze.

"Just want to look nice, Dad," he said. The story was that he and the other kids were going to a club. They wanted to celebrate Ares, Dorian, and Sloane after the party their parents threw earlier.

I wasn't sure about that, and, if I knew any of our kids,

they were up to something. I think the general consensus in my group chat with my friends was the same. We, their parents, weren't idiots, but we also knew they were adults. If they were getting into something, we could trust them... I guess.

"Make good choices," I said, sounding like a fucking *dad*. I hadn't really grown up with one and cringed every time I sounded like one.

I still loved my dad, though. We'd gotten really close over the years, and I respected him. Even still, I didn't want to *sound* like him. He was really fucking serious, and I prided myself on never sounding too serious.

I think Wells got that from me, and he laughed until I pushed that tie right up to his neck. I wasn't joking about making good choices.

"Don't I always?" he stated before loosening the tie a little from his neck. I wasn't sure about that either, but I did know he'd changed so much over the last few months. For starters, he'd actually be graduating next year as long as he continued to do the work. He'd managed to get his grades up, and I knew a lot of that had to do with Bow. Between her and Bru, who was also brilliant, my son had managed to make a great turnaround.

Because of that, I pulled something out of my pocket.

"What's this?" Wells asked, opening it. His dark brows jumped. "Are you serious?"

I nodded. I pointed at him. "You still have to put in the work though. Graduate."

His hustle really showed me what he could do. I wasn't going to cut him off, and I also was going to give him the thing he wanted. I knew he really didn't want to follow in my footsteps with the family business. I was a businessman through and through, and, though Wells had gotten some of that, he had more creative pursuits. I respected it.

"You're paying for my culinary school... Full ride?" He

stared in awe at the check made out to the school I knew he wanted to go to. He had pamphlets of the place everywhere and always talked about it. He smiled. "Thanks, Dad."

I shook my head. "You put in the work."

My son hugged me. I didn't get a lot of hugs because we just didn't really hug a lot, but when we did, it was like this. It was a father and son. It was respect, but most importantly there was love.

Knock. Knock.

Wells and I turned to see my wife at the door. She wasn't alone. Bru was with her, and he was just as dressed up as Wells.

I watched my son hug the guy he loved, but not before giving some love over to his mom. Cleo squeezed Wells so tight. I was so lucky to have her. She shouldn't love me, but something I learned over the years was to take a blessing when it was gifted. Cleo was a part of me, and I was literally a part of her. I donated a kidney to her once, and we both had the scars.

I put my arm around her as I watched Wells and Bru leave. The boys mentioned needing to pick up Bow, and it was like watching my kid go off to prom.

"You know they're up to something, right?" Cleo said to me, and I laughed. Our kids were one hundred percent up to something.

Let's just say they better hope we didn't find out.

Cleo

"I'm going to kill him, but that's only if my buddies don't kill him first."

Jax's hand gripped the steering wheel after what he said, and I took one of his hands. I was mad too, but I knew I had to be the voice of reason for my husband.

Placing Jax's hand in my lap, I rubbed it. "It's going to be okay."

"It'll be okay if my friends and I make it to Vegas in time," Jax grunted. I'd never seen him so red. The flush actually made its way to his dark hairline.

Despite his anger, my husband looked so handsome. His hair was moussed, and he wore a suit he purchased for the last charity event we both attended. I'd found a formal gown in my closet that sparkled and complemented his suit. I'd even been able to fashion my hair into a nice chignon despite how rushed we'd both been leaving the house.

Jax bared his teeth. "Royal and Ramses are furious."

I didn't blame them. It was *their children* getting married.

Jax and I knew Wells had been up to something tonight. Even still, this particular something surprised us. It was only by the grace of God Jax happened to be scanning our bank accounts this evening. Wells had made the transaction to his bank card only recently. He purchased not one but several tickets to Las Vegas, Vegas! It didn't take a rocket scientist to figure out why, when the number of airline tickets he purchased matched how many close friends he had.

It was well known Royal's son, Dorian, and Ramses's daughter, Sloane, had gotten engaged recently. We obviously couldn't guarantee that was why the kids were hopping a last-minute plane to Las Vegas, but them doing so was too coincidental.

Jax and I were silent the rest of the way to the airport. Well, I was silent and Jax was doing all he could to keep the cursing at bay. He knew I didn't like it.

I couldn't help but smile, seeing him so angry. Nothing about this situation was funny, but what the kids were doing was kind of sweet. Wells's role in it all showed me what kind of friend he was. He knew his dad and I would be angry, but he was okay making the charge for his friends, even though his dad hadn't cut him off and that was a serious risk to take.

But he did it for his friends, so it was hard not to be proud of the man his father and I had raised. Seeing Wells had found happiness with not one but two people made me happy as well. Anyone with eyes could see how in love with Rainbow Reed he was, and I knew that even when they'd been kids. Wells was a veil of protection for Bow, but I knew things changed after that terrible summer they both had.

I didn't know how that all played into his and Bow's relationship, but I did know they stopped being so close after that. My son had gone through a lot of therapy and healing after that summer, but, even so, he never was completely himself again. In fact, it wasn't until recently that Jax and I started to see that boy he used to be. The one who was happy and carefree, light.

Bow and Bru were so good for Wells. Ramses and Brielle had a good son, and I knew in my heart that all three of them would take care of each other.

"I'm going to kill your kid," Royal said, pointing at Jax as soon as Jax and I arrived at Maywood Heights's Airport.

Royal's nostrils flared. "But that's only after I kill mine. I knew Dorian was up to something. I freaking *knew it.* Especially after he purchased that new suit from Armani."

Apparently, all our boys had purchased suits from Armani. It was something all us parents realized after we checked our credit card statements and bank accounts.

December, Royal's wife, was calming Royal down just like I was calming Jax. December was lovely and reminded me of Snow White. She had dark hair and fair skin which was the exact opposite from Royal who was blond and had the tan/physique of a Ken doll. Together, the two looked like a prince and princess out of a fairy tale.

December frowned at her husband. "We're going to make it in time."

"Dorian better hope we do. It's one thing to do this to *us,* but to do this to Ramses and Brielle? For them to miss their daughter's wedding?" Royal said, and I understood.

"We're actually kind of excited," Ramses said, chipper as he entered the conversation. He and Brielle had just arrived; Knight and Greer, Thatcher and Bow's parents, were right behind them.

The men of the group wore suits while the women were in lovely gowns of various colors and lengths. We all definitely looked like we were attending a wedding. In an airport where everyone was wearing sweats and neck pillows, we were the outliers.

Ramses touched Royal's chest. He was a tall man who resembled Aladdin from the movie. The only difference was that he had shorter hair, and Brielle definitely looked like Princess Jasmine. Ramses grinned. "Come on, Prinze. Our kids are getting married. It's a happy time."

Honestly, I wasn't surprised to see this reaction from Ramses. He was always more glass half full, like me.

Really, everyone else looked mad for him, but even Brielle didn't appear angry.

"Is it weird that I am excited?" Brielle asked me later, on the plane. We were seated across each other in first class. The husbands had made sure all the wives were comfortable, so basically the entire first-class section was all us parents.

I bit my lip, fighting a smile. I nodded. I was only really upset for her and the Prinzes' benefit. I obviously wasn't thrilled my son lied, but Dorian and Sloane were like my own kids. I was happy to see them happy and tying the knot.

I took Brielle's hand across the aisle. "I'm excited too, knowing you are."

"I think we all are," December said from in front of us. She spoke between the seats and had to whisper because Royal was sleeping. Funnily enough, all the men were knocked out beside us. I think they'd exhausted themselves in anger. December snickered. "I can't believe my son is getting married."

It really was crazy. All our kids were no longer kids. They'd always be our babies, but they were growing up.

Brielle reached over and took December's hands. "We're going to be in-laws."

This made December smile. They both looked really happy, which made me happy.

"I can imagine it'll be my kid next," Greer said from the aisle seat across from December. Greer grinned. "Thatcher is head over heels for Aspen. Or maybe Bow, Wells, and Bru will surprise us."

It was weird to think Greer, Brielle, and I could be family

one day. I wasn't sure about the logistics of all that, but our kids did have a way of surprising us.

I think all us moms loved surprises. We loved our children, and the four of us held hands before we lay back and closed our eyes. When we woke up, we'd be in Vegas, and I knew we all had a lot of people to report back to. Our kids had so much family. They had so much love; my son's god-dad, LJ, and his wife, Billie, would be joining us in Vegas as well. The couple had headed out of the country after the kids' graduation for business, but they were hightailing it back after we told them the situation. The first of our children were getting married.

And so the next adventure began.

CHAPTER
THIRTY-SEVEN

Wells

My friends were getting married tonight.

I thought about that as I straightened my cuffs, then took a breath. It was my turn.

I headed down the aisle of a little white chapel off the Las Vegas strip. The shotgun wedding was Dorian's idea. He and Sloane had only been engaged for like a second, but, according to him, he'd waited long enough to have her as his wife. He'd been in love with his girl since high school and only waited this long out of formality.

He wanted Sloane to have more time with her family. There was a history there, where she'd been separated from them for a while.

Dorian beamed from the front of the aisle. Well, "beaming" for Dorian Prinze was a strong smirk. Dude smiled, but not a ton, and he was giving the grin from up front. He rocked black on black but the rest of his groomsmen, Thatcher, Ares, Bru, and I, all wore differently styled suits. Dorian wanted us to be comfortable up there with him.

Dorian had no best man tonight. We were all his best men, and I was last to head up the aisle to join the groom. Bru waited for me behind Dorian, Ares, and Thatcher, and the moment Bru and I locked eyes, a heat rushed to my dick. His suit was ridiculously snug and hit his broad shoulders and brawny frame just right. He had his hair swept back, and he had the classic look of a nineties Val Kilmer on the red carpet.

Yeah, I was taking that ass tonight.

He appraised me too, an appreciation ringing his brown eyes as I made my way toward him. I smirked, but it slipped when we broke eye contact for a second during my strides. There were other people in the audience.

Our parents looked pissed.

I was aware the cat was let out of the bag about this event the moment my phone started blowing up after my flight to Vegas landed. Literally, my phone (and my friends') started chiming off. Our parents, all our parents, including my god-dad, LJ, and his wife, Billie, were aware of this wedding. But not only that, they were coming to Vegas to see it.

They were obviously all here now, and, straightening my tie, I tried not to buckle at the looks I knew I was about to get.

Dorian and Sloane planned to have a larger affair when they got home. That affair included all our parents of course, and, though the couple hadn't gone out of their way to *not* have them attend, they also didn't want our families to talk them out of things. This wedding was spur of the moment. It was about Dorian and Sloane, and, of course, the guys and I aided them in their pursuit of that. We all knew the risks. Especially me. Had I wanted to test my father so soon after he *didn't* cut me off? No, but it was a risk I was willing to take. Fuck, I was willing to possibly lose out on a full ride to culinary school, and everyone knew what that shit meant to me.

Dorian was my brother though, and I'd do anything for him. So, with those thoughts in my mind, I made sure there was confidence in my strides as I continued to make my way down the aisle. I saw LJ and his wife, Billie, first. LJ definitely had a look of judgement in his eyes, but Billie was smiling. I honestly couldn't believe they were able to come. They'd been on their way out of the country after all the graduation stuff.

Swallowing, I caught the eyes of Thatcher and Bow's parents next. Right away, Mr. Reed gave me *a look*, but I had a feeling that was equally for flying his baby girl out of town as it was for keeping this wedding a secret.

Mr. Reed crossed his arms in my direction, but Mrs. Reed didn't look too pissed. If anything, there was a peaceful look on her face as she studied me, and was that a gentle nod?

I had to be imagining that, but I got a similar nod from all the mothers in attendance as I passed them, including Dorian's mom, Mrs. Prinze, and that was crazy. I even got an eye crinkle from her. Sloane's mom too: Mrs. Mallick's eyes were definitely warm as I passed her, but what was crazy was my mom. My mom *grinned*. She even put her hands up to cover her mouth.

Something inside me bounced a little that I might have gotten away with this secret shit, but then I caught my dad. He brought his fingers to his eyes, then pointed them both at me. Like he was watching me, but then he smirked and took my mom's hand. For some reason, my parents didn't look totally pissed.

"Apparently, your mom got him to come around," Bru whispered to me when I finally got to the front. The guys were all up there with a well-dressed officiant. I mean, the guy had nothing on all us dressed in Armani, but whatevs. Bru eyed me. "And I totally want to fuck you right now, by the way."

That fucking heat returned to my cock, something I passed a discreet hand over before leaning toward him. I grinned. "I just may let you later if you're a good boy."

I felt Bru shiver. His big body eased out a breath before he straightened and passed the moment off.

I didn't usually let him fuck me. I liked control and domination, but I found myself submitting to Bru more and more. I was gone when it came to him.

But I was *done* when it came to her.

Bru and I both were, and I felt his breath leave again when a tiny woman made her way down the aisle in a soft pink color. My breath left too.

Bow still had a bandage on her head from the accident, but that didn't matter. She was still the most beautiful thing in this room right now.

The smooth material Bow wore was modest, as it came down to her ankles, but the dress had a slit that went up to her mid-thigh. This exposed her fair skin every step she took. Like a peek at the treasure that led up between her thighs, and my cock could fucking split wood thinking about the heat there, her smell there. I squeezed Bru's other side, and I felt a rumble in his back against my chest. Bow *would* be in an ankle-length dress and turn us on.

She was heaven.

The need to protect this girl, her innocence, overtook us both. I didn't regret previous actions when it came to her, and I know Bru didn't.

None of my brothers did either.

We all did something not long ago to someone who hurt one of our own without shame or hesitation.

"I want you to hunt him down."

We all did what Bow asked us to that night. *I* avenged her, and I had Bru by my side.

I'd done some dark things with my friends before. We'd all gotten our hands dirty in the past making people pay, but taking a life was a new level, for me in particular. I had blood on my hands, but I'd never played jury and executioner.

Patrick Donovan had begged in the end. He'd *begged for*

his life, and even brought our parents into it. He said we'd never get away with what we were about to do and threatened there'd be consequences from our parents if they found out.

I'd smirked at that because I knew our parents. I knew *my father*. I knew for a fact what my dad and his friends would have done had they actually found the man who almost killed Bow and Sloane.

They would have made him suffer. They would have ended him.

Just like my friends and I did.

We were the men raised by our fathers, and we were proud to be their sons. We also didn't want to burden our dads with this, and didn't need to. We took care of it.

We took care of Bow.

It wasn't hard to make things look like an accident, since people got lost in those woods all the time. I was sure they'd eventually find Donovan's body at the bottom of a ravine in Grimwood Hollow, and his death would look like an accident. Like a man who went on a walk behind his property and got lost. Even his maid didn't know he went out that night.

As it turned out, he abused her too, often, and she had no problem telling anyone that she had no idea her boss left on a walk that night. She also had no problem backing up the story that her boss had no visitors that evening.

My friends and I made some calls to ensure that she already had a new, better job.

All of that was history now, or we were moving toward that, at least. The wounds were still fresh, and Bow would always have them. A part of that fucker would probably always remain as a cloud over her life, and how could it not?

We'd make it easier for her, though. All of my friends would, yes, but especially Bru and me.

A flush bloomed in Rainbow Reed's cheeks, and every

parent she passed wore the same warm, adoring smile toward her. I knew it'd taken a lot for Bow to keep this wedding a secret. She obviously didn't like lying to our parents, since she was such a goody-goody. She was also loyal, and I knew she'd take all our secrets to the grave no matter how dark.

Bow's goodness only made me love her more, but my smile fell a little noticing Mr. Reed's eye twitching. He obviously saw my attention on his daughter. I stood up straight. Bru did too, and I assumed Mr. Reed also caught him looking at Bow.

Clearly having noticed her dad wanting to murder us with his eyes, Bow shook her head a little. She mouthed, "Dad," to Mr. Reed, and, right away, his hard expression softened. Only she and Mrs. Reed could get that huge dude to bend and ease up.

Bow made it about three-quarters of the way down the aisle before Bru and I left the ranks to give her our arms. Each of us guys did that when our girls came down the aisle, which was why Fawn and Aspen were already standing up front on the bride's side of the officiant.

Fawn and Aspen were also in that soft pink color, but my focus was on Bow and how she smelled like a flower just as soft as the color she wore. A hint of cinnamon backed the scent.

"You guys look so handsome," she said to Bru and me.

"I have no words," Bru said, his gaze sliding down her pink dress, but only in the most respectful of ways. That was just Bru though. Even if our parents weren't here, he'd be that way. He put his hand on top of hers before he leaned down and said, "I'll settle for 'you're one of the most beautiful things I've ever seen,' Bow. Seriously, stunning."

His compliment voiced my thoughts, and I was happy he was the one to speak. If it were up to me, I'd end up saying something very inappropriate in front of our entire family.

The flush in Bow's cheeks hiked up a thousand degrees at

the compliment, and, before I could give her mine, we made it to the altar. I supposed I had to hand her off to the bride's side now, but not before I passed her some parting words.

"Later," I said, kissing her hand. There was a promise in my word. Later, she would be with me. Both of them would be.

In case my promise wasn't clear, I slid my gaze over her. She only gave us a peek of tits, but it was enough to charge blood to my cock again. I held Bow's hand until I was forced to let go of her. I noticed attention from both our fathers in the moment. Dad's eyes on me were in warning, but Mr. Reed had his own promise in his eyes. Mr. Reed loved me like a son, but he would definitely kick my ass if I didn't let go of his daughter right now.

Knowing that, I gave him a wry grin and his daughter a parting wink before returning to the groom's side with Bru.

Dorian fought a chuckle behind his hand. He obviously saw the exchange between myself and Mr. Reed, and Ares and Thatcher sported their own grins. I had a feeling their future fathers-in-law would be a lot easier to deal with, and I knew Dorian's would be. Sloane's father, Ramses, was nice as hell.

Whoa… I realized the words *father-in-law* were in my head. Like one day, it'd be Bow walking down this very aisle. She *would* be, if Bru or I had something to say about it.

Those were thoughts for another day though, because today was about my friends. I was sure we all would be doing this again soon for Dorian and Sloane, a big wedding with all the pomp and circumstance. Our parents would see to it that Dorian and Sloane got a proper wedding when we got home.

Sloane looked beautiful at the front of the chapel. She wore a white suit which was so like her. She was always going against the grain.

Dorian loved Sloane's grit. He loved her strength, and he

sucked in a breath as soon as he spotted her. I'd never seen such a look in my buddy's eyes. His future wife completely consumed him.

I knew the feeling, and couldn't help sliding my sight over to Bow. She stared at Sloane with a sheen in her eyes; those were probably the first tears of many, knowing her. She had an ability to be constantly vulnerable, and that was something I could take a note from.

Bru also noticed the tears, his grin on Bow shortly before going back to his sister, Sloane. Bru had so much pride on his face. He and his sister had certainly come full circle. I knew they both had so much tragedy in their lives, but that wasn't today. Today was a new beginning.

I squeezed Bru's shoulder, his grin widening. It managed to get even bigger when he noticed someone stand up in the crowd. It was his dad, Ramses, who had his own prideful grin as he left the pews and headed to his daughter. He put out his arm for Sloane to walk her down the rest of the way.

This really was a full-circle moment.

I think we all choked down a few tears that day, Ramses taking Sloane up to the altar, then later, handing her off to Dorian. I think the only moment that was more emotional was when Dorian received her, and the two started their vows. I'd never seen my buddy so earnest, passionate. He spoke with so much love in his heart.

A pin could have dropped in the room while the couple exchanged their vows, but the space also exploded in applause when they finally sealed the deal. The kiss between them was legendary and was followed by Dorian dipping his new wife. My friends were married, and their family got to be a part of it.

We were family and always would be. A legacy couldn't be broken.

It was forever.

CHAPTER
THIRTY-EIGHT

Bow

My best friend got married today, and it nearly killed me to keep that secret. It was worth it though, and everything turned out great in the end. Our parents all got to be there, and it was perfect.

Sloane looked beautiful.

I could only hope to one day look as lovely as her on my wedding day, and she and Dorian together were magic. Dorian was one of my big brothers, and it was so special to see him so happy. Everyone was happy.

One couldn't help but be in a complete sense of euphoria that night. Everyone was gathered around the happy couple, showering them with love and praise. There was so much love in the air.

"Thanks for today, little rabbit," Sloane said to me later that night. Our parents had bought out a restaurant on the strip for Dorian and Sloane's reception. There'd been dancing and a full four-course dinner before Sloane and I hopped onto the dance floor ourselves. She hugged me there, her smile wide. "Today was so special."

My best friend had asked me to be her maid of honor, and, though I'd never done it before, I did what I could for her today. We couldn't do much with the time crunch, but I did arrange for someone to come in and do our hair and nails before the wedding. Fawn and Aspen were there too, of course. We had a fun time with just us girls.

I did make Sloane a promise that I would do more for her once we did this whole thing again back in our hometown. Our parents wouldn't stand for such a small event here in Vegas, and we all knew that.

As far as I was concerned, my best friend's wedding needed to be as big as it possibly could be. I hugged Sloane tight. "I love you."

I never had a sister. I always had brothers growing up, so when Sloane came around, it'd been something I never knew I needed. She was beyond my bestie. She took care of me. Especially after I told her about the baby.

Our group left what happened at the hospital there that night. They didn't make me talk about it, and Bru and Wells didn't talk about what happened after they showed me my abuser's face one last time. They just came back to the hospital and stayed there until I left. I was still healing from everything, but the healing process was easier with them. I didn't need to know what happened with Professor Donovan, but I could assume.

Again, all that stayed at the hospital.

I ultimately left on the arms of two men and felt more powerful than I ever had. It wasn't because of Bru and Wells though. My power finally came from me, and it always would, from that day forward. It was a promise I made to myself and would forever keep.

Bru and Wells were at the bar while Sloane and I danced. Everyone else was either full at their tables or already headed back to their respective hotels. The majority of our parents had cut out since it was so late, but a small group of them stayed.

The guys smiled at me from the bar and I smiled back. I loved them both so much.

"I love you too, sis," Sloane said to me, and she grinned having noticed my attention on Wells and her brother. Wells and Bru were both still looking at me. In fact, they hadn't taken their eyes off me tonight, though I tried to ignore the fact. It always made me so shy when they looked at me, and that couldn't be helped. The guys didn't just *look* at me. It was like my presence consumed them, and they could never get their fill.

"Bow, do you mind if I have this next dance with my little fighter?" Dorian asked, suddenly appearing in his dark suit. He looked so handsome. He always called Sloane his little fighter which was terribly cute. He grinned at her. "That is if my wife wants to dance with her husband."

It was rare I saw Sloane blush, but she did then. My best friend was married, crazy.

"I suppose I don't mind," Sloane said as Dorian lifted her hand and kissed it. Together, the pair looked like an ad for complete and utter happiness.

I backed away as Dorian pulled Sloane in. He tucked her body into his and so much warmth consumed me. It was like I felt the joy physically coming off them.

I wasn't sure how long all of us stayed at the restaurant. I just knew that, after the last of the parents headed back to their hotels, all us kids continued to use the music for as long as we could. The restaurant stayed open for us, and we took advantage of it.

We all danced together that night. We were Legacy in a big group of joy and celebration. Dancing with my friends actually reminded me of prom night back in high school. A bunch of us were about to graduate then too, and we partied like our lives depended on it. *I* partied and the night ended with all of us jumping into the pool at an after-party. I'd been furious about that, my dress all wet, but it'd somehow been perfect.

Tonight felt perfect. Tonight felt like the beginning of so much more than Dorian and Sloane's nuptials. We all really weren't kids anymore. We were headed out toward that next chapter, and, for me, that meant so much. I felt a freedom I hadn't had at the beginning of the year. Like life and its prospects could really be anything I wanted it to be. Like *I* got to define who I was and my own future.

And that felt pretty goddamn cool.

EPILOGUE

Bru

I thumbed my King ring, the eyes of the gorilla black diamonds. It matched my sister Sloane's ring even though she didn't really wear it anymore. I didn't either, but, for some reason, I wore it today. It was a symbol all my friends wore. At least, we used to. We got the rings by being in the Court. It was like a community club or whatever in our hometown.

None of us wore them anymore really, but today, I thought it'd give me some strength. Wells and I prepared for weeks for this, but still, this was a big step.

I let go of the metal face of a gorilla to grab on to the balcony. The house overlooked the hills of Maywood Heights and was a beautiful view of the city. Maywood Heights wasn't a huge town, but it'd been home for so long. The house also gave views of both my parents' house and Wells's parents' house.

It overlooked Bow's parents' house too.

My phone buzzed in my pocket, and I was anxious,

thinking it was Wells. He was close. He was close *with her* but imagine my relief when I saw my sister's face.

I smiled at the picture of her and Dorian on the beach. They were honeymooning in Bali, and she sent all kinds of pictures. Apparently, the Prinze family had a private island there, and Dorian took Sloane there. They'd been there for weeks and had plans to be there quite a bit of the summer.

If my new brother-in-law was one thing, he was extra, and how crazy that *Dorian Prinze* was my brother-in-law? We had a tumultuous history he and I, but I loved that guy. He was also good for my sister, great for her.

My smile was big on the picture, but it managed to get bigger with the words below it.

Sloane: Good luck today. She's going to love it!

Leave it to my sister to settle my stomach a little. I also heard from Fawn today. She was my brother Ares's fiancée, but she was also one of my best friends. She and I didn't talk as much since we were both so busy, but she sent me a text this morning.

Fawn: I'm so happy for you, friend! Make sure to tell me all about Bow's reaction.

She would definitely be hearing from me. My brother, Ares, also reached out about today. In fact, I'd heard from all our friends at one point. They wanted to know Bow's reaction to everything.

Their support made me strong, but my stomach flip-flopped again as I read the text I just got.

Wells: Almost there. Look out.

I braved my shit up in that moment. I told myself it wouldn't freak out our girlfriend that we bought her a house before any of us graduated.

Me: Lead her upstairs.

We had been planning this meticulously, but still things could go wrong. I mean, Bow could say no to moving in with us.

My dad didn't think I was crazy, but he did ask if I was sure I wanted to use a healthy part of my trust fund to buy the house. Wells did the same, but his dad *did* think he was crazy.

Funnily enough, neither of our moms had. They said we were our fathers' sons and it didn't take a scientist to know what they meant by that. All our parents loved hard, and when we found the one, well, we went all in.

"What is this?" Bow asked, giggling. Wells had his hands over her eyes, which was hilarious. He could have just had her wear a blindfold. She touched his hands. "Come on, Archer. Tell me."

The grin that split Wells's face was crazy. These two had a history I'd never been a part of, and, though I never would, that didn't matter.

I got behind Bow. I put my hands on her trim hips, and she jumped a little. She was wearing this short little skirt that teased the fuck out of me. It'd been *killing* me not being able to touch her properly lately. She'd been recovering from her accident, and the three of us actually hadn't had sex since *before* the accident. Wells and I hadn't wanted to hurt Bow.

Yeah, that shit had been killing *all of us*, but we'd gotten by. Let's just say the three of us got… creative sometimes.

Bow was fully healed now, and my cock twitched seeing the effect my hands had on her. She braced my hands on her hips before sucking in a breath.

"Bru?" It was crazy how she knew my touch from Wells's. She guessed it was me all the time when we were in the shower and I tried to surprise her. We were never in there long before Wells came in. Again, no sex was had, but things got pretty steamy before Wells and I forced ourselves to stop for Bow's sake.

Bow leaned back into my arms. "Why am I not surprised you're here too?"

Maybe because Wells and I never did anything without the other.

"We've got a surprise for you," I said, enjoying her smell. I hugged her close. Honestly, once I had her sweet smell in my nose, I didn't want to let go of her, but Wells eyed me. He could be possessive when it came to her, and I loved that because I got to break him down. I got to test his boundaries, which was always fun.

"The kid and I have to show you something," Wells said as he uncovered her eyes. Bow had her hair down today, her beautiful dark waves shining in the setting sun. The view was *perfect* out here now, which was why we waited to show her the place we bought for this exact time.

Bow's mouth parted, and she stared off into the horizon of Maywood Heights. It was all rolling hills and beautifully scenic with its lush green trees combined with the cityscape. Bow turned toward us, a gleeful look on her face. "What is this?"

"This is the view from your new house. Well, our new house," Wells explained, then dropped an arm around my shoulders. "The kid and I bought it for you. For us."

"That is, if you want to move in with us," I said, taking Bow's hand.

"Move... in?" she questioned, shaking her head. "You guys bought me a house. *Us* a house?" Her mouth parted. "When would we move in?"

The fact that she didn't say this all was crazy...

She wants this too.

Honestly, it hadn't felt like Wells and I were rushing when he initially proposed the idea of moving in together on the day of Dorian and Sloane's wedding. The fact I literally hadn't gone a day without seeing either Bow or Wells since we got together was a sign of what was to come. I was addicted to these two.

They were my forever.

I doubted Wells was shocked either by what Bow said. Even still, he had a bit of awe on his face when he took her hand. He held it up. "Whenever you want, Squeak. We could move in fucking today if you want."

"What about school?" she asked, knowing our university was a couple hours away. She eyed Wells. "You'd be willing to commute?"

"Hell yeah, if I can with you and that asshole of course," he said referring to me, and my eyes lifted. Wells chuckled. "Seriously, it'd be fucking awesome. I can't think of a better way to literally spend hours each day than going back and forth to campus with you guys."

"You sure you want to be trapped in a car with him every day?" I asked Bow, and Ambrose nudged me. I shoved him back, and he made a maneuver to get me in a hold. I was quick though, and got him first. He easily slid out, but I got him.

"Your ass is going to pay for that later," he promised me, and my dick kicked in my boxers. I could only hope. I needed them both so badly.

Bow ended up coming between Wells and me when we refused to break our roughhousing up. She was always the softness to our roughness, and she kissed our cheeks before pulling us in to kiss us both. It was a long kiss with just as much teeth as tongue, and *she* was the one to make it happen. Our timid little Bow had no problem controlling both of us. She was our strength, the core to our unit of three.

I'd like to say I didn't know how it happened. How we all ended up upstairs in what was going to be our furnished bedroom. At present, there was only a bed in there, sans the sheets. Maybe Wells and I were a bit presumptuous ordering that for the house. It was literally the only thing we'd bought so far.

Maybe we were just hoping to break it in after showing our girlfriend our new home.

Either way, we all ended up on the bed. We left a trail of our clothes in the house along the way, and there was nothing like seeing this girl naked, spread out on a king-sized mattress. Without the sheets, Bow was like her own piece of art. Her legs were open, pussy wet, and I swiped a lick before drawing one of her chocolate-colored nipples into my mouth. That shit tasted just as sweet, and she squeaked out a sound the moment my tongue swirled around it.

"Oh my gosh, Bru," she said, grabbing my hair and clawing at my back. Again, I felt like I hadn't gotten to touch her properly since she got hurt. Those dark days were between all of us, and, though they never truly would go away, Wells and I could make things easier for Bow. We could make her feel loved and give her all the attention.

I squeezed her breast, sucking her nipple so hard, and Wells was suddenly beside me on the other. He was just as naked as Bow, and, if I hadn't been distracted by her, I would have realized what a work of art he was too. His cock hung heavy between his firm legs, and he fisted himself while his tongue lavished Bow.

"Wells, I can't," she squeaked out again. Wells always made fun of her for that sound, hence his nickname for her, but it was so goddamn cute I couldn't stand it. She gripped a hand in his hair. "Harder."

Harder.

We both went hard, Wells and I. We hadn't gotten to *love* her right in so long, and I took full advantage when Bow opened her legs for me again. Hunkering down between her thighs, I sucked her pussy lips into my mouth, and that cute-as-fuck sound left her lips again.

"I want you both inside me," she said, and it was like a kill switch hit the moment. I stopped eating pussy, and Wells stopped sucking Bow's tit.

"You sure, Squeak?" Wells asked the question I'd been

thinking. I mean, she could definitely take both of us inside her.

Again, we'd all gotten creative.

Since Bow's accident, neither Wells nor I had physically been inside her. We just didn't want to chance it, but we had done other things.

We'd done lots of other things.

Some of those other things consisted of the plug we all damn well knew was in her ass right now. It was actually Bow's idea to wear the butt plug after Wells and I started doing some ass play with her.

I think we'd all been preparing for this moment.

Lying on her back, Bow was playing with Wells's hair. Her beautiful skin was flushed and perfect, hot, and her perfectly pouty lips were just as red. She chewed one. "I can handle it, and I want to."

Her face blasted hotter in color. Bow still did the shy thing every once in a while, but in the next breath she was asking us to purchase a butt plug for her. She was getting more comfortable with telling us what she needed, and I loved that.

Reaching up, I pushed my hand in her hair. "Where do you want me?"

My place turned out to be between her legs, and how I missed that heat, her heat. I'd only gotten that the one time after we'd all been at the cabin. Wells had been inside her then, but we all made love again when we got back home. I'd gotten to have her then.

I guided her on top of me once I sheathed myself, and she hugged my dick like a *fucking* glove. I actually sucked in a breath as I gripped her hips. I was afraid to move and come prematurely.

"Are you all right?" she asked, looking like she thought she'd done something wrong. She started to move her hips but stopped. Her mouth parted. "Bru—"

"Fine," I said, so fucking fine it wasn't even funny. I

pushed my hand between her breasts. "Arch back. I want to do this right."

I didn't want to hold back, and, when her back bowed right away, I knew I could. She was giving me permission to fuck her, take her.

I didn't wait. I slammed my hips up with intension, purpose, and the noise that left Bow's mouth wasn't a squeak this time. She *called out* and screamed so hard I thought I hurt her at first.

"Don't stop," she said, obviously feeling the resistance in my hips. I'd slowed down, but I started again when she continued to move hers. Her tits bounced with every rock of her trim hips, her dark hair back and brushing my thighs. That was how far she arched back, and I almost did come at the sight of her. She was an erotic vision incarnate.

"You both look so hot like this," Wells said, and I came out of my sex-induced haze enough to watch him watching us. He looked hot too, his hand on his cock, his body golden. He pumped his thick length once before putting a hand on my chest. That made me fuck Bow harder. Especially when he pinched my nipple.

Christ.

He kissed me, which was so good, but it was even better when he tugged Bow's head back and gave her the deepest kiss I'd ever seen. It was like he was physically fusing himself to her.

I picked up my pace watching them, seeing fucking stars at this point. Bow's tits continued to bounce, and I played with them. I pinched one, and she cried out in Wells's mouth. My dick twitched. "Bro, you need to fuck her before I come."

I was so fucking close, but we told Bow she could have us both. Knowing that, I slowed down, which was *agony.*

"So eager," Wells said to me, and I wanted to punch his lights out for playing with me. He was also playing with her.

He put his hand between her legs and pinched her clit while I fucked her.

"Please," Bow said. I think she knew how Wells operated by now. He'd draw this shit out if we let him, but he always listened to Bow. He was a sucker for her, and I saw that when she shoved her hand into his platinum hair and forced him to kiss her. Wells growled in response and resistance was forgotten when he grabbed a condom out of his jeans.

"You'll let us know if either of us should stop, Squeak," he said to her, his kiss on her lips slow as he sheathed himself. It was so beautiful watching him submit to her. It was so beautiful watching *them*. The love I had for the two of them should scare me since it was so intense, but it didn't. It just made me hungrier for them. I was hungry for their love and connection. I lived and breathed by these two, and that was definitely a good thing.

Bow nodded during her kiss with Wells, and he was gone after that. He was behind her like she was his own personal siren. He pulled out her butt plug, and the minute he filled her, I felt it.

It was goddamn wonderful.

It was goddamn *full*, and I watched both Bow's face and Wells's transform at the connection between all three of us. Bow's mouth went so wide, and Wells's eyes rolled back in his head. He completely lost himself in the connection, which wasn't like him. He liked to be the one in control.

"Fuck, you guys. Fuck," Wells growled, holding tight to Bow's hips. I knew the hold was tight because I was already holding Bow's hips. That meant Wells was holding *on top* of my hold, and he gripped my hands so hard I thought he'd cut off the circulation in my hands. "I can feel you both. It's so fucking good."

It was good. It was *euphoric*.

We moved together. All three of us were grinding, fucking

and in the middle of it was Bow. She was our passion, our pleasure.

"I love you both," Bow said. She had Wells's hands on her breasts. Her flesh was pooling so hotly between his fingers. He was hugging her and kissing her back. The two were so close, but she let me be a part of the moment when she bent down and kissed me.

Her mouth was like home to me, and Wells's was too when he kissed me after my lips parted Bow's. He had his hand in my hair, gripping the shit out of it. "I love you guys."

Wells's tongue flicked mine. He kissed me with Bow between us. All three of us in this intense, all-encompassing position.

"You guys are my everything," I said, and I was so happy not to do this shit alone anymore. Life. I had family, friends, but something was missing. That something turned out to be two things. Two people.

Bow watched Wells and me. She smiled before kissing my chest, and that did me in. The curse left my mouth as I stiffened, came, and Wells wasn't far behind. He actually bit my tongue with his release and drew blood.

"Oh my God," Bow called out, the last to come, and I was glad. Wells and I had both finished by then, and we just got to watch her. We got to watch her be beautiful and sacred between us. She was *perfect*.

I had no idea how long the three of us lay in that bed without sheets. It shouldn't be comfortable, but it was actually the most comfortable thing there ever could be with Bow lying on my chest. I got to hold her while Wells had an arm around us both. It was literally heaven.

"You think you guys could show me the rest of the house now?" she asked, and her cheeks brightened. I think she secretly liked telling us what to do even though she acted shy about it, and I guess we all had gotten a bit distracted.

After getting our clothes on, Wells and I showed her the

house's various floors and how it gave views of the houses belonging to the people we cared about the most, our parents. Thatcher, Ares, and Dorian had all bought houses in the same cul-de-sac as ours to surprise their girls with too. We'd probably all be raising families here one day. We'd be starting our own legacy, and we had some pretty great fucking role models. I think we all aspired to be like the men and women who raised us. They showed us strength and love, and, if there was one thing this huge fucking family had, it was an abundance of the latter. There was never a shortage of that.

And the next generation, our generation, would make sure there never would be.

The End.

Want a bonus deleted scene from the book that may or may not have some spice? ;) You're in luck because there's a bonus chapter to *A Little Bit Reckless*! This is a FREE download and it's available exclusively to my newsletter subscribers!

Join my newsletter today to get your free deleted bonus scene told from Bow's POV!

Get here:

https://edenoneill.myflodesk.com/alittlebitreckless

Acknowledgements

I want to take a moment to thank all my patrons on Patreon for all their support! I appreciate each and every one of you. Thank you so much for supporting me and my work <3

My Lovely Patrons:

A
abbycadabby
Aiden
Alex J
Amanda
Amanda S
Amandha K
Amber D
Amber R
Amie N
Amy
Amy R
Angeli
Annalisse G
Ashley P
Ashley R
Aubrie O
Becky B
Bethany
Breanna
Breanne T
Brenda H
Brianna L
Brianne
Brittany
Brittany E
Brooke E
Brooklynn P
Bryn M
Carrie
Charlotte K
Christina
Christine McA
Chyana S
Coffee Break with Bc
Danielle B
Delayne
Devonne H
Diana C
Elissa C
Emi B
emily
Emily Alfin D
Emily C
Emily K
Gemma
gigi moonchild
Grace
Heather L
Heather M
Hissa A
Jacquelynn R
Jamiese
Jasmine O
Jen74
Jennifer
Jessica C
JRea
Justice
Kari
Kari K
Katelin
Kay
Kelsey G.
Kirsty A
Kittycat
Kristina
Kymmie G
Leah Apil
Leah R
Leighton G
Lexi F
Lilian
Lis
Lisa A
Lisa G
Liz
Madison G
Maleny
Maria D
Marianela V
Melissa
Melissa
Meri M
Micaiah W
Michaela P
Michelle
Michelle
Michelle M
Milly B
Mona B
Ms. Diamond
Naomi
Nichole T
Nikki St. Crowe
Ofelia F
Olivia K
Paige L
Pippa S
Rachel
Rebecca C
Rebecca F
Robin
Rosa M
Rose-Mari
Samantha
Samantha
Samantha M
Sara S
Sarah J
Savanna L
Schella D
Shaunna D
Shekinah K
Shyla M
Sophie
Sophie E
Stassi
Summer M
Sunni
Tammi
Tawnya M
Taylour K
Tommy59
Tristan P
Verrell
Vieve
Violeta W
Xen G

If you'd like to join me on Patreon (and be listed in the acknowledgements page in my next book!) You can join me at the link below:

https://www.patreon.com/edenoneillwrites

Thank you so much for reading A LITTLE BIT RECKLESS! Did you know I've written books about Bow's parents as well as Bru's adoptive parents? I've also written stories about Wells's parents and his god-dad LJ! You can check them out on Amazon today!

Brutal Heir (Court University Book 1)
Knight and Greer's story (Bow's parents)

Kingpin (Court University Book 2)
Billie and LJ's story (Wells's god-dad)

Beautiful Brute (Court University Book 3)
Jax and Cleo's story (Wells's parents)

Lover (Court University Book 4)
Ramses and Brielle's story (Bru's adoptive parents)

www.ingramcontent.com/pod-product-compliance
Lightning Source LLC
Chambersburg PA
CBHW070237200726
48293CB00005B/1657